BEACON STREET MOURNING

"Day's astute descriptions of the social mores and day-to-day life in Boston in 1909 are as entertaining as the characters she creates and give much more added pleasure to the reader." —*Publishers Weekly*

DEATH TRAIN TO BOSTON

"Fremont Jones is a laudable and attractive heroine. . . . Ms. Day has done her research and readers who relish being transported to another time will find this an extremely appealing book. Every facet of the novel—the writing, the characterizations, the suspense, the history—provides knowledge and just plain good storytelling."
—*The Book Report*

EMPEROR NORTON'S GHOST

"Fremont is a spirited young woman ahead of her time and her adventures make enthralling reading."
—*The Purloined Letter*

"[An] appealing portrait of a spirited, irrepressible heroine." —*Publishers Weekly*

"Fremont is . . . [a] delightful, feisty, independent adventurer . . . [who] exhibits a wry sense of humor."
—*Southbridge Evening News,* Southbridge, MA

THE BOHEMIAN MURDERS

"Thrill to the third in this exciting series featuring the liberated Fremont at her bravest. . . . This knockout setting draws you in like no other. *The Bohemian*

Murders conjures up the murkiest mystery—you can just hear the waves and smell the fog. Bravo."
—*Mystery Lovers Bookshop News*

"Delightful."
—*San Francisco Chronicle*

"A plucky heroine, a darkly handsome suitor in the wings, and a glimpse back into history all add to the charms this series has to offer."
—*Alfred Hitchcock Mystery Magazine*

"Light, entertaining and ever-so-slightly racy, *The Bohemian Murders* is perfect summer reading."
—*Wisconsin State Journal*

"An attractive and involving historical."
—*Library Journal*

"Fast-paced machinations keep the reader turning page after page with anticipation."
—*The Carmel Pine Cone*

"By the third book in a new series, most new sleuths tend to flounder. Not that plucky Bostonian Caroline Fremont Jones . . . The strong-minded Fremont surrenders neither her independence nor her intelligence. . . . This liberated woman has come too far ever to go back."
—*The New York Times Book Review*

FIRE AND FOG

"A winner." —*Monterey County Herald*

"Day's decorous, spirited heroine is as charming as ever as she picks her way through a world of rubble where every acquaintance could be a killer."
—*Kirkus Reviews*

"The strong-willed, intelligent Jones shines, whether she's helping her friend, fending off suitors, or fleeing the clutches of ninja smugglers." —*Publishers Weekly*

BEACON STREET MOURNING

A FREMONT JONES MYSTERY

DIANNE DAY

Bantam Books

NEW YORK   TORONTO   LONDON   SYDNEY   AUCKLAND

This edition contains the complete text
of the original hardcover edition.
NOT ONE WORD HAS BEEN OMITTED.

BEACON STREET MOURNING
A Bantam Book

PUBLISHING HISTORY
Doubleday hardcover edition published October 2000
Bantam mass market edition / November 2001

ISBN 0-553-58061-2

Reprinted by arrangement with Doubleday.

Published simultaneously in the United States and Canada.

Bantam Books are published by Bantam Books, a division of Random House,
Inc. Its trademark, consisting of the words "Bantam Books" and the portrayal
of a rooster, is Registered in U.S. Patent and Trademark Office and in other
countries. Marca Registrada. Bantam Books, 1540 Broadway, New York, New
York 10036.

PRINTED IN THE UNITED STATES OF AMERICA

OPM   10   9   8   7   6   5   4   3   2   1

To my father,
who died when I was an infant,
and
to my mother,
who lives on

ACKNOWLEDGMENTS

I want to thank Barbara and Rudi Franchi for their hospitality and for sharing historical and background materials, documents, and photographs of Boston; their daughter Susan Frank for being an excellent West Coast source of the same; Karen Levin of Salem, Massachusetts, for patiently driving me many places when I was doing research; Kate of Kate's Mystery Books in Cambridge just for being there; the Boston area DorothyLers, ditto; Bob Smith for the history of Locke-Ober and knowledge of Cape Cod; and last but far from least, Luci Zahray for her expertise on poisons, without which this book could not have been written.

—D.D.

BEACON STREET
MOURNING

ONE

WITH THE TURN of the New Year came, as always, a time of resolutions and new beginnings. No more could I afford the vaguely pleasurable limbo in which I'd lately been floating. So I took stock and began to deal with feelings of guilt I had metaphorically swept under the carpet.

Since my return to San Francisco in early December from a certain trip I didn't even like to think about, I'd allowed myself to luxuriate in feelings of safety and belonging. I was daily overwhelmed with gratitude at simply finding myself alive—especially considering a number of things that had happened while I was away that might have produced quite the opposite result. There were times when to be alive and in love with my partner Michael Kossoff was almost more happiness than I could bear. Of course there were also times when I wished I were strong enough to throw him off the roof of our house at the top of Divisadero Street, but that's another story.

If I were honest, I had to admit that underneath my happiness ran a subterranean vein of the most profound disquiet, and in this vein lay the source of my guilt: deep concerns about my father. I was worried about his

health and general well-being, certain I had good reason
for worry, and yet I had done next to nothing.

Oh, I had a good excuse for my inaction: two broken
legs that were excruciatingly slow to heal, and some unpleasant mental and emotional aftereffects of that
aforementioned trip. I would have denied having any
problem other than my legs if anyone had asked, especially Michael; lacking control over one's thoughts and
feelings can be most distressing. My legs were stronger
now—I had recently traded my crutches for two
canes—and even though I was less sure about strength
in the rest of me, I could not wait any longer to do
something about Father.

Ever testing limits, I tucked one cane under my left
arm and, leaning only upon the other one, started
across the sitting room. Three steps: drops of perspira-
tion broke out on my forehead. This was agony—not so
much physical, although there was pain. The embarrassing truth was, ever since giving up the crutches, I'd
been afraid of falling.

Breathing hard against fear's chill, I thought: Why
push myself too far? I needed both the canes, for balance as well as support. Even so, I forced one more step
before allowing the relief that flooded me as soon as I
put that second cane to the floor.

If I hadn't known better, I could've sworn this house
had grown larger during the time I was away. It took a
ridiculously long time to cross this room. Or any room.
Finally I reached the other side, as sweat-drenched as if
I'd run a race in midsummer rather than walked a few
steps indoors on a gloomy, rainy San Francisco winter
day.

Taking a seat at a little antique writing desk that had
been a welcome-home gift from Michael, I heard the
telephone ring right beneath my feet. Downstairs on my
side of our double house is the office suite of J&K, the
private investigation agency that Michael and I own
and operate together. Not that I had lately been of any

use to our operation whatsoever. I sighed, and reached
for writing paper.

The telephone rang three times before it was picked
up, then faintly I heard the inimitable tones of Edna
Stephenson's voice. She has a large voice for such a
small woman, yet I couldn't make out her exact words.
Never mind, she always said the same thing anyway:
"The J and K Agency. This is Mrs. Stephenson, the re-
ceptionist, speaking. May I help you?"

I smiled, then frowned, straining to hear even though
I knew the chance of my being able to make out the
words through the thick walls of the house was slim to
none. Lately my pleasure at being safe and sound has
been regularly outweighed by a strong desire to resume
all my normal activities, such as snooping. As an eaves-
dropper I excelled, in large part due to my unusually
acute hearing. But here the walls defeated me; in the
world at large my physical limitations did the same.
What good is a detective who cannot walk unaided?
For whom a flight of stairs presents a formidable obsta-
cle? How long, oh how long before I would be myself
again?

My present routine had me going downstairs to the
office twice a day, once in the morning and once in the
afternoon, to meet with the others and hear what cases
the agency had going. These two trips up and down
were all I could physically handle.

Sitting in on case discussion was not enough for me.
I wanted to do more. I might have stayed downstairs to
do typewriting in the mornings, I was physically capable of that—but Edna had become quite a good type-
writer. She could run the office alone. She did not need
me, and after a few minutes I inevitably felt like an intruder. The office was no longer my territory, I had
made myself into a detective, or an investigator, and if I
could not detect or investigate then I felt useless.

Downstairs the sound of Edna's voice ceased; involuntarily I winced as she banged the earpiece back on its

hook, a gentle hang-up not being Edna's style. For a moment I pictured her slipping out of her chair—she is a short woman whose feet do not quite reach the floor when she sits at her desk—then tottering on tiny feet across the front office, through the conference room, and then into the kitchen. I glanced at my pendant watch—another gift from Michael, who has been showering me with entirely too many presents lately—to confirm the time. As I'd thought, it was about 4 P.M. In another hour I would make my way down the stairs to follow the same path Edna had just taken in my mind's eye, back to the kitchen where she and Michael and Wish and I would discuss what they had done today. Wish Stephenson is our other investigator, and Edna is his mother. The others would talk and I would listen; greedily, enviously I would drink in their words along with Edna's scalding coffee.

But right now I had a letter to write.

I had been thinking about this letter for a long time. It was the sort of letter that would start something, would lead to irrevocable consequences—and so I hadn't dared to write it until I believed I could handle those consequences. This letter would say words that, once said, could not be taken back. It would bring an outside person into a situation that, thus far, had been private. It was a difficult and possibly a dangerous step to take. Yet I hesitated no longer; words flowed from my pen.

The sound of a pen moving across paper is irresistible to a cat. Sometimes to my detriment I forget this. I was completely engrossed when Hiram leaped upon the desk, tucked his haunches under and sat on a corner of the paper, his golden eyes tracking the moving pen with a born stalker's fascination. Uh-oh. I put the pen down just in time. He blinked at me quite crossly for ruining his fun.

I have not had Hiram for very long; I acquired him as a tiny kitten on that trip I do not like to think about. To say that he is growing rapidly would be an understatement. I suppose in cat time he must be entering adolescence; certainly he has the cat version of that gangly look, as if the rest of him may never catch up to the length of his legs and tail. He has become somewhat clumsy as well. I clapped one hand over the inkwell before we could have a nasty accident.

"How kind of you to join me," I said acerbically, as I picked Hiram up and tucked him in my lap beneath the fold-down panel of the desk. "If you want to stay, then you must sit there quietly and behave yourself."

He stretched his neck and stared at me upside down as if to judge whether I meant what I'd said. "Really," I added for emphasis.

This apparently convinced him, for he stretched once and then shaped himself into a purring ball of sleek black fur. I stroked him for a while, rereading what I'd written thus far; then I caught my lower lip in my teeth (which somehow facilitates thought) and continued to write. I did not stop until I had finished the whole letter. Then I read it through. Though the paper trembled in my hand, I was satisfied that I'd said what needed to be said:

> *Divisadero Street*
> *San Francisco*
> *January 10, 1909*

Mr. William Barrett
Great Centennial Bank
Boston, Massachusetts

Dear William,
  I write to ask for your assistance in a matter pertaining to my father, Leonard Pembroke Jones. I do hope you will forgive my presumption in approaching you after an absence and silence of so many years. My memory of your past kindness prompts me to do so. I have such a warm recollection of your solicitousness on those occasions when, after my mother's death, I served

*as my father's awkward young hostess. You made
things easier for me then, and I hope now you will be
able to do the same—although the present situation is,
alas, far more serious. In truth, William, I do not know
where else to turn. I trust I may rely on your discretion,
as this is a matter of some delicacy.*

*Before proceeding with an explanation, I should say
I am well aware that Father is no longer at the bank,
that he is "retired," though in Father's case I am not
sure what the exact meaning of that word would be.
While I am sorry on his account, as he was always a
man whose work meant much to him, I do hope his departure may have meant promotion for you. I know he
would have thought you a worthy successor.*

*In essence my dilemma is this: I have been lately un-
able to make contact with Father. Over the past two
months I have sent him three telegrams. Only the first
of these was answered, by Father's faithful secretary
Gladys, who told me he was no longer at the bank due
to his (aforementioned) retirement. The two subsequent
telegrams, sent to him at the Beacon Street residence,
have gone unanswered, though Western Union has assured me they were delivered.*

*If I may speak plainly: I suspect the intervention of
Father's wife, Augusta (as was) Simmons. I cannot
imagine any circumstance under which Augusta would
have any right or reason to intercept a communication
from me, or indeed from anyone, to my father. If Father
had received my telegrams himself, I am certain he
would have replied. Because I know the telegrams were
delivered to the house but Father has not replied, I can
only conclude they were delivered into hands other than
Father's. Whose else but Augusta's? I do not wish to be
unfair, but I can reach no other conclusion.*

*I know that when I left Boston and came to San
Francisco without Father's prior knowledge or consent
four years ago, it may have looked as if I were deliberately disowning myself. But such was not my intention,*

as Father eventually understood. He and I are not estranged. Last April he came here to San Francisco for my twenty-fifth birthday, and I was on my way to Boston to visit him in October when a rather nasty incident interrupted my trip. As I explained in those two ill-fated telegrams, I am still recovering from injuries suffered at that time. Father would never fail to reply to a letter telling him I had been hurt, as I am sure you will agree.

William, if you would be so kind as to go to the Pembroke Jones house, I know Augusta could not refuse to admit you. You could say you had come on bank business, could you not? Would you please go and tell him that I am alive and well, and longing to see him again? That I will come to Boston at the earliest possible opportunity? And would you then write and let me know how he seems to you, if he be well or ill or at any stage in between?

I await most eagerly your reply.

Your friend always,
Caroline Fremont Jones

There, it was done. I read it over a second time and was satisfied. The letter could go out today—if Edna were willing to take care of it on her way home.

Yes, asking Edna to mail the letter was a good idea. That way Michael would not have to know I'd written it. He would not approve; he would say I was not yet well enough to be thinking about these things. His protectiveness could so easily cross an invisible line and become stifling to me.

MY TOO PROTECTIVE LOVE came bounding up the stairs shortly before five o'clock. Edna had already left on my letter-mailing errand, and Wish was not yet back from wherever he was working; I'd been hoping to get downstairs before Michael's return, but no such luck.

"Fremont," he called out when he was only perhaps halfway up, "are you alone? And if you are, why was the door unlocked? I've told Edna and Wish never to leave you in the house alone with the door unlocked."

By the time he reached the last part of this complaint he had burst into my sitting room, where I stood in the middle of the handsome Chinese rug that had been my first purchase of furnishing for this place—back when money had been hard to come by.

"I am glad to see you too," I said, "and how nice of you to knock before entering my part of the house."

"Oh, piffle." Michael kissed my cheek. His own cheek, which he laid against mine for a moment, was cool, his hair felt damp, he smelled of Pears soap and something else, something slightly smoky—I supposed just of having been out in the City.

"Piffle, my foot. And you wonder why I don't want to marry. Perhaps it is because I would like to have a little privacy now and then."

"Married people can have privacy. Married people can live just the way we live—each in half a house. And in fact plenty do live that way, with far less intimacy than you and I have achieved in spite of the ridiculous lines you draw, Fremont."

I smiled. This was an old argument, its permutations as familiar as the forms of a dance. The only new addition to our established pattern was Hiram the cat, who twined himself in and out of Michael's legs, purring loudly.

"Edna needed to leave early," I said, resuming my stately pace across the floor, "and Wish is not back yet, so I told her to leave the door unlocked because I'd be downstairs directly. I'm surprised you didn't pass her on the sidewalk."

"I was driving the Maxwell—I expect I came up the hill from the opposite direction."

"I see."

Since giving up the familiar crutches for the unfamiliar canes, it was hard for me to walk and talk at the same time, so I said no more, although I did wonder where Michael had been.

In the opposite direction lay the Presidio. I did not want Michael going there because it meant the likelihood of the Army pressing him into more intelligence work. Intelligence—a fancy name for pure and simple spying. Well, not so simple: Michael wanted out but they would not let him go. They'd say he was free but then they would call him back, again and again, always with the same lie: "Just one more time."

I felt Michael's eyes boring into me as I approached the top of the stairs. More than once we'd fought over this, how he wanted to help me on the stairs, and how strongly I felt I must do it alone; how nervous I became, how much more likely to lose my balance, when he was watching.

I hooked the cane that had been in my right hand over the top of the stair rail—I kept another cane at the bottom—and then grasped the banister with that hand.

Michael cleared his throat. "You're going right on down, then."

"Obviously," I said, looking back over my shoulder, trying to keep a note of exasperation out of my voice and facial expression. "Why?"

"I, um, took the liberty of looking into something we won't want to discuss in front of either of the Stephensons. I thought perhaps there'd be time to tell you before we went downstairs."

"Will it take long to tell me this, whatever it is?"

"No." Michael ruffled his hair, a nervous mannerism that was not a particularly good sign. "No, it won't. You go on down. I'll wash my hands in your bathroom, if you don't mind. See you in the kitchen?"

"Yes," I said gratefully, "I'll see you there shortly." Then I tightened my grip on the banister, got my balance, and started down.

One step at a time, one leg and then the other. The

descent required every ounce of my concentration. For
the minutes that it took, there was nothing else in the
world but me and those damn stairs.

"YOU HAVE ROSES in your cheeks," Michael said
later on joining me. "Physical exertion becomes you."

"Hmm," I said, cocking my head to one side and
studying his handsome, bearded face, "I will admit
some kinds of physical exertion are more fun than others. The stairs would not be my first choice."

"Fremont, you are wicked. I can read your mind."

I smiled. "Yes, I expect you can."

Michael busied himself with pouring the coffee Edna
had made earlier into the pottery mugs he and I both
prefer to china teacups. "Maybe later?" he inquired,
raising his eyebrows a couple of times in a comical way
that was anything but seductive.

I laughed. "Maybe."

He placed a mug on the table before me, then sat in
the chair nearest mine.

I said, "Now, tell me this bad news."

He blew across the top of his mug. "How do you
know it's bad?"

"I have powers of mystic divination. Now, tell."

Michael's blowing became a heavy sigh. "It's about
whether or not your legs are healing properly. I saw a
doctor today who works with the X-ray."

My breath caught in my throat. The X-ray was an
experimental procedure sometimes exploited for sensa-
tionalism, as if it were a form of entertainment. But I
knew it had been used on people for serious medical
reasons. I had read about these medical uses in a newspaper not long ago and had become quite excited. With
X-rays, which were discovered about ten years ago, it is
possible to see the bones beneath the skin and muscles
and everything. Supposedly it is like looking at your
own skeleton—hence the macabre attraction, X-rays as

entertainment. Yet the medical information such a procedure might give me seemed of such obvious value that I craved it.

"And—?" I urged.

"And it is too dangerous. Doctors do not know how to control the X-ray. Sometimes people are horribly burned. The doctors who have been working with it the longest have suffered most. Their skin reddens, then blisters, and erupts with sores. I don't imagine you want to hear any more than that, do you?"

I didn't, yet I did. "I still have questions. If it's so harmful, then why are they still doing it?"

"Because they—well, this doctor I talked to anyway—believe the medical benefits of X-ray will eventually be great enough that they must learn to control it. Just think, Fremont, to be able to see inside a person without cutting through the skin!"

"That is precisely what I had hoped might be done with my legs," I said rather bitterly, "yet you tell me this doctor will not do it."

"I know you're disappointed." Michael reached over and covered my hand with his on top of the table.

I nodded, not looking at him.

"Perhaps it will be of some consolation to you that this doctor said the same as the other two."

"You mean," I said into my lap, as this subject to me was unpleasant in the extreme, "that my bones may have been broken in more than one place, even though no bone protruded through the skin. And that is why the healing process is taking so long."

"Yes. Fremont, he also said that ten to twelve weeks is not an abnormally long time for such an injury to heal—even though it undoubtedly seems so to you."

I raised my head and looked into Michael's eyes. His eyes are blue but changeable, like sea and sky in different weather; now they were deep and dark, like a pool in a forest clearing. "My fear is that I walked too soon, made my legs bear my weight before they were ready.

So by my own actions I may have disrupted whatever goes on when bones grow back together, and now my legs will never be right again."

"Fremont, my dearest"—Michael stroked my face with the back of his hand—"be patient with yourself."

"I just thought, if I could *see* . . ." I didn't bother to finish the sentence. What was the point? Yet it was so hard to give up. "He, this X-ray doctor, he wouldn't do it for me once, just once? I would pay—"

"No." Michael shook his head. "I did say we would gladly pay any cost, but he still declined. He asked me if your legs were misshapen, and I said no, only somewhat wasted. He said muscles grow weak and thin from lack of exercise. If you don't have too much pain, he suggested you should walk with your canes, increasing the time and the distance a little each day."

I sighed. That at least was something. One of the two doctors I'd seen since my return had told me the exact opposite—he had wanted me in a wheeled chair, like an invalid, until I felt no pain whatever on standing.

I said, "Michael, I do not believe the doctors really know very much at all about what goes on in the human body."

"My dear Fremont, you are quite, quite right." He put one hand behind my neck and drew my face close, until he could kiss me. We were still kissing when we heard the front door open and Wish's voice sing out. Then we pulled apart, blushing like guilty children.

TWO

------◆◆◆------

Great Centennial Bank
Boston, Massachusetts
January 23, 1909

Miss Caroline Fremont Jones
Divisadero Street
San Francisco, California

Dear Caroline,

Although I gather you go by your middle name now,
it will always be difficult for me to call you anything
but Caroline. I cannot tell you how happy I was at first
to have your letter, and then how shocked as I read its
contents. It seems that last year was not a good one for
the Pembroke Joneses, if you and Leonard are any example. I am so very sorry, and I hope that you are well
now. I do not think we will be able to say the same for
your father, at least not any time soon.

Here is the situation: Having been alerted by your
letter, I put together a portfolio of material that I
could legitimately discuss with Leonard and went calling at Pembroke Jones House on Beacon Street. At first
Augusta Simmons Jones—who does know me on sight,
by the way—insisted on calling the bank to verify my

errand, as if I were some underling. I gathered from the
redness of her face that she was soon set straight. Next
she claimed your father was too ill to receive visitors.

Caroline, I was harsh with her. If I had not been, I
do not believe she would ever have allowed me to climb
the stairs. I said if Leonard were too ill to sign his sig-
nature to some bank business that required it, I would
have to hear as much from his doctor. I mentioned
Searles Cosgrove by name, as I assumed he would still
be the family's physician; I had recalled Searles being in
attendance at the time of your mother's death.

Upon my uttering Searles Cosgrove's name, your
stepmother went quite pale in the face, for a reason I
can now surmise, although it baffled me then. She did,
however, take me upstairs a short while later, after leaving me alone for a time, during which I suppose she did
her best to make poor Leonard presentable.

I will not write out the details here for you, but will
say only that they are shocking, and it is a good thing
your letter to me arrived when it did. I cannot say for
certain that Augusta has neglected your father; it may
be that she is telling the truth when she says she believed there was no medical hope for him, and that the
best she could do was to keep him comfortable until the
end came. She says she did not give him your telegrams
for the same reason, that is, their contents would have
upset him, and as he was too ill to do anything himself,
it was best for his peace of mind that he not know.

I can say, however, that I felt most strongly Searles
Cosgrove should be called in immediately. I was able to
bully Augusta into calling him without threatening her
outright—but I want you to know, Caroline, I would
have threatened her if I'd had to.

Leonard is now in Boston Priory Hospital under
Cosgrove's care, more comfortable than he was at
home, and of course he is in a private room. He wants
to see you, and has asked that I tell you so. I hope you
will be able to come as soon as possible. Meanwhile any

correspondence you wish to have with your father, if you will send it to me, I will put it in his hands myself.

In closing, I see upon reading again what I have written above that I have not mentioned the prognosis for your father's condition. If you are still of as inquisitive and insistent a nature as I remember you (and if I may be so bold, I hope you have not changed!), then you will wonder. Cosgrove says Leonard's condition is "guarded"—that is to say, he may regain some of his former strength or he may not, we must wait and see. He is gravely ill, of a wasting disease that has attacked his gastrointestinal system, so that his appetite is affected along with his ability to draw nourishment from food. That is the extent of my knowledge.

Hoping to see you again in the near future, while distressed that our reacquaintance must occur in such a sad situation, I remain—

Your obedient servant,
William Barrett

Upon reading William's letter I felt a wave of anger like nothing I had known before. This was primal fury, such as I expect a creature feels when its offspring are threatened; that I should feel the same for a father now rendered helpless and childlike by illness was not hard to understand. If Augusta had been in the same room with me at that moment, I expect I would have physically attacked her. Luckily for her, she was a whole continent away.

But not for long.

I TOLD THEM all together the same afternoon I received William's letter, as the four of us—Michael, Edna and Wish Stephenson, and I—were sitting at the round kitchen table for our end-of-day discussion. This was a ploy on my part, I admit; and it played out much as I had thought it would.

I read the letter to them in its entirety; they heard me out in complete silence, even Edna, who would ordinarily have been given to little gasps of indignation and flurries of fidgeting in response to such news. When I was done I refolded the letter and said, with my eyes cast down, seemingly intent on getting the paper folded just right:

"Of course I must go immediately. I think it best I should go alone."

Edna drew in her breath sharply, but no words came out. Not a word from Michael or Wish either, at least not immediately. Then:

"You can't—"

"Do you really think—"

Michael and Wish both spoke at the same time. I raised my eyes and looked at them in turn, but in the meantime Edna had gotten herself together. She leaned over and touched me lightly on the arm.

"Of course you gotta go, dearie," she said.

I turned my head quickly to look at her and saw that her eyes were bright with unshed tears. Such a capacity for empathy was, I admit, something I had not expected in her and it touched me deeply.

"Thank you, Edna." I placed my hand over hers. "I should have known you would be the first to understand."

"Mama," Wish said urgently, "just think what you're saying!" He glanced at me, saw how I frowned at his remark (but hopefully did not realize how calculated that frown was), then returned his attention to his mother. "If this was, well, in the usual way of things, then maybe, all right, I could agree and all."

"But what we have here is far from the usual way of things"—predictably, Michael took up the argument— "because Fremont is a long way yet from regaining her full strength and physical ability."

"He's her daddy," Edna insisted stoutly, sitting as tall as she could in her chair, her small chin thrust out, curls wobbling with the vigorousness of her defense of my position, "so she's gotta go. 'Specially on account of Fremont's got no brothers nor sisters. I'n't that right, dearie, you're the only one?"

"That's right, Edna. I'm my father's only child. He has no one else but me."

"He has a wife of his own choosing," Michael said darkly. This utterance was followed by a moment of silence in which one might have heard a pin drop.

I had known, of course, that Michael would fight me on this. Not that he didn't want me to go to Boston to be with Father, but that he would not want me to go at this particular time. He and I had become lost from each other during the incident when my legs were broken, and though Michael would deny it to this day, in some deep part of himself he'd believed me dead. Michael is of Russian ancestry, and he has that passionate temperament that on its dark side is brooding and fatalistic. Sometimes that dark side takes him over; I was watching that happen now, I could see it in his eyes.

When Michael is working out of his dark side, he is dangerous.

I straightened my spine and, like Edna, drew myself to my full seated height. "Anyone can make a mistake in choosing a mate," I said. "Father should not have to pay for it with his health, and perhaps with his life."

"You have been determined to dislike that woman from the start," Michael said, his eyes flashing and his fingers spread wide upon the tabletop as if he were readying himself to leap across it at me. "You have not given her a fair chance. Your friend, this—this Barrett fellow, he says himself he is not sure that he can fault Augusta. Most likely she was taking care of your father to the best of her ability. At any rate, now that he is in a hospital he will be well tended. You need to get your full strength back, Fremont, before you can go anywhere."

After a moment I said to Michael, "Are you finished?"

He didn't reply, merely glowered beneath his black eyebrows.

"I will take that as a yes," I said, dipping my head in a nod. "There is no point in my arguing with you, Michael; or in your arguing with me. I am going to Boston and that is that. Now, as I said a moment ago, I think it best I go alone. There is the matter of who will look after Hiram in my absence, as I cannot possibly take a cat with me. I expect, at least as long as Father is in the hospital, I will be staying in a hotel and I'm not at all sure a Boston hotel would allow a cat in the room. Michael, if you don't want to take responsibility for my cat, perhaps—"

"Oh, for God's sake, Fremont!" Michael exploded. Unable to contain himself, he popped up from the table like a jack-in-the-box. Wish drew back, and Edna's eyes went wide.

"Lord have mercy!" Edna said, crossing herself. I knew she was a good Catholic—why else would anybody give her son a name like Aloysius—but I'd never seen her do that before!

Michael targeted me with a gaze so blazing I was surprised not to be singed by it.

He thundered: "If you must go, if you cannot be persuaded to take better care of yourself, if not for your own sake then for the sake of those of us who . . . who love you"—he gestured to include the Stephensons—"then you cannot go alone. I absolutely will not allow it!"

Aha! I thought.

Edna, bless her, jumped right in. "Now you wait just a minute, Mr. Michael Archer Kossoff. Don't you go includin' me in your hoity-toity objections. I toldja right off, I'm with Fremont in this, if she wants ta go to her daddy then she should go."

"But, Mama, Michael is right," Wish said earnestly.

Wish Stephenson is the most honest man I know. Both Michael and I, when need be, can tell convenient lies, whereas Wish is uncomfortable with anything but the complete truth. His face used to reflect everything that passed through his mind, which was a great detriment in his days as a policeman; but since coming to us he has learned to guard his facial expressions. I believe, in fact, that Michael has worked with him on this point. However, when he is with people he trusts, Wish's face is as open as ever, and now the conflict he felt inside showed upon his visage.

Wish pleaded with me; as he spoke his eyes wavered, and I knew he was resisting an urge to dart glances at Michael. "You mustn't go alone, Fremont. You must have a traveling companion. Someone to look out for you on the trip, and to . . . to see to things when you've arrived."

"Nonsense. I shall be perfectly safe on the train. The culprit who caused so much trouble before cannot harm me—or the Union Pacific Railroad—again. I will have to change trains once, in Chicago, but I daresay that will not be a problem as there are plenty of redcaps to handle the luggage. And once I'm in Boston there will be any number of people I can call upon for assistance if need be. After all, I spent my whole life there until just a few years ago."

"I will go with her," Michael pronounced, in a tone of complete finality.

Edna gave a sigh of relief. "I'll look after yer cat, dearie. Best you let Michael come along."

I appeared to hesitate. To Edna I remarked aside, as if just between the two of us, "I don't know what makes him think he can decide just like that, and assume I will fall in line with his wishes."

"He's a man, that's all it takes. Besides, if he stays here he'll drive me and Wish crazy, that's a fact. We won't get a lick of work done what with him fussin' and fumin' all over the place. Best you take him with you." She nodded vigorously, the tight curls of her old-fashioned hairdo bouncing.

Now I glanced back and forth, from Michael to Wish and back again. "What about our business? At present I'm contributing nothing, so I won't be missed.

But, Michael, you haven't been putting much time into J&K lately. Wish can hardly be expected to continue to do everything all by himself."

"Don't worry about it," Wish said.

"Now you're just being stubborn," Michael pointed out.

He was right. I had what I'd wanted. The whole reason I'd brought this matter up with all of us present, and had started from a position of insisting I must go alone, was so that Michael would feel he'd won some sort of victory when I agreed he could come with me.

My ploy had probably saved me at least two hours of the particularly awful kind of disagreement that can happen between two people who know each other too well. I was, therefore, most pleased.

"I was merely trying to be prudent," I said, but weakly, as if I knew the battle was lost and I was conceding gracefully. "We do have a business to run, and it's hardly fair for you and me to keep going off and leaving Wish and Edna to run it alone."

"Now, now, we don't mind a bit," Edna said. "Do we, boy?"

"No, Mama, we don't. Of course not." Wish's honesty caught up with him again. "Well, we do like it best when you're both here"—he bit his lip and his high forehead wrinkled—"and I'd be very happy to be your traveling companion myself, Fremont, if Michael were unable to go, but—"

"But I have said I'm going with Fremont to Boston, and that is that!"

"Very well," I said demurely. "More coffee, anyone?"

LATER THAT NIGHT, when we lay in bed together, I wondered if Michael had figured out my ploy. He did seem unusually ruminative.

"There will be snow on the ground in Boston," he said, "and ice. Had you thought of that?" He was winding a strand of my stubbornly straight hair around his finger.

"Well of course there will be snow and ice, it's wintertime. I lived in New England for twenty-two years, how could I forget something like that? And your point is—?"

"My point is, if you will forgive me for making a point out of your infirmity: Considering that you have a hard enough time walking here in San Francisco, where we have no obstacles—"

"Except hills," I interrupted.

Michael pulled his expressive eyebrows together in annoyance. "All right, no obstacles other than a few steep hillsides; nevertheless I shudder to think of you trying to walk unassisted in the ice and snow."

"I do not walk unassisted. I walk with two canes. And I have improved a great deal in the past two weeks, since you told me that doctor said exercise would be good for me. He was right, by the way—as I thought you'd observed. I grow stronger each day."

"I mean, my dear Fremont"—Michael let go of the strand of hair he'd been twisting and it unraveled without a kink, just as straight as ever it had been—"you need a person to hold your arm on the icy streets. To make sure you don't fall and injure yourself again. To catch you if worse comes to worst and you lose your footing. You are an intelligent woman. Surely that would have occurred to you?"

I reached out and stroked the short hairs at the back of his neck. Yes indeed that very thing had occurred to me, but I wasn't going to admit it. I wanted him to think his coming with me was all his idea, just as I'd wanted our argument to be on the point of whether or not I was to go alone, rather than on whether or not I was to go at all.

I said, "I'm glad you're coming with me. Really, I am."

Then I kissed him, and he kissed me back, and one thing led to another as often happens in such a situation, and so we were occupied with one another for a while.

Eventually Michael turned out the light for good,

and I snuggled in the crook of his arm. My body was re-laxed, but my mind was not yet ready to let go. Nor were my thoughts anything I could share with Michael, because they were in a vague way about him. Some-thing was working its way up from deep inside me, and it was disturbing; something that suggested there might have been more truth behind my ploy than I'd intended.

This disturbing suspicion grew stronger as I lay there in the dark listening to Michael's breath lengthen into the long, regular exhalations of sleep. Grew stronger until it became a full-blown premonition: I had been more right than I knew when I'd said I should go alone—in the weeks to come, Michael would prove to be a problem or a complication, and I would wish that I had gone to Boston alone.

THREE

ONCE UPON THE train we were engulfed by winter. Living in the northern part of California where the seasons are softer, more forgiving—one hears the same of Florida, although I have never been there and so cannot say firsthand—I had gradually forgotten the hard beauty of the cold season. But I soon became reacquainted with it during the course of this cross-country train ride.

To see our country unfold before you—through mountains, over plains, through towns small and cities large—is to know the vastness of Nature and how puny by comparison are we humans who seek to tame it. The ultimate futility of such an endeavor, particularly in the wintertime, is inescapable. A humbling experience, to say the least.

On our way through the Sierra Nevada the train was delayed for a fall of snow and rocks to be cleared from the tracks—the first of several such delays over the course of the entire journey. While we were waiting there in the Sierras I thought of the Donner Party, who had become lost in the nearby place that has since been named for them, Donner Summit, and had starved to death; except for a few who had eaten the flesh of their dead companions, if the stories told were true. Those few flesh-eaters had survived but they had gone mad, all but one, who both bravely and ashamedly lived to tell the tale.

When our train was traversing the state of Utah, I felt decidedly unwell and stayed in my compartment with the shade pulled all the way down on the window. I could neither put a precise cause to this sickness nor define its symptoms, which seemed multiple and variable—one moment nausea, another weakness in the knees; at some times a headache and at others the chills. It was really most odd, even a little frightening. To stay in bed seemed best, and so when the porter came to convert my bunk back into its daytime configuration, I told him I was ill. He offered to summon a doctor, which I declined, saying I believed a day of bed rest would make me right again.

Later in the morning I said the same to Michael when he came knocking at my door. I did not leave my compartment until night fell and I could no longer see those mountains, the Wasatch and the High Uintas, out any of the train's windows. On joining Michael in the dining car that evening, I was not unduly surprised to learn that the train had left Utah for Colorado almost simultaneously with my beginning to feel better. The body remembers, I suppose, what the mind tries to forget; it was in Utah that all those things I prefer not to think about had occurred.

The next day we traveled over a great expanse of flatland, acres and acres, miles and miles of snow. It was very beautiful. We even lowered the window for a time in order to smell the clean, cold air. But then the wind shifted and we got smoke from the locomotive instead, and quickly closed the window before any sparks could fly in.

The farther east we went, the more my anticipation rose, and my heart lifted too.

"I've stayed away too long," I said to Michael as we approached Chicago, where we would be changing trains. The one we'd taken across the country to this point would continue on without us, making a southerly swing down to New York. On a different train we would follow a more northern line of tracks, skirting the edge of the Great Lakes and on across the widest part of New York State to Albany, then into Massachusetts and the Berkshire Mountains, and finally to Boston. Though I had been this way only once before, and in reverse at that, I'd traced the route on the map with my fingertip until I knew it by heart.

"You never said you wanted to return home," Michael remarked curiously, "never once in all the years I've known you. Until now."

"My *home* is in San Francisco. That is, if home is where one's heart is. Yet I must admit, I do *feel* as if I am going home." I looked deep into his eyes and my heart turned over; I was both happy and unhappy at the same time, which was more than confusing. "I've never felt quite this way before."

Michael and I were at that moment together in my compartment; he had come to carry our hand luggage in anticipation of the train's imminent arrival in the Chicago station. Sensing a degree of distress in me, he sat down for a moment and took my gloved hand.

"Fremont, I was born at Fort Ross in California and lived there until I was nineteen years old. Yet when I went to Moscow for the first time at twenty, I felt as if I were going home. And in a way, I was. There must be something inside us that makes us this way, creates these ties. Perhaps it's in our minds, or in our blood . . ."

He looked away through the small window, silent for a moment, musing. "But how could that feeling have been so strong in me, when I myself had never been in Russia at all? I do not understand it now, any more than I ever did."

"Yet it's real, is it not?" I asked, but it was not really a question.

The train had slowed. The rotation of the wheels no longer went *clickety-clack, clickety-clack,* but rather *clack . . . clack . . . clack,* each clack farther from the one previous.

"Yes, it's real," Michael said. He gave my hand a squeeze, then got to his feet and went on, looking down at me: "You're a Bostonian for many generations back, and I'm a Californian with strong Russian roots. We won't either one of us get away from that. Everyone in America is from somewhere else—"

"Except the Indians," I interjected.

"Very well, except the Indians who were here all along. Leaving them aside, the point I was about to make is that you New Englanders have been here longer than the rest of us, which I suppose accounts for a certain proprietary attitude I've noticed among Bostonians during my own travels."

The train lurched to a stop. Michael took up my small valise and his own portmanteau.

"Ah," I said lightly, "then you will understand why Boston is called the Hub of the Universe, and why a certain elderly Aunt Pembroke—she was my father's mother's sister—"

"Spare me recitations of relations," Michael complained lightly.

I went right on: "As I was saying before I was so rudely interrupted, Aunt Pembroke maintained that the Wild West begins on the other side of Framingham."

"Doubtless she would consider the entire state of California to have fallen off the globe."

"I am certain of it," I agreed, "consigned to that part of the map marked *Here there be monsters.*"

A cane in each hand, I preceded Michael out of our compartment and into the narrow corridor where others were already passing. "But then we need not be concerned, because Aunt Pembroke is long since dead."

As soon as those words were out of my mouth I wished I had not said them. Yet I had uttered the word—*dead*—and it set up a resonance, a vibration inside me that turned my spine to a column of dread.

Numbly I nodded when Michael brushed by me, saying quietly as he passed, "Let me disembark first, Fremont, and give me time to put down the bags. I want both hands free to help you."

I did not protest when he placed those strong hands under my arms and lifted me from the train's steps as if I were light as a feather. Instead of protesting I was praying silently, to the God I believe in now more than I used to, even though I haven't a clue to understanding what the true nature of this God may be: "Please let me reach Boston safely before my father dies. And if it isn't too much to ask, please let him not die but live, and be healthy once again."

BOSTON · FEBRUARY 7, 1909

FATHER KNEW THE DATE of our anticipated arrival, and so did William Barrett, but I'd told Augusta nothing, not even that we were coming. I'd taken a suite at the Parker House, as that hotel, though old, is still quite respectable and not too far from our house—generally called Pembroke Jones House as Pembrokes too lived there in the previous century—on Beacon Street.

Michael had reserved a room for himself on the same floor as my suite. We do not travel as husband and wife, nor do we live that way openly; in the eyes of the world I hope Michael and I appear to be close friends and business partners, no more. If our friends conclude we are also lovers—for I suppose we cannot conceal the fact all the time—then they must think what they will.

What Father would think . . . well, that was a bridge I would cross when I must, and not before. Father had said, when he was in San Francisco last year for my twenty-fifth birthday, that he wanted to see me married. He'd hinted broadly that he wished to examine Michael as the most likely prospect; but Michael had been, by design, away at the time.

Today, as I looked around the Boston train station for the first time in five years, gazed up at the familiar ribbing of the roof that had so often protected me along with other arriving and departing passengers, my old stubbornness hardened again in my heart. I wanted to be a single woman, a woman alone and independent. This I had wanted for as far back as I could remember. Yet now I was in love and loved. Was it fair to want to love and be loved yet still prefer my essential aloneness, and my independence?

It would be best, I knew, not to think on this subject any longer. I had never found the solution, the answer to that question; and dwelling on it tended to make me crazy.

Michael provided a welcome distraction by grumbling about our hotel reservation, and the crowded conditions in the station, and the consequent difficulty we'd most likely have in finding a taxicab, either auto or horse-drawn.

I placated him, though I supposed he had cause for grumbling, at least about our hotel rooms. Due to bad-weather delays we'd missed our anticipated arrival date by one full day. From Chicago we'd wired ahead to ask that our rooms to be held for us, but being unable to receive a reply when on board the train, we did not know if the hotel would do as we'd asked.

"I expect the hotel will honor our reservation," I said, "even if we are arriving a day late."

Michael said, "Humph."

That response is a slightly disgusted version of the same thing he means when he says, "Hmm." It neither merits nor requires a reply.

I was walking slowly along the platform toward the main station, watching my balance in the perilously crowded conditions, when over the general hubbub someone called out:

"Caroline? Caroline Jones?"

I had the oddest visceral reaction to hearing myself called by my old name for the first time in so many years: I shuddered, and the bottom dropped out of my stomach.

Yet there was an eagerness in me, too, as I searched for the owner of that masculine voice. I didn't see a recognizable face in the crowd, not a single one.

"Who is that?" asked Michael on a suspicious note.

"I don't know. I didn't ask anyone to meet us," I said quietly, scanning the thick stand of black bowler hats that surrounded us for one familiar face.

Then suddenly I saw him. And though my stomach did something peculiar again, I smiled, shifted one of my canes so that I could wave a greeting, and said aside to Michael, "It is William Barrett, the family friend who has been assisting me with Father. Unless he told people at the bank, no one else knew I was coming." Then I raised my voice and called, "Hello, William!"

I started off in his direction as he also headed toward me through the crowd, but he was in a sense swimming upstream; thus I made better progress with my canes than might have been the case otherwise. Burdened with our hand luggage, Michael still managed to stay right on my heels—and he was throwing some kind of protective mental armor around us so thick I could feel it, even if it was invisible to the eye.

"Welcome home, Caroline," William said a moment later when we converged. He snatched his hat off his head and kissed my cheek, which was how he had always greeted me for as long as I could remember; then he quickly stepped back, his face reddening. "I beg your pardon, you are a woman now, I forgot myself. I didn't mean to be overly familiar."

I smiled and murmured some words designed to put him more at ease. William Barrett had a nice face, clean-shaven and fair, with a narrow nose perhaps a trifle too long, and clear gray eyes with long, light brown lashes to match his light brown hair, which was thinning on top. He seemed not as old as I remembered him to be, which greatly surprised me. In fact, he was most likely no older than Michael.

Now it was my turn to think, but not to say: Hmm.

I roused myself to make the introduction. "William, may I present my business partner, Michael Archer Kossoff? Michael, this is William Barrett, a colleague of my father's, whom I have known for most of my life."

Michael put down the bags and he and William exchanged handshakes and greetings warily, in a way that put me rather in mind of two seals taking each other's measure at the beach. I suppose one must be grateful that in the course of our evolution human beings have lost much of our sense of smell, or else males in particular would forever be sniffing each other out, as do the rest of our animal kin.

The male inspection ritual over, William rubbed his gray-gloved hands together and said, "Well then. I have brought my automobile and will be happy to drive you to Beacon Street."

"That's very kind of you," I said quickly, before Michael could speak, "but you must drive us to School Street instead. We are staying at the Parker House. I didn't want to inconvenience Augusta."

"Oh, I see."

But by his puzzled expression I could tell that he didn't see; well, I was not going to enlighten him.

"Of course I'll be glad to take you wherever you want to go. Your, uh, partner too, naturally."

"Good of you. Appreciate it," said Michael gruffly.

We entered the station's great main hall and I took a seat in the waiting area while the two men went about the particulars of retrieving both our baggage and William's automobile. Meanwhile I was content to breathe Boston air, and to allow fragments of memories to flit through my mind. Such as the times my family had been to New York, or down to Princeton; once to Philadelphia, where we'd seen the Liberty Bell with its famous crack. Then I realized, with a jolt: All those trips had been when I was quite young, before my mother died. Father and I had never traveled alone together, anywhere.

And now most likely it was too late. I'd never be able to take a trip alone with my father, never ever. It seemed a great loss. Why had neither he nor I ever thought of it before?

Eventually Michael came back for me, and said William and the auto were waiting. As it had turned out, the automobile could not accommodate three passengers plus the luggage, so Michael had hired a man with a horse and cart to follow us to the hotel.

The air outside was so cold, it was like breathing shards of ice. I was glad to be wearing a muffler of Russian sable that Michael had insisted I take from a supply of furs handed down in his family. (The Kossoffs had made their fortune in the fur trade between Russia and California, and Michael has great stores of such furs put away in trunks lined with a certain wood that discourages moths and other ruinous critters.) In fact, as I felt my nose redden and my ears go numb, I wished I were also wearing the matching hat. Generally I detest hats and so had left it packed in my trunk during the train trip.

As was considered polite, Michael allowed me the more comfortable front passenger seat in the auto, while he himself took the back seat. I sat next to William and felt Michael staring at the backs of our heads. But I ignored him, and as soon as the auto was put-putting down the street, I asked the question uppermost in my mind.

"Have you seen Father recently, William? How is he?"

"He continues to improve."

I waited for more.

After an uncomfortably long silence, during which I could not help noticing from the corner of my eye how high the snow was piled on either side of the street, and how dingy and soiled it looked, William said in an overly solicitous tone, as one might use with a child or a very young person, "Your father will be greatly changed from what you remember, Caroline."

I blinked. Lowered my head for a moment, rubbed the cold tip of my nose with one hand. "William, Father is not the only one who has greatly changed."

Michael made some kind of sound in his throat, as if he were inhibiting a word or more. Fine, let him inhibit.

I continued, looking resolutely at William Barrett's long-nosed profile: "I wonder if you could possibly call me Fremont, not Caroline. I know it will seem odd to you at first, but I really am no longer Caroline Jones. I am not the girl you used to know, and if you will call me Fremont, then perhaps the changes in me may come as less of a surprise."

"Very well then: Fremont."

"Thank you. I assure you I'm prepared for the worst. So I ask you again, how is he? Really?"

"He is conscious most of the time. He can take nourishment. He is alive, when if he had not gone into the hospital at the time he did, Searles Cosgrove says he would almost certainly have died. So all of this is to the good, Car—I mean, Fremont."

"He knows I am arriving today, and Dr. Cosgrove knows too?"

"Yes. Your father is anxious to see you. As is Augusta."

"Augusta! But I didn't tell her I was coming! I didn't want her to know. In fact, it was crucial that she *not* know. Oh, this is terrible. I wish you hadn't told her. William, how *could* you?"

The auto had stopped at a busy corner, a significant corner where I could feel the weight of colonial history all around me, but for the moment I would neither look nor pay it any mind.

William's gray eyes met mine, and he looked wounded. "If what you mean is, how could I tell her—I didn't. I expect your father did."

"Father? Father told her? But she shouldn't be allowed to *see* him, nor to speak to him, not after the way she neglected him. Surely Dr. Cosgrove must know, he must have sense enough to see that Father's condition is Augusta's fault!"

"Fremont," said Michael darkly from the back seat, "we discussed this. How it is not wise to make accusations."

"Oh *bother* what we discussed. Really, William, Augusta should be kept away from Father."

Traffic began to move again. There were more horses than autos on the streets, and far less order to traffic procession than we usually had in San Francisco. Part of the muddle was due to the rutted, icy road surface. Animals and machines alike had problems with traction.

For a few minutes William paid close attention to his driving, but I could see he was also gaining control over himself. He was angry and it showed in the heightened color of his pale skin, and in the tightly clenched muscles of his jaw.

Finally he said, "Augusta Simmons is your father's wife. Legally she is his next of kin. It's natural enough, I suppose, that you should blame her since Leonard was so ill, so far deteriorated, in her care. But as I think I explained to you in a letter, it's impossible to say that she wasn't doing the right thing. He might, Leonard might—"

"Well, go ahead," I insisted impatiently, "whatever it is, say it."

"Leonard might have suffered less if he had been allowed to die. We may not have done him any favors by putting him into the hospital. Searles has said as much."

"Yet it was Dr. Cosgrove who ordered Father taken to the hospital, who was shocked that Augusta had not called him or any doctor in. You told me so yourself."

In the back seat, Michael cleared his throat. I glanced over my shoulder and saw him raise his eyebrows—a warning, as in: Fremont, do not go too far.

"Yes, that is so," William said. "But I believe Searles

has changed his mind about the neglect, and so have I. Your father has his wits about him most of the time now, and there is no indication that he mistrusts his wife. Far from it, he welcomes her. His eyes light up when she comes into his room, I have seen this myself."

I had seen that too, his eyes lighting up for Augusta; no question but that Father had been besotted with the woman. But he'd seemed much less so during his visit to me last April. I had to find out why. I had to know what was really going on here. And it was going to be much, much more difficult if Augusta knew of my presence in Boston. I had hoped for a few days, at least, to talk to people without her being aware—not to mention wary.

We had reached the Parker House, which looked exactly the same as it has always looked for as long as I can remember: a huge stone structure in a sort of French rococo style, with cupolas and towers and chimney pots, and the occasional arched or odd-sized window; a building that might have seemed more at home on the streets of Paris than here in the Home of the Bean and the Cod.

William stopped the auto but did not take his hands from the wheel. "You'll want to hear this from Searles, from the doctor's mouth—but given your unfounded suspicions of your father's wife, I think it best I tell you first so that you'll have more time to absorb it: Your father is dying, Caroline. Or Fremont, as you prefer. Three weeks of constant nursing care have brought improvements, but they are only temporary."

"You sound so sure of yourself," I said bitterly.

"I'm only telling you what Cosgrove has told me— much of it while you were en route and could not be reached for me to pass the information along to you."

While William and I had continued to verbally hammer at each other, the doorman had come to the edge of the curb and was waiting for some sign from us. Michael had inched forward and was perched on the edge of the back seat. Clearly it was time to move on. I took the hint.

"Thank you," I said, gathering my skirts and reaching for my canes.

"Wait," said William, holding out his hand in a palm-down gesture, "there's more, and you may as well hear it all. Later you can get Searles Cosgrove to confirm it: Leonard has a wasting disease that has affected his ability to digest food. All those with this affliction will die, it is inevitable. And so will Leonard, sooner or later. By bringing him to the hospital we were making a choice for him to die later. When you see him for yourself, you will know what I mean when I say I am not sure we did him any favors by taking him out of Augusta's care."

I was shocked, through and through. My body went numb and my ears rang. I was only dimly aware of Michael reaching around me to open the door; instead I stared at William Barrett, my supposedly good old friend, who had, I felt, betrayed my trust.

"You are saying," I said hoarsely, a sudden tightness in my throat preventing me from speech much above a whisper, "that because I contacted you, you visited my father, and then out of concern called in the family doctor, and, as a result, Father has gone through unnecessary suffering?"

"I am only saying it's possible. I'm saying you should not blame Augusta, who was doing everything she believed was best for Leonard. By not having the doctor, she thought she could shorten his time of pain."

Michael was standing by the auto's open passenger door; he had climbed out around me and was now waiting—and not patiently. The horse-drawn cart had come up behind us with our luggage, and from the corner of my eye I saw my trunk being unloaded. These things were going on but my brain was locked in some separate and coldly calculating place.

"It would be Augusta, I suppose," I said, "who convinced you of this. That my father would have suffered less if he'd never been taken to the hospital but had been allowed to die quietly at home. For his own good."

William squirmed a bit, then seeing there was no way out, he nodded. "Yes, it was Augusta, but Searles Cosgrove agreed with her. That is, he said he could not disagree."

"And if Father had been allowed to die at home, without our intervention, which resulted in his being taken into the hospital, would he have been dead by now?"

"I don't know. I suppose so, but I can't say for sure. You must ask Searles when you see him."

"Oh, you can be certain I will."

FOUR

———◆◆◆———

"Y OU FORGOT TO thank him," Michael said, turning to watch William Barrett drive away.

"No," I said, not wanting to deal with the hotel doorman and on my own steam pushing through the newfangled revolving door of the Parker House, "I didn't forget."

I was burning with . . . with something—I supposed it was hatred, or something very akin to it. All I could think was that Augusta was having her way with my father *again*. Again and again and again. Only this time, it could cost him his life.

TWO HOURS LATER, having unpacked, rested, and changed my clothes, I exited the hotel not through the revolving thing but by a more normal sort of door to one side, this one manned by a uniformed doorman with epaulettes on his shoulders dripping gold braid. He inquired if I wished transportation.

"Soon," I replied, "but I am inclined to walk a little, and take the air."

"As you wish, madam," he said, touching the brim of his cap, which sported more gold braid, and I continued on to the corner of Tremont Street. There I paused to get

my bearings. Slowly I began to *feel* my way back into
Boston.

Cold: that was my first and most predominant impression. All of Nature seemed so cold and white and
barren. I shivered, feeling the cold all the way into my
bones, from the tip of my nose down to my very toes.

Except for a few yards here and there where the side-
walks had been scraped bare—in front of the Parker
House, for example—every horizontal surface was covered with snow. The snow had packed down hard and
flat on the streets and walkways but piled up elsewhere,
in mounds of every size, from tiny ones in the crooks of
tree limbs and atop window moldings, to some formidable streetside barriers. Icicles hung from the eaves
of buildings and from the limbs of trees. As my eyes
adjusted and began to discriminate, all that snow no
longer seemed so white but took on a more realistic and
often sullied appearance.

Directly across Tremont Street from the corner
where I stood was the entrance to the Old Burying
Ground, which occupies a kind of excrescence of land
off Boston Common—that is, the area is attached but
not a part of the Common proper. There, tall skeletons
of ancient trees raised naked branches to the mottled
gray sky, guarding the old graves as they have done for
more than two hundred years. But I did not cross
Tremont Street, although I felt those trees beckon to
me; instead I crossed School Street with the intention of
paying my respects at King's Chapel.

My father has always been fond of King's; when we
attended church, which after Mother's death was not often, this was where we came. As one might surmise from
the name, King's was founded as an Anglican church,
but ever since the Revolution, they have held Unitarian-
Universalist services there. King's has a graveyard too,
and it was there I went, passing first along the portico
beneath the heavy columns of the small but substantial
church building, which is made entirely of local granite.

They had run out of space for burials here at King's

long ago, or else I supposed this might be where Father would want his bones to lie for his eternal rest—if there is such a thing. Instead he would be buried next to my mother in Mount Auburn Cemetery, across the Charles River in Cambridge. Mother—who had known for a good many months before it finally happened that she would die—had made that choice herself.

I walked back and forth among the graves, forcing myself to accept the likelihood that Father would die. The thought weighed on me. Indeed, in this place, with its tombs of John Winthrop and Paul Revere and such venerables, one felt the whole heavy weight of history. That weight is part and parcel of Boston, it was what I wanted to feel.

"Fremont, you are not in San Francisco anymore," I said softly to myself. Stating the obvious, yes, but I needed the reminder. San Francisco ways of thinking would not work for me here, nor the more open, casual manner of dealing with people. Boston was everything I'd run from four years earlier, that was true; yet this place was in my blood, my origin if no longer my home.

Surely if I remembered to draw upon the maturity that had become mine through experience during those four years I'd been away, I could do well in the difficult time I knew lay ahead of me. I might have been a child here—even here in this very graveyard where I used to come out of morbid curiosity—yet I did not have to let this city evoke in me the frustrating, helpless paralyses of childhood.

Slowly I raised my gaze from a tombstone I'd been contemplating, whose principal decoration was a skull with wings where its ears should have been, and looked toward the New State House. "New" it is called, though it was built in the 1790s or thereabout. Different from San Francisco indeed.

Across a few blocks of rooftops I could see architect Bulfinch's golden dome of the State House glowing like a beacon, making its own light in spite of the grayness of this cold afternoon. All the buildings around were

equally old and equally different from what my eyes
had become used to during the past four years. Dark
red brick and stone formed the predominant materials
here, with roofs being made of even darker slate.

In this part of Boston—even on my own street,
Beacon Street—the architectural style is most often
plain; the buildings, whether designed as places of business or family dwellings, are flat-fronted and without
ornament, save for the occasional pediment or pilaster.
Pembroke Jones House was no exception. I used to
know the name of the architect who designed the family
home, someone famous; but such things were never
very important to me and I had forgotten. The style of
architecture, that I could remember: It is called Federal.

I stood in the graveyard a few moments longer,
breathing more easily and deeply of the cold air as my
body adjusted to a changed clime, and my mind did too.
I was wearing both the fur hat and the muffler, and
leather gloves of course, though they were not lined. My
full-length, fitted coat of burgundy wool was the heavi-
est available ready-made at San Francisco's best (at least
in my opinion) department store, the City of Paris—yet I
feared it was not really warm enough for Boston. If we—
if I—stayed here very long, I would need something
warmer. And perhaps of better quality. I should have to
see what Augusta and others were wearing.

I sighed. I had to think about these things again, and
I didn't like it. Clothes and fashion and style and such
trivia can clutter up one's mind interminably once one
lets that sort of thing get started. Yet I had a purpose
here, things to prove, points to be made; and if I must
dress and act the part of my father's daughter, his only
rightful heir taking her place in society, in order to
achieve my purpose, then most assuredly I would.

Perhaps I could even convert these damnable canes
into a kind of dignified accessory, I thought as I returned to the hotel. I walked as tall and straight as possible, with an almost normal gait. If every now and then
I felt a twinge that caused a hitch in my step, I stopped

to stare at some detail of nearby scenery as if my pause
had been intentional. I was not fast but I was becoming
more and more surefooted with each passing day. The
Parker House being so near the Common and the
Public Garden, I would be able to take my daily exercise easily. A considerable bonus: There were no hills to
climb. Even Beacon Hill, which rises between Beacon
Street and the Charles River, is nothing compared to the
steepness of our San Francisco slopes.

Nor was the Charles much compared to San
Francisco Bay. I would miss my City by the Bay, but I
had work to do here, and I was about to begin it. The
things that would happen in the next few weeks might
prove to be the most important things I would ever do
in my entire life.

I SIGHED. It was extremely ungracious of me, perhaps
even rude, but I could not help it.

"Michael," I said, trying hard to keep the exasperation out of my voice, "did you even bother to read the
note I left you?"

His eyes flashed blue fire, like the hottest part of a
flame. "Yes, I read your note. But surely you don't expect me to let you go off by yourself like that! Why do
you think I came all the way across the country with
you? Go ahead, that's not a rhetorical question. Answer
me if you can."

"Shush! You are embarrassing me in front of the
doorman, not to mention the passersby." I answered his
question, if only tangentially, in a low voice: "I know
you came to be of assistance, but there are times—this
first visit to my father in the hospital being one of
them—when I absolutely must do things by myself."

Intent on his own agenda, he ignored everything I'd
just said and ranted on:

"What if you'd fallen? The doorman told me a woman
of your description—and I ask you who else could that
have been, even considering that I did not know precisely

what you would be wearing—had gone for a walk a full half hour ago. I was beside myself with worry."

"I have no sympathy for you. If you had paid attention to what I said in the note, you would be in your room, or perhaps in the hotel bar, right this very minute. All safe and sound and tranquil as a . . . a bug in a rug. A poor metaphor but the only one that comes to me at the moment."

"How can I be tranquil as bugs in rugs or whatever other ridiculous ideas may enter your head for the moment, when you're out doing unwise things that may—probably will—result in your getting hurt again?"

I moved farther along the sidewalk in the other, less traveled direction, away from Tremont Street, where there were fewer pedestrians passing to overhear this argument, which was vexing me more with every passing minute.

"Michael," I said insistently, "in the first place, I didn't get my legs broken because of anything I did, any mistake I made, or the least bit of carelessness on my part. My injuries were not my fault, any more than the broken collarbone that plagued you for quite some time was yours. You and I and many other people were victims of a violent criminal act made to look like an accident, you know that. So just stop trying to make me feel guilty."

He nodded gruffly, but didn't say a word. His eyes were still flaming blue in their depths and a nerve jumped in his cheek, evidence of—or perhaps a protest from—a tightly clenched jaw. He wore a black bowler hat pulled down almost to the black arches of his eyebrows, and his breath came out in visible puffs like smoke on the cold air.

As he did not choose to speak, I continued: "In the second place, you can just think of it this way: Have I ever complained, even once, about all the times you disappeared out of my life, just went away, sometimes for weeks and sometimes with no warning? Come on, tell me: Have I ever complained?"

He scratched one eyebrow with a black-gloved finger. "Well, no. But this is different."

"Yes, it's different all right. It's different because instead of weeks or months—which is how long you tend to be gone—I'll be away only a couple of hours. It's different because I wrote you a note explaining in some detail just exactly where I'm going, how I plan to get there, when I expect to return—things you have seldom if ever done for me. I did all that, but you still couldn't trust me, could you?"

I was getting wound up, my cheeks were hot, but I couldn't stop myself, the words came pouring out. "Oh no, you had to come down here and hang around the hotel entrance, waiting for me as if I were some recalcitrant child. Well, I'll tell you this right now, I won't have it! I'm not a child and I'm not your wife, and I'm going to do this my own way!"

"God!" he exploded. "You are the most stubborn woman!"

We stood inches apart, glaring at each other, both of us breathing hard and creating clouds of steam that rose between us like a two-headed dragon.

"Go back inside the hotel, Michael," I said after a few moments.

The tension between us broke. He took a step back. "Allow me to assist you into your carriage and see you on your way first. Please."

"That would be most kind of you."

The doorman had been properly trained for his role at a good Boston hotel: If he had been the least bit shocked by our bad manners, airing a disagreement in public, his face did not betray it. He simply summoned a horse-drawn cab for me and I was soon on my way.

THE PRIORY is an old, private hospital overlooking the Charles River, not too far from Massachusetts General Hospital. One hears the latter is becoming rather well known for medical breakthroughs.

At least, I mused as the cab bumped through the ice-rutted streets, I had not been accustomed to keep up with such things in the past, but perhaps I would be wise in the future to change that. In my present situation I would have liked very much to have acquired some base of knowledge, so that I might better understand what was happening to Father. I wished too that I had known more about the nature of my own injuries when they occurred, and what I should have expected in the healing process—what a lot of agony some knowledge might have prevented!

I sighed. As they say, there is no use crying over spilt milk. For me it was too late now. Either my legs were mending properly or they were not; there was nothing to be done except I must continue to rebuild my strength and take care to do no further damage. But perhaps it was not too late for Father. Perhaps William Barrett—that traitor—had not really known what he was talking about when he said all who suffer from what ails Father will surely die.

One can always hope.

I clung to that thought as I alighted from the cab, paid the driver, turned toward the hospital, and immediately found myself confronted by a distressingly steep flight of steps. It appeared that the main entrance of this place was on the second floor!

Surely that could not be right. Sick people cannot be expected to climb or descend so many steps—this was my reasoning, and it turned out I was right. Perhaps those steps were meant to present an impressive appearance, but fortunately they also concealed a large pair of doors right at ground level, the threshold perfectly, reassuringly flat. I entered through these doors with ease, and inquired at an information desk for the number and floor of my father's room.

"I am his daughter," I added, "Caroline Fremont Jones."

I had not told anyone, including Dr. Searles Cosgrove, that I would be visiting this afternoon, but that did not seem to matter. The sweet-faced, gray-haired woman who manned the desk smiled when I said I was Leonard Jones's daughter, and provided me with the room number and a set of thorough instructions on how to proceed.

Hospitals always seem to me like a foreign land with laws that are incomprehensible to the average person, ruled by a corps of white-coated dictators, all male, usually bearded. That these dictators are generally served by attractive handmaidens does not further endear them to me.

Also, hospitals smell peculiar.

Getting into the elevator with two of the handmaidens, otherwise known as nurses, reminded me that Priory is a Catholic institution. The nurses were nuns; I must remember to address them as "Sister." I did not think I would have any trouble remembering—their headdresses, which were shaped like wings, made it hard to forget they were not ordinary women.

As I followed two of the wing-headed creatures of this alien land off the elevator, I had a sudden, stabbingly sharp mental image of the winged skull on the tombstone in King's Chapel graveyard.

I could have done without that, I thought—mentally, as it were, shaking myself to dispel the unwelcome sight from my mind.

Yet I could not make it go away. And so it was that I approached my father's hospital room with a vision of Death, in the stark form of a skull with wings to either side of its hollow eyes, floating in the air before me.

FIVE

———◆◆◆———

I STOOD IN the open door of my father's hospital room. He appeared to be sleeping. He lay on his back with his mouth open, his breath coming in gasps that did not sound at all normal. I could hear him better than I could see him because of the light from the windows beyond, which cast his form in shadow.

It was late afternoon; ironically, the sun had chosen this time of day to escape from the sky's heavy gray cloud cover, and now blazed forth in brief glory. Father had one of the better rooms in the hospital, with two windows side by side on the far wall, overlooking the Charles River; which is to say, the windows faced northwest and thus had a view of the setting winter sun. I saw his face in profile against the sunlight, which made a nimbus of his hair—hair that had once been dark and thick but was now sparse and pale. Thus haloed, my father looked like an ungainly angel. If not for the harsh, irregular sound of his breathing I might have thought him already dead.

The Sister behind me gave a little nudge. "It's all right, you can go on in," she said.

"But he's sleeping," I whispered.

Now that skull with the wings was floating over

Father's bed. I could see it—only in my mind's eye, I knew, but still I could see it.

"Then wake him." She had a smile in her voice—I didn't have to see her face to know that smile was there. "He will want to spend every possible minute with you. I know he will, for he has talked of you often."

Her warmth gave me courage, and I entered the room. I walked around to the other side of the bed, so that I would no longer have the sun near-blinding me. I heard the Sister close the door . . . and then I was alone with my father.

I had a lump in my throat the size of China.

Oh, he was so dreadfully different from the father I had always known; different even from the greatly changed man I had last seen less than a year ago. He looked a hundred years old. No, more than that, he looked as if he were already partially in the grave. Even worse, his body bore a faint odor that seemed on the edge of decay—even though one had only to glance at him to see that he was being scrupulously cared for, his nightshirt and bed linens pristine. His skin had an alien yellow-brown cast and lay slack upon his bones, as it does with people who have once been full-fleshed but have morbidly wasted.

I moved closer and bent down, wanting to kiss his cheek, but at the last moment I found myself afraid to do so. My presence suddenly seemed an intrusion. For a few moments I felt almost as if I should leave, or as if I should not have come—this chilled me. I backed away from the bed.

I stood there horribly confused, not knowing what to do, to stay or go. But then, through the confusion came a faint glimmer of understanding: My mother had died in this lingering way. I'd been only fourteen then, and had to watch uncomprehending as slowly her life, all that remained of her existence, became focused more on something or someplace beyond, than on the room in which she lay, or with the people—my father and myself—to

whom she was so dear. I'd felt held at a distance from
Mother as she died, by some invisible force; nothing I
could do would bring her closer to me. Inexorably she'd
drifted farther and farther away until finally one day my
mother was not there at all. Her death had been a bitter
lesson.

My impulse to go away now and leave Father to his
dying was selfish—I only wanted to spare myself the
pain of that slow yet final separation. But I was not
fourteen anymore. Nor was Father dead yet. He needed
me for a while longer, and I would stay. But I did not
want to wake him, simply being in the room with him
was enough for now—so I refrained from kissing his
cheek.

Father was dreaming, or so I fancied, for his eyes
were moving back and forth behind his paper-thin eye-
lids, as if he were watching something only he could
see. What else could that be but a dream? I hoped the
dream was a good one, for it was clear that Father's life
outside of dreams was not good, not now.

Once again I silently cursed William Barrett for
planting in my mind the insidious thought that I was responsible for causing my father additional suffering.
Then I cursed Augusta Simmons for being the origin of
that idea in the first place. Who knew but what, if he'd
had proper medical attention in a hospital months ago,
he might not be in this condition now? For at least the
hundredth time I wondered how much of his illness was
Augusta's fault, and hers alone.

Father had not moved. His breath, though full of unhealthy noises such as wheezes and an occasional whistle, came at reassuringly regular intervals. I adjusted the
slats of the window blinds so that the sinking sun's light
was directed upward, where it might bounce off the
ceiling and fill the room with a mellow glow. Then I
took off my hat and muffler, hooked my canes over the
arm of a chair placed near the bed for visitors, sat
down, and began to unbutton all the buttons down the
front of my burgundy wool coat.

This took a while. When I looked up from undoing the final three buttons nearest the hem, my father had opened his eyes.

"Is it really you?" he said. "My girl has come at last?"

"Yes, Father," I said, biting my lip, which suddenly quivered uncontrollably. "I came as soon as I was able."

He opened his near arm to me, and I rose, forgetting everything except an overwhelming desire to feel that arm around me. I do not know how I got to his bed without my canes, nor do I remember what I said to him or he to me in the first overwhelming joy and pain of that meeting.

But I do remember the sunset on that February day in 1909, how brilliant was its light, how red it glowed off the ceiling and walls of my father's hospital room, like being bathed in blood.

"AUGUSTA WILL BE here soon," Father said much later, after we'd talked and I had shed a few unavoidable tears. "She generally arrives when they bring the evening meal. She'll make it her business to see that I eat. I'd far rather she didn't—" He paused to cough, a painful process obviously, which racked his thin chest and left him shaking.

"How soon do you suppose that will be?" I asked as soon as the coughing spell had passed. Glancing around the room, I did not see a clock. Nor was Father's pocket watch on the table at his bedside. I supposed he could tell the time as I had done during my own period of invalid's incarceration, by an internal clock that takes some of its cues from things like the rising and setting of the sun, and certain noises that come regularly from the world outside the doors, and eventually—when one is well enough—from cycles of hunger and sleeping.

Father said nothing for a moment. Then he turned his head on the pillow and said, "Perhaps it would be best if you were to open the door now. She could arrive at any minute. It is positively uncanny how the woman—I mean Augusta—and the Sister with the dinner tray arrive most nights simultaneously."

I got up, walked across Father's room using both canes, and opened the door. I could not help being excruciatingly aware of how closely he watched me. Indeed, at Father's insistence we had talked more about my recent calamities than about his much more serious condition.

Because I was unhappy to hear of Augusta's imminent arrival and did not want my father to see that on my face, after opening the door I went to the window and tweaked the blinds, so that I could see the river and the scattered lights of Cambridge on the other side. While doing these things I composed myself.

"You won't need those canes much longer, I think," said Father.

I turned, forcing a smile. "I hope you're right. It seems a long time I've been unable to walk the way I used to."

"Raise the blinds all the way, if you'll be so kind, daughter. And leave the curtains open. I like to look out at the night."

I did as he asked, then returned to my place in the chair once more. Previously I'd pushed it as close as possible to the bed, so that I could hold Father's hand as we talked.

"Fremont, who used to be Caroline, my daughter," Father said. I waited for him to say something more, but he didn't, only my name. His eyes shone even though the whites were clouded. I took his hand again and he placed his other hand on top of mine. His were cold and bony, but there was warmth in his shining eyes.

It was hard to look directly at him for very long. I think he knew it. He said, "I'm dying, you know."

I bit my lip and nodded my head. I wanted to protest, to deny, but somehow I could not.

"They're trying to make me well in this place, but they can't. It's too late. Even for Searles Cosgrove, who thinks he knows everything. Always has thought that ever since I've known him. Heh."

Father tried to laugh at his mild gibe, but only succeeded in coughing more. I tried to smile, with not much more success.

"Perhaps you are wrong," I said, suddenly finding my voice, along with a store of denial—or was it hope?—I had not known I possessed. "You're stronger now than when you were brought to the hospital, or so I've been told. So perhaps you will regain more strength, and then who knows what may happen!"

"I'm not wrong."

In spite of those discouraging words, Father smiled. His smile brought back so much. For a blessed, fleeting moment I could see in his face the father I'd relied on throughout my childhood, the father I'd loved so much, still loved too much to lose him.

"But you're too young to die! You're not yet sixty years old, and many people live to be much older than that."

"Dearest daughter, I don't mind. I'm going to be with your mother. But I'm glad I'll have a little time with you, at least, before I go—now that you're here. Thank you for coming. Now give me a kiss and be on your way. You'll be here again tomorrow?"

I supposed he wanted me to go back to the hotel now so as to avoid a confrontation with Augusta. I gave him the kiss and my promise to return soon, and then I left as he'd asked.

SEARLES COSGROVE kept an office in Back Bay, on Commonwealth Avenue. Somewhat in the manner of the house Michael and I shared on Divisadero Street, Dr. Cosgrove had his suite for seeing patients downstairs and his own private quarters upstairs. However, Cosgrove's house was far larger—a full three stories—

and far more impressive than the residence of Jones and
Kossoff and the offices of the J&K Agency.

"Commonwealth Avenue," Michael said as he assisted me up the few stone steps from the sidewalk to
the arched front door, "looks more like Paris than any
other place I've been. Do you suppose they planned it
that way?"

"Without doubt."

"Except perhaps for St. Petersburg"—Michael carried on with his thought as if I had not spoken—"which
would look a good deal more like Paris without its
canals."

"Paris has canals? That's the first I've ever heard
of it."

"No, St. Petersburg has canals. I must take you there
sometime, Fremont."

"To St. Petersburg or to Paris?"

I had reached the top of the steps, largely without assistance, because Michael had stopped to give all his attention to the view. I did not mind this in the least,
because now I could congratulate myself on having done
well alone. I was a little out of breath, that was all.

Flushed by this small victory I added, "I think I
should like to see both."

"Then you shall. It's hard to believe you've never
been to Europe. Your education has been sadly neglected, Fremont."

"If Mother had lived, she would have accompanied
me to Europe. Father never had time, and of course I
could not go alone."

Michael waved his arm in continuing appreciation:
"Just look at all those mansard roofs. I think a mansard
gives a handsome look to a house. But it is the use of
stone, really, that gives such a feeling of elegance. We
don't quite achieve this kind of thing in San Francisco."

"You know the story of Back Bay's development, I
suppose?" I asked, then turned and rang the bell. If we
were to be on time for my appointment, then Michael
would soon have to place some limits on his enthusiasm.

"No," he replied, "I can't say that I do. My first trip
to Boston was—hm, let me see—I believe it must have
been around fifteen years ago. I must say I never wondered about this part of the city. I suppose I assumed it
was always as it is now."

"No, Back Bay was literally that—the back end of
the bay, and none too pleasant. It was a swamp until
about fifty years ago. The Fenway is named for the Fens
in England."

I pushed the buzzer again, then tried the door and
found it unlocked. I should have thought of that—
Cosgrove would no more lock his office than we'd have
locked the offices of J&K in the daytime.

I said, "Michael, no one has answered the door but I
think we are supposed to go in." Then I gathered up my
skirts, preparing to do exactly that.

"Wait just one minute." He bounded up the steps
and tugged lightly at my elbow, an indication that he
wanted me to turn around. "What is that big place
across the street there, on the corner?"

The building he indicated was most definitely big—it
occupied fully half the block, starting at the corner
where Commonwealth meets Dartmouth Street. It was
also a strikingly handsome piece of property.

"That is the Hotel Vendome," I said, "and as you
mentioned, it is probably the most French-looking
building around these parts. Now come, we really must
go inside."

"A hotel," Michael muttered. He sounded disappointed.

"It used to be more fashionable in the last century
than it is now. I believe the Vendome has become rather
run-down. There are apartments within the hotel where
people live permanently, in addition to the usual sort of
guest rooms. I haven't been in that hotel more than once
or twice in my life. I don't remember much about it."

"Perhaps I'll take a look some afternoon when
you're doing other things."

Now *that* was an excellent idea, though I couldn't

imagine why the Vendome had so captured Michael's fancy. But never mind, if it kept him busy on his own, that could only be to the good.

I made no comment, but pushed open the door and proceeded on through, with the assumption that Michael would catch it and follow. Which was exactly what he did.

I had not wanted him to accompany me on this appointment to talk to my father's doctor, but I hadn't tried too hard to stop him, either. The truth is, although he bothers me beyond belief sometimes, Michael is an exceptionally good observer and judge of people—better than I am most of the time. We have these qualities in common; in fact you might say they are what binds us together.

I tell myself Michael is only better at these things because I'm twenty years younger than he is, and when I've been doing them as long as he has, I will be equally good at them. But alas I cannot know this for a fact, and so for the moment, as well as for the foreseeable future, I was glad enough to have him with me.

Immediately inside the door we encountered a vestibule, and another door, as is often the case in New England dwellings; the double door arrangement serves to keep the heat in and the cold out. The space between the two doors also provided a place to leave one's boots and umbrellas. Since we had neither, we went on through the second door and into the building proper.

Focused on my goal of talking to the doctor, I did not pay much attention to the marble floor in the hallway, or to the wood paneling on the walls, or the staircase that ascended on our right toward the upper floors—but Michael made up for my neglect by providing running commentary. If I hadn't known better I might have thought he'd never seen civilization before. Or that—God forbid—San Francisco was not civilized enough for him. I might have to give him a talking-to on this subject at some point, but now was not the moment.

A quick glance up the hall confirmed the likelihood of the main office being on our immediate left, so that was where I went.

Searles Cosgrove had a nurse—not a nun but the regular sort, who looked rather dull, actually, after one had become accustomed to the rather spectacular headgear of the nuns at Priory. Dressed in an unfrilly white pinafore over a dark blue gabardine dress, with a small white cap on her head that looked incongruously as if it had been folded in the manner of a child's paper boat, she sat at a reception desk with a ledger open in front of her.

"Good morning," Michael said, stepping around me and taking the lead. He removed his hat politely and continued: "My partner has an appointment with Dr. Cosgrove at ten o'clock."

Now the nurse looked up, first at Michael—she smiled; then at me—she frowned; then she looked around as if she had been expecting someone else entirely. Finally she settled on Michael, who was apparently more pleasing to her eyes. Women often have that reaction, I have found, sometimes to my amusement and sometimes to my chagrin.

"Your partner has an appointment?" she inquired.

"Miss Jones"—Michael gestured toward me with the hand that held the hat—"is my business partner. My name is Michael Kossoff."

"Oh. How do you do, I am Nurse Anna Bates. Yes, Caroline Jones, that would be Mr. Leonard Jones's daughter."

"Yes indeed," I said, wanting to contribute something to this fascinating exchange we were having. I did not correct her by saying Caroline *Fremont* Jones, but as soon as I'd let it go by I wished I had.

The nurse seemed friendlier now that she had a category in which to place me. She popped up. "I'll tell Doctor you're here. Just have a seat."

A fire burned in a fireplace against the outside wall of this rather large wood-paneled room, throwing off so much heat that it felt a bit uncomfortable when one had just come in from the cold. Once again I was in fur from the neck up, and all buttoned down in wool over the rest of me. One forgets how bothersome, not to mention heavy, all these winter accouterments can be.

I settled for sitting in the chair farthest from the fire, and removing my hat. I'd forgotten that I had not put my hair up but rather had simply pulled it back in a clasp and then piled it on top of my head beneath the hat, so I was rather startled when it came tumbling down.

"Very fetching," said Michael, smiling, as he removed his gloves one finger at a time.

"Shush," I said affectionately, smoothing the hair over my ears and refastening the clasp, which was the best I could do; it would have to suffice. By the time I'd done that, Nurse Bates had returned and indicated we were to follow her.

Back we went into the hall with the slippery marble floor, to the farthest door, which she opened without knocking. "Here's Miss Jones and Mr. Kossoff," she said, and stood back to let us enter.

"Miss Jones," said Searles Cosgrove, indicating the chairs in front of his desk with an open hand. "And Mr.—uh, again, please?"

"Kossoff, Michael Archer Kossoff." Michael offered his hand, which Cosgrove shook briefly, and then both men sat. I had already done so and was removing the fur muffler.

Cosgrove's eyes lingered speculatively on Michael, but then he turned his attention to me.

"It's nice to see you again after so many years, Caroline. I trust you don't mind my use of your given name?"

"I prefer my middle name, Fremont, Dr. Cosgrove," I said quickly. I wanted to establish my adult identity and encourage a different attitude in him from the start.

Searles Cosgrove had known me too long and too

well to give me the respect I desired—or so I feared. He had dosed me with cough syrup and other vile-tasting concoctions, had looked in my ears, up my nose, and down my throat, perhaps had even examined my little private parts back in the days when they'd been hairless—thankfully I did not remember the last, whether he had or not. But now I wanted him to forget all that.

And so for emphasis I added, "Since I left Boston four years ago, I've been known as Fremont Jones."

"I see." He frowned slightly, then turned his attention to Michael. "And you are the business partner of Miss Jones, is that correct?"

Michael had unbuttoned his long overcoat and now crossed his legs at the knee, giving a smart, sharp tug to the crease of his trousers. "That is correct."

"What sort of business, may I inquire?"

"An agency of private inquiry," Michael said, with a faint smile, "a detective agency."

Cosgrove's eyebrows went up. He said, "How extraordinary."

Ignoring all that, in an attempt to steer this encounter the way I wished it to go, I moved immediately to the matters uppermost in my mind. "I saw my father briefly yesterday afternoon."

"So I was told by the nurses when I went by to check on him this morning." He leaned back in his high-backed leather chair and commenced tapping his fists together at the knuckles in a rhythm, as if itching for a fight. A curious habit, I thought. But then as I recalled more about him, I thought perhaps not.

Searles Cosgrove had not changed much in my time away, only acquired a bit of gray at his temples. He is a small, dark, neat man, almost a miniature male—my guess would be that he is not more than five and a half feet tall. I had topped him in height by the time I was twelve. Perhaps to compensate for his stature he can be overly aggressive, sometimes to the point of obnoxiousness. Yet he is, at least by reputation, a good doctor. For

as far back as I could remember, most of the people we
knew in Back Bay and on Beacon Hill had been his patients.

"And how was Father this morning?" I inquired, determined to keep this discussion going my way.

"He seemed a bit improved over yesterday. His color
is better. Augusta told me he ate almost half his dinner
last night, and a bit of breakfast this morning. That is
an improvement, certainly."

"Augusta was there?" I felt my heart thump, but I
was determined to appear cool.

"Yes. After the first few days, when I kept your father isolated until I felt I understood his condition, she
has been there most mornings and evenings."

"I see." I did not voice any objection to her presence.

I had reasoned all this out the night before: Since Dr.
Cosgrove had already given permission for Augusta to
visit, there was no point in my insisting he change
his ruling. To insist would suggest that I questioned his
judgment, which could only alienate him. If eventually I
did have good cause to question his judgment—as I suspected might happen—by that time I would have engaged another doctor. Until then, I preferred to have
Cosgrove on my side for as long as possible.

I went on: "Doctor, if you would please tell me exactly what my father's condition is, and what we can
expect for the future, I'd be most grateful."

He left off bumping his fists together and opened a
folder on his desk, which I gathered contained Father's
medical chart. With only an occasional reference to its
pages he recapitulated what I had already heard from
William Barrett. I had not expected anything different,
but I'd had to hear it from the doctor himself.

Then at the end, Searles Cosgrove surprised me.
"Your father wants to return to Beacon Street, and I
have approved his discharge. He will be released from
the hospital tomorrow morning."

SIX

After a stunned silence I asked, "Dr. Cosgrove, are you sure it's wise for Father to return home?"

"It's what your father wants. He wants to die at home, and I don't believe he's going to improve any further by being kept in the hospital."

I couldn't meet the doctor's eyes, or Michael's. This was a completely unexpected development, another one; just as Augusta's having been told—and by my own father!—that I was in Boston had been unexpected. All my plans were going awry. I felt as if some prankster god were throwing rocks in my path.

Michael, although surely he knew the gesture was unconventional between one business partner and another, reached into my lap, where my hands were tightly clasped, and closed his hand over mine. I appreciated his gesture, but could not allow his hand to remain there so intimately. I moved my fingers restlessly under his; he understood, and the awkwardly revealing moment was over.

Dr. Cosgrove cleared his throat.

When I looked up, I saw that he was again bumping his fists together at the knuckles. He narrowed his eyes at me and said, "Caroline, what are you thinking? I've known you since you were about three years old. I suggest you just come out with it."

I shook my head from side to side, to indicate no. I couldn't trust myself to say anything yet.

"For heaven's sake, young woman, I'm your family's doctor. If you can't trust me, then whom can you trust?"

I supposed that was a very good question. My dilemma was that my family's doctor had announced his intention to discharge my father from the hospital before I could possibly find another doctor, suitably highly recommended, to give me a second opinion.

Perhaps too late I realized he might have taken the shaking of my head to indicate that I didn't trust him, rather than simply that I did not know whom to trust. I was not yet ready to burn this bridge, so to speak, and so I began to speak even though I was not prepared.

"I beg your pardon, Dr. Cosgrove," I said. My voice wobbled, so I took a deep breath and tried again. "I didn't mean to imply that I don't trust you. It's rather that I . . . I'm in a quandary."

Beside me Michael recrossed his legs. I could almost feel the intensity with which he was scrutinizing Dr. Searles Cosgrove. And then, suddenly, I knew what I had to do and how to do it: I would treat Cosgrove as if he were involved in one of our investigations. I would interrogate him. With my partner by my side during this interview, I would glean all possible information. That way, if I missed something Michael might pick up on it. Yes! Instantly I felt a thousand times better.

I sat up straighter and leaned forward in the chair.

"Dr. Cosgrove, in April of last year I saw my father face to face for the first time since I left Boston in 1905. I was shocked to see how much weight he had lost, by the pallor of his skin and, in general, how much he seemed to have aged in so short a time. I would like to know: Had Father been to see you regularly during those three years?"

Cosgrove's dark eyes flashed. Then he too sat forward. He turned some pages, going backward through the papers in Father's medical records. But he disappointed me; he didn't read aloud what he had written there. Instead he read silently, nodding to himself, then looked at me and said, "Yes, I had seen him. But in all honesty I cannot say that I saw him regularly after the first two of those three years."

"What do you mean, precisely?"

"Your father's medical records—and all medical records, in case you didn't know, young lady—are confidential. You may be his daughter, but that doesn't give you the right to pry."

So much for feeling like an adult, professional investigator!

I shot a quick glance at Michael, to find him already watching me, and I inclined my head all but imperceptibly.

He immediately picked up my subtle cue. "What Miss Jones is trying to ascertain is whether or not you treated her father in the past for this current illness, which seems—from all I can gather, I have not yet seen the man myself—to have become terminal."

"Thank you, Mr. Kossoff," I said. He had given me the respite I required, and I was able to go on forcefully. "My partner is quite right. I would appreciate an answer to that question."

Again, Cosgrove made fists of his fingers and pounded them against each other; really it was the most irritating habit. I stared at him as intently as I had ever stared at anyone in my life, as if with my eyes alone I could force him to tell me—as they say in court—the truth, the whole truth, and nothing but the truth.

Finally he said, "I treated your father for a condition he was much concerned about during the first two years of his marriage, that would be 1905 and 1906. A condition that is peculiar to males of the human species, and which I am certainly not going to discuss with a female, particularly not when the female is the patient's daughter. Nor will I discuss it with Kossoff here, no matter that he is your business partner and appears to be a gentleman."

Cosgrove paused, raised his eyebrows in a supercilious expression and added, "Although one would have to question the gentility of anyone whose business is a so-called detective agency."

Oh really? I sat straighter. My chin came up. "Dr. Cosgrove, do you want me to tell my father that you have insulted me, and my partner as well?"

Cosgrove sniffed. "Frankly, Caroline, I feel *you* have insulted *me* when you question my ability to care for a man who has been my patient over so many years."

Once again I took a deep breath in order to better control myself before replying. "In that case, I apologize. It was not my intention to insult you."

"I accept your apology."

But he couldn't very well say he hadn't intended *his* insult, could he? Because it had been very obviously deliberate. I ground my teeth together and kept silent. So did Michael, though I thought I detected a certain heat of anger radiating from him as well.

Cosgrove bowed his head briefly, which I took to be a conciliatory gesture, and said, "Perhaps we can start over."

"That would be an admirable course," Michael agreed. I had seldom heard him speak so formally. I wondered what Cosgrove would think if he were to find out that in Russia, where Michael has citizenship as well as here in the United States, Michael is an aristocrat, a duke I do believe. And then I wondered if it might be possible for me to make sure Cosgrove did find out.

On the other hand, Michael was well able to take care of himself, and I knew he would; he certainly wouldn't tolerate being taken for less than a gentleman just because of his profession.

"All right," I said. "I agree, we can start over. However, if you didn't treat my father for the illness he has presently, then . . . then I am at a loss for information."

"So was I, when your friend William Barrett called me. I was indeed shocked to find poor Leonard so sadly deteriorated. Leonard and I are of an age, did you know that? He was at Harvard when I was at Princeton. We—"

He stopped abruptly and threw his hands up in dismissal. "Ah, what does it matter? It's possible, I suppose, your father may have been unhappy with my inability to help him in that matter I mentioned."

"The one peculiar to males," I said quietly.

"Yes. And he may have gone to someone else. If so, then he is the only one who knows whom he consulted. Augusta does not know, for I have asked her. The day I examined your father at Beacon Street and ordered him brought immediately to Priory, Leonard was so badly dehydrated and malnourished that the powers of his mind had deserted him. It was no use questioning him."

"In other words," Michael said sharply, "you had to base your diagnosis of his current condition on your examination alone. You could not ask for history of the complaint, because the patient was unable to give it to you."

"I could ask his wife, and I did. What do you take me for, man?"

"Dr. Cosgrove," I intervened, making a quick decision because Michael's tone indicated he was ready to pick a verbal fight, "I believe we can save a great deal of further misunderstanding if I will simply be blunt. I realize how this is going to sound, but I am going to say it nevertheless: For me, Augusta Simmons is a problem. Perhaps even *the* problem. I believe she may have been, and may still be, poisoning my father."

To my absolute horror and complete surprise, after a moment in which he opened his eyes almost comically wide, Searles Cosgrove laughed. He threw back his

immaculately combed dark head, swiveled his chair
from side to side, and laughed.

I looked at Michael, Michael looked at me; we were
both stunned and perplexed.

Then Michael said in his darkest, most compelling
voice: "I fail to find the humor in this situation."

"You're quite right, of course." Cosgrove's laughter
stopped as abruptly as it had burst forth. "It's just that I
wondered the same thing myself, at first, and here we
three have been tiptoeing around the subject, creating a
misunderstanding to the point of trading insults."

"You, too, thought she might be poisoning Father?"
I heard a little-girlish eagerness in my tone that might
be deplorable, but I couldn't help it.

"Yes, Caroline, at first I did wonder, because your father had never before shown any signs of having a weak
gastrointestinal system. When I quizzed his wife as to
whether or not Leonard had seen another doctor since
his last visit to my office, which was—hmm, let's see
here"—he consulted the chart—"in December of 1906,
she claimed that he had indeed gone regularly to a doctor but she did not know the man's name, or where his
office was located. I asked her to look for some record,
such as a bill that had been paid, but she said your father took care of all his bills through his office at the
bank, and had continued that practice even after his retirement."

"Gladys," I murmured.

"I beg your pardon?" Cosgrove inquired.

"Nothing important. Please, go on."

"Very well. Under the circumstances, I thought it
would be best if I dropped that line of inquiry."

"Yet," Michael prompted, "you suspected poison."

"Well, yes, initially I thought perhaps arsenic, because Leonard had always been in good physical health
up to that time, at least so far as I knew, and some of
his symptoms did fit."

He hesitated, bumped his fists together a couple of

times, then seemed to come to some decision and went on: "I was somewhat influenced in my suspicions by the fact that Augusta Simmons is not—that is, she has never—well, no one in our circle knows her very well, anything of her background and so forth. However, I did not want to be unfair to the woman in so serious a matter, and once I had Leonard in the hospital for a thorough examination, I was able to rule out arsenic. Primarily through examination of skin, hair, and fingernails—there are tests that can be done, you understand, which will determine if residue of arsenic is present."

"And it was not, I take it?" Michael inquired.

"It was not."

"Might there have been something else, some other poison?" I asked.

Dr. Cosgrove shrugged. "I dropped that line of thought, because almost as soon as the Sisters of Charity—they are the religious order of nuns at Priory Hospital—began to care for your father around the clock, he showed improvement. He rallied, and since then I've been concerned with helping him maintain. At least his mind is clear most of the time now. As for his physical condition—"

Cosgrove broke off, turned his chair to one side, and gazed out of his window, deep in thought. Michael and I waited politely. When he was ready, the doctor faced us again and said, "I got to know Augusta Jones better, and that made all the difference. That woman could never poison Leonard. She adores him."

I blinked, as if that might remove the skepticism from my eyes.

Michael said, "Is that your professional opinion, or merely a personal one?"

"Both. I do not believe Leonard Jones was poisoned, by Augusta or by anyone else. I do believe his health began to fail, and because he had been, um, offended and perhaps discouraged with my treatment of that other matter I mentioned, he either did not seek medical help or went to an inferior physician with this illness he now has. I cannot say that I could have helped him myself. These diseases of the stomach and intestines often do not respond to treatment. By the time the liver is chronically affected—as you can see by his skin color it is in Leonard's case—it is too late. A slow death becomes inevitable."

On hearing those words, I felt a shudder begin somewhere down deep inside of me. It traveled up my spine, turning each vertebra to ice along its way. I gripped the arms of the chair in which I sat with both hands as hard as I could and prayed that I could keep my body outwardly still while inwardly I was experiencing my own personal earthquake.

I felt Michael glance at me even as he continued to engage Searles Cosgrove's attention, for which I was most grateful. Michael said, "So we are to understand that you're allowing Mr. Jones to return home, in essence, because there is nothing more to be done for him in the hospital."

Cosgrove nodded. "That is essentially correct."

"Yet I'm puzzled by something that appears to me a contradiction. Perhaps you can clear it up for me, Doctor." Michael paused, then went on. "Mr. Jones's health improved when he was taken from his home and brought to the hospital; now you intend to return him to his home because you say he cannot improve any further. Do you not have any concern that he will deteriorate to his former state when he is taken home again?"

"Augusta did not know how to take care of him properly before. I have instructed her, and I will stop by from time to time to see that she is following my instructions."

Aha!

My shuddering stopped. I saw an opening, a possibility, a glimmer of hope, and I plunged into it: "May I suggest a kind of compromise? I would be much happier if Father could remain at Priory, but since that is not what he wants, nor what Augusta wants, I'd feel much better if you would order, Dr. Cosgrove, a trained nurse to be on duty in his room at home twenty-four hours a day."

"An interesting suggestion," Cosgrove said. "But expensive."

"We can afford it. You know that," I said.

That is, I thought, we could have afforded it in the past, and so should we be able to still, unless something had changed dramatically without my knowledge.

"Augusta will not be pleased," Cosgrove said. "She wants to care for him herself."

I was adamant. "Augusta Simmons has been my father's wife for four years, but I have been his daughter for far longer than that. I want Father to have a nurse at his bedside when he returns home. For his care, and for my own peace of mind. You can do that for us, you have only to write the order. Will you, please, Dr. Cosgrove?"

Searles Cosgrove acquiesced, bowing his head rather more gracefully than I would have thought possible. "Very well. I will write the order."

"Thank you, Doctor," Michael and I said simultaneously.

There was little left to be said, other than a bit of inconsequential small talk. We were soon shaking hands with the doctor and saying goodbye to Nurse Bates.

For me it was a considerable relief to leave that elegant house and office on Commonwealth Avenue. We took our time, the fresh air feeling good if rather cold, as we walked to the corner. Chances of hailing a cab, either horse-drawn or motor-driven, would be better there than in the middle of the block.

Along the way Michael commented, "There was something rather remarkable about that whole thing with Cosgrove. I wonder if you noticed."

I thought for a while, and finally admitted, "Other than what we discussed, no. I don't think I noticed anything else remarkable. This whole situation is bizarre enough, I think."

"I don't disagree with your assessment. However, I still think it's remarkable that not once did your family doctor say anything, or ask a single question, about the fact that you are walking with two canes. For a doctor, I do think that is odd."

SEVEN

━━━◆◆◆━━━

THAT AFTERNOON MICHAEL accompanied me to the hospital and I introduced him to Father. It was a bittersweet experience.

Oh how much I wished I had not waited so long to bring together these two men I love most in the world! Now Michael could never know Father as he'd been when he was healthy, vigorous, and full of life. That wasted shell, that pale shadow of a man who lay in this hospital bed—surely that could not be Leonard Pembroke Jones.

Yet within minutes of my having made their introduction, Michael had engaged Father in a conversation on the subject of the monetary situation in Europe—a topic I had never heard Michael mention before, and had had no idea he knew or cared anything about. Of course Michael and I do not discuss money unless in connection with the running of the agency, so how would I have known?

Father being a banker, he warmed immediately and leapt right into a spirited discussion, seemingly unembarrassed by his occasional hesitancy and groping for words. Obviously he'd been hungry for male companionship—especially from someone who knew the world of finance, in which he'd spent most of his professional

life. Now, to see Michael satisfying my father's need
flooded me with a kind of warmth I had never felt before. It was really quite extraordinary.

Yet I did wonder once more about William Barrett,
for I'd been assuming that he was visiting Father right
along. Surely William would have filled this need?

In addition to his profession as a banker, Father
was for one or two terms an elected member of the
Massachusetts Commonwealth's legislature—which
was how he came by the honorific he seldom uses: The
Honorable Leonard Pembroke Jones. I had not had
cause to remember my father's political career for years,
but now I saw it again, however improbably, as from
his sickbed Father charmed and manipulated the unma-
nipulatable Michael Archer Kossoff.

What a curious pleasure it was for me to watch them
together! I relaxed and let this new experience warm
me, leaning back in my chair, not really part of the conversation, and not minding that a bit. Gradually my attention wandered, and I fell to thinking about what
Michael had told me earlier over lunch at our hotel.

While we were waiting for our food, I had asked
Michael if he could explain to me the "condition peculiar to males of the human species" that Dr. Cosgrove
had thought so unsuitable for my delicate, feminine
ears. Naturally enough, I had already surmised this condition must have something to do with either the sexual
act or the male genitalia.

Michael initially had difficulty answering me. This
came as a surprise since he usually doesn't mind explaining such things to me—in fact, there have been plenty of
times when he has positively enjoyed it—but this was,
apparently, quite different. He had to ruffle his hair and
clear his throat a time or two before he got started:

"I believe, given the doctor's report that your father
consulted him for this condition soon after marriage, and
persisted with the treatments—whatever they may have
been—over a period of almost two years . . . Oh, damn!"

At this inconvenient juncture, our waiter had arrived with shallow bowls of lovely, fragrantly steaming she-crab soup, and a basket of the freshly made rolls the hotel is famous for. I will admit so much mouthwatering stuff took an edge off my curiosity. Michael must have used the time to consider what he might say, because eventually he tackled the topic again, though in a somewhat backhanded manner.

"Look here, Fremont, I'm beginning to think Cosgrove may have been right. Your father's privacy should be protected. And respected, as well."

"Michael, please, you're talking to *me,* not some stranger," I said softly but urgently, giving his knee a nudge with mine beneath the table to emphasize my point. "I'm my father's daughter and his only child. No one could possibly respect him more than I do. There is certainly no need for you to hold back or to be shy about anything."

"But the man is your *father,* Fremont, and men are, well, sensitive about this particular . . . um, thing."

I studied his face, which was slightly flushed. I noted as well the presence of a little crease that has recently begun to show between his eyebrows when something troubles him.

"Granted. But still," I said, matching my low tone of voice to his, "you must agree it's important I be able to understand everything that has happened to Father in relation to his health. If you think you know what Dr. Cosgrove refuses to tell me, then you *must* do it. Truly."

His eyes, darkening as he gazed at me, were like the rings that spread after a pebble has been dropped in the water, going deeper and deeper. I felt as if he wished to see not just into my soul but rather all the way through me. The intensity of that gaze both thrilled and chilled me.

However, I was not going to let him see through me; at least, not this time. I gazed implacably back, and willed my eyes and my soul to become opaque.

I must have succeeded, because finally Michael

asked, "Do you know the meaning of the word 'impotence'?"

"Yes, of course. It means weakness, powerlessness."

"Have you ever heard the word 'impotence' applied to a male's ability, or lack thereof, to perform the sex act?"

"No," I replied.

These things might be discussed in some circles, but lately I hadn't been a member of any circle of females. My good friends Meiling Li and Frances McFadden were both so involved in their own concerns that I seldom saw them. Leaving females aside, there was only Michael with whom I might converse on such a subject.

"No," I said again, "I confess that is a subject to which I have not given much thought."

Now I *did* think about it . . . and in a few seconds I was glad I had not had these thoughts in the doctor's office. I mean, considering the mental images that came to mind. I felt my cheeks flush.

"Oh," I blurted, somewhat too loudly, then reflexively covered my mouth with one hand. I lowered my voice again: "You mean—sometimes it doesn't *work?*"

For some reason this struck Michael as funny. A sort of smirky grin spread across his face. "That's right, Fremont. Sometimes it doesn't work."

"Good heavens," I said. "How distressing."

Michael's grin faded. "An understatement."

"How perfectly awful." I really had never even considered such a thing. But then I'd never been with anyone but Michael, and he—well—he was just always *there.*

"Especially for the man," Michael said gravely.

"And for the woman too, surely," I said, then quickly lowered my eyes.

Uh-oh. That had made Augusta barge into my mind in the most unpleasant sort of way, and I wished I hadn't thought of her, or any of this.

"Not necessarily," Michael said, a statement which

rather puzzled me, but as I was preoccupied with erasing Augusta from my thoughts I let it go by. Eyes still modestly lowered, I returned to spooning up my soup, which was now only lukewarm but still delicious.

As uncomfortable as this whole topic had made me—and Michael too, I supposed—I knew it was important, and not just in and of itself. Exactly how or why, I didn't know; it was what we in the detective business call a hunch. So I filed it away for later reference.

The main course had arrived at about that time, and as we'd finished the meal Michael had gone on to explain in a matter-of-fact way the consequences of impotence for a man of Father's age, and for a marriage.

Now in Father's hospital room I watched the two of them talk—Father propped up against pillows in his hospital bed and Michael with his chair pulled close, leaning forward with his elbows on his knees. And I wondered if I was really better off knowing those consequences of impotence as Michael had detailed them:

Father, finding difficulty in satisfying himself and Augusta in the bedroom, must have gone to Searles Cosgrove for medical help. But nothing Searles had done or suggested would suffice. Poor Father—for two long years he must have struggled and tried Cosgrove's nostrums only to meet with frustration.

So eventually Father had gone elsewhere and kept his own counsel about it. What had happened then? Whatever it was, had it any bearing on what ailed Father now? Would we ever know? Was there any way to find out?

I couldn't ask Father, that much was certain. And I didn't think Michael would do it, either, because the questions would only embarrass them both. No one wanted to cause Father the least discomfort. We all wanted him to be happy for however many days he had left. Surely we all wanted that.

Even Augusta. Or so one hoped.

Suddenly I realized the conversation over the bed had taken a turn that required my attention.

Father was saying, "You will stay with us at Beacon Street, of course, Michael."

Michael glanced at me quickly, then replied before I had time to react: "I'd like that very much, sir. Thank you for the invitation."

"Separate rooms, of course," Father said.

To my utter astonishment, my father winked!

"Of course." Michael grinned.

"Well then, that's settled. Good." Father pushed back into his pillows, though his head had never really left them. As much as he'd enjoyed it, the conversation had visibly tired him.

Even so, I couldn't be letting these men decide things without so much as an inquiry into my wishes on the matter. "I seem to have missed something," I said.

"This is a fine fellow you've found yourself here, Fremont. You should marry him," Father said.

I resisted the urge to roll my eyes. Instead I simply ignored the remark and pushed on with my own agenda. Though I rather doubted I was going to get anywhere, I had to try. I had not the slightest intention of staying in our house with Augusta Simmons in charge. I had *never* wanted to be under the same roof with her; in some respects I'd gone all the way to California to avoid that very thing. So I said firmly:

"Father, Michael and I are staying at the Parker House."

"Ridiculous to spend that amount of money when there's no need. Plenty of rooms at Beacon Street, not to mention it's your home, girl. No matter whether you call yourself Caroline or Fremont, it's still your home."

I refused to show any reaction, although the words "your home" did give me a pang. Any argument with Father has always been a contest of who can stay the course longest, and so I must not let him distract me.

I heard myself say, "If we're here for an extended time, I thought we might rent a small apartment. For perhaps a month or two," though I had not thought any such thing until this very moment.

"Oh. So were you planning to get married while you're here then, just to please your dear old dad?"

I blinked. I hadn't seen that one coming. I said, "I beg your pardon?"

"You said 'an apartment,'" Father replied. "That means one for the two of you. And of course I could see why a newly married couple wouldn't want to be in the same house with a sick old fogy like me."

He winked at Michael again, and Michael winked back, as if there were some kind of silent conspiracy between them.

"Father, really"—I stretched out my hand to him, and he placed his cool, bony fingers in mine—"I hadn't thought about any of that! And I don't want to. I only thought that Augusta would not want the extra work of having me and Michael in the house. That is why I made reservations at the hotel."

Half my statement was a lie, but a kind one.

Michael raised one eyebrow, in a certain quite effective way he has of doing that. "Your father's point is well taken, Fremont," he said. "I think we should discuss it further."

Fortunately for me, at that moment Father had one of his fits of coughing. A Sister, passing in the hallway, came in and administered a glass of water as if it were medicine.

"He coughs because his mouth and throat get too dry," she said, glancing at me and Michael in turn, "particularly when he's been talking for a long time. He doesn't produce much saliva anymore."

"I'm going home tomorrow," Father said, looking up at her as she took the glass away. He had dribbled a bit of water down his chin and the nun wiped it away with a clean cloth that she took from a pocket hidden somewhere in her voluminous skirt. "I can talk as much as I want then."

"You can talk as much as you want here too, Mr.

Jones." She smiled, tucking the cloth back among her
folds. She was pretty when she smiled, with cheeks as
smooth and clear as porcelain; but how she could stand
to do a day's work in that winged hat and huge skirt
was completely beyond me.

The Sister had not quite finished with her patient and
went on to say, "But when you become uncomfortable
and start coughing, it would probably be best to rest,
don't you think? You can see your daughter and her
husband more another time."

Egad. The nun already had us married.

Michael smirked.

With the way the conversation was going, it was
high time we got out of there anyway. I took up my
canes and got to my feet.

"You're right, Sister," I said. "Father, we'll finish this
discussion later." Much, much later. If ever.

The nun smiled and gracefully slipped out of the
room, the points of her hat just barely clearing the
doorframe.

"I've already told Augusta to expect you at the
house," Father said to me pointedly. When he spoke in
that tone of voice even I could not dissuade him, and I
knew it, so I remained silent.

He said further, "I'll tell her to get that maid of hers
to make up another bedroom for Michael. Six bedrooms in the house, no point in a hotel, none whatever.
Waste of money."

Father coughed again, and this time it was Michael
who offered the water glass, with a tender care that
touched me deeply.

I sighed. Wasting money offended Father's Yankee
sense of thriftiness. Money belonged in banks, in his
philosophy; in fact, one should spend as little of it as
possible—given the demands of a certain lifestyle.

"Yes, Father," I agreed.

"That's my girl," he said. He reached up and I bent
down to kiss his cheek. For a moment, with his hand on
the nape of my neck, he held me there with his cheek

next to mine. A tear slipped from him to me and made a tiny wet spot on my temple.

"My girl," he said again, whispering into my ear.

BACK AT THE HOTEL I wrote out a note on Parker House notepaper. It was most fortunate for me that the hotel came better equipped for the niceties of genteel living than I myself did these days.

Dear Augusta, [I wrote] *as Father has told you, I am in Boston for an indefinite period of time. I have come primarily to be with him as much as possible while he recovers his health. While I don't wish to impose on you, I do want Father to be happy, and as you must know he is insisting that my partner, Michael Kossoff, and I stay at the house on Beacon Street.*

I would appreciate an opportunity to discuss this privately with you, since I recognize our presence in the house will make extra work. Father's discharge from the hospital tomorrow morning makes it urgent that we resolve this matter as soon as possible. Therefore, I would like to call on you at home tonight after supper. If you prefer to come here to the Parker House, kindly have the desk clerk phone up for me when you arrive and I will come down. We can talk over tea in the lounge.

I will ask the messenger who delivers this note to wait for your reply.

I had signed: *Yours most sincerely,* a bald-faced lie.

The reply came promptly:
Caroline, I shall be happy to receive you here at eight this evening. Augusta S. Jones.

MEN ARE PERVERSE. I daresay they are all that way, there is simply no getting around it; but there are times when I swear to you Michael Archer Kossoff must be

the most perverse of them all. He would not go with me
to speak to Augusta that evening.

"Honestly, Michael!" I stamped my foot, which I
should not have done because I felt it all the way up
past my knee, but I was so exasperated I could not help
it and almost welcomed the pain. "I cannot understand
why you won't do this for me. Why you are always insisting on coming along when I'd rather be by myself,
but refuse when I want you to come because I *don't*
want to be by myself, is completely beyond me!"

He calmly stroked the silver streaks in his beard,
which run from the corners of his mouth down past his
chin in a pleasingly symmetrical manner. "I wish to remain neutral in this matter."

"You can't," I stated unequivocally. "I need you on
my side."

"I *am* on your side, but in order to be of greatest use
to you I must remain objective. Therefore, I will not accompany you this evening. You and Augusta must come
to whatever understanding you can reach between you
in order to allow a reasonably peaceful sharing of space
in the house. You know you must, for your father's
sake. As for me, your father has extended his invitation,
I have accepted, and that is sufficient."

"I hate it when you sound so reasonable about
things that are inherently maddening."

"Fremont, come here. Please." He held out his hand.
He sat on a small sofa in the sitting room of my two-
room suite. I had been pacing back and forth because I
could not sit still; I told myself it was a useful form of
exercise.

I sighed and went to him.

One by one Michael took the canes from me and laid
them on the floor. He put his arm around me and drew
me close.

"Your body is taut as a bedspring," he said.

I hunched my shoulders. I could not think of any re-
joinder since it was true, my muscles and nerves and
everything felt stretched to the breaking point.

He placed his fingers under my chin and turned my face to his. Softly he said, "Forget Augusta for now. It's two whole hours before you must deal with her. Let us talk about something else, something much more pleasant."

"Such as?"

He kissed me, a soft and lingering kiss of the sort it is impossible to resist, the sort of kiss that has one's lips parting, wanting more, no matter what one's mind says.

"Such as your father's wish to see us married."

Before I could react, while the softness of his kiss and the wanting more were still upon me, Michael's lips came over mine again, this time offering the taste of his tongue . . . and I was lost in him.

EIGHT

P EMBROKE JONES HOUSE is on Beacon between
Charles and Arlington streets, directly across from
the Public Garden. The house was built in the previous century, sometime prior to 1850; just as I had not
been able to recall the name of the architect, I also
couldn't remember the exact date of its construction.
Perhaps it was time I learned both these things. I wondered if they were recorded somewhere for posterity or
if I would have to confess my ignorance to Father—
more evidence of my shocking lack of concern for
things most Bostonians of our ilk are supposed to hold
sacred.

The facade of the house is brick and stone and has
remained unaltered all its many years, save for a few ne-
cessities such as replacement of the outside shutters.
Like all the others along the old stretch of Beacon Street
from Arlington up past the State House (that's as op-
posed to the new part of Beacon on down through Back
Bay), these houses in our block were built flush to the
sidewalk with no front yard or even a strip of grassy
verge to call their own. Nor do they have much space in
back, though ours has a tiny walled garden where one
may sit out in summer. The builders must have assumed

that anyone desirous of outdoor activity would go across the street to the Public Garden. Why then waste valuable lot space that could be used to enclose more rooms?

The house does have many rooms, on three full floors plus a top floor of tiny rooms with low ceilings and dormer windows that stick up through the sloping slate roof. There is also a basement scarcely worth mention, as it has never been much more than a stony hole in the ground.

The driver of the hansom cab had assisted me out of his vehicle and I'd paid and tipped him handsomely, with the promise of more to come if he would return for me in an hour. Now I stood on the sidewalk gathering my composure and contemplating this place where I and so many generations of my paternal family had lived the majority of our lives.

I had to admit it was rather imposing. In part this was due to the cumulative effect of so many tall houses taken altogether, their appearance similar yet not identical, each as large and handsome as the ones on either side, and all bathed in the mellow glow of evening's gas lamps. These old Federal-style houses were plain when compared to the Victorians and Edwardians of San Francisco; yet they seemed somehow both more substantial and more elegant. Beacon Street commanded respect—even from me, though I had never thought or felt this way before.

I slowly climbed the seven steps from the sidewalk to the front door and rang the bell. Lights glowed behind the drapes of the first-floor windows, but the upper floors were all dark. My heart began to beat faster as I stood there waiting to be admitted to the place where in the years of childhood my little feet had once run freely in and out.

The woman in servant's dress who answered the door was completely unknown to me, and I to her. But apparently I was expected and she was well trained, because she did the little dip that passes for a curtsy these days and said, "Evening, Miss Jones, please come in."

"Fremont Jones to see Augusta Simmons Jones," I said, perhaps unnecessarily. But I wanted the maid to announce my arrival to Augusta as Fremont, not as Caroline.

"May I help you with your coat and all, miss?"

I acquiesced to this offer, and while divesting myself of all the layers of outdoor wrappings, I remarked, "Your employer is my father. I grew up in this house. Did Augusta—Mrs. Jones—tell you that?"

"No, miss. Only that you'd be Miss Jones and you was expected."

"I see." Well, that was a place to start at least.

Propriety notwithstanding, I had always been inclined to talk freely with the servants, mine and other people's, because, for one thing, they are people too and deserve to be treated as such, and, for another, because they generally know much more about what is going on in any house than anyone else. But in this instance, with a maid handpicked by Augusta, I must remember to be wary.

"How long have you worked here, may I ask?"

At closer range she was even younger than she had appeared when she first opened the door. Her skin was so fair that it bordered on the unhealthy, a bluish-white like skim milk. But her fingers were red, especially around the knuckles; Augusta was working this girl hard.

"Few months, miss," she replied, her pale eyes flickering as she counted up in her head, "going on five, I reckon. Would you like me to undo your coat buttons?"

"No, thank you, I can manage. What is your name?"

"Mary."

"And do you have a last name, Mary?" I asked gently, with a smile.

"Mary Fowey."

Mary Fowey could scarcely stand still while she waited for me to undo the buttons all down the front of my coat. I was deliberately taking my time, not to torture poor Mary, but because Augusta had not seen fit to come into the hall and welcome me properly, with the warmth due a family member—or even a close friend. She should not have left me for her maid to handle like any old evening caller. I tried not to mind, for after all, I no more wanted to be there than Augusta wanted me, but still it did sting.

"Well, Mary," I said as I finished undoing the last few buttons, "perhaps you can tell me if Ralph and Myra Porter are still working here?"

Ralph and Myra between them had looked after this house inside and out for more than twenty years, and they had been very much in residence when I'd left for San Francisco four years earlier. They lived not in those little dormer rooms on the top floor but in their own suite of rooms on the third floor, convenient to the back stairs; my mother was the one who had made this change, declaring it was senseless for Ralph and Myra to squeeze themselves into those tiny rooms on the top floor when the whole rest of the house was occupied by only three people. I'd unthinkingly assumed the devoted servant couple would be there forever—or at least until they died. This house had always been their home as much as it was home to me and Mother and Father.

Mary ducked behind me to take my coat as it slipped off my shoulders. Her hands trembled, and were so cold I felt their chill through the fabric of my dress when she touched me briefly.

"No, Miss Jones," she said. "There's never been anybody here by that name since I come. Nobody here but me takin' care of the missus."

"I'll need my canes," I said quickly, as she was about to store them in the umbrella stand. "I'm sorry to hear about the Porters. They were here for a long time—and I expect sometimes you must wish you had some help."

At this Mary's eyes widened. "Anything you say, miss," she blurted, and then scurried off down the hall. She was several steps along before she thought to turn

and say, "Mrs. Jones is in the library. If you'll just follow me."

Interesting, only the one girl for this big house. No
wonder her hands were red. Even given that recently
Augusta had been the only person living here, it was
still a lot of work for one maid. I imagined she would
just get through the rooms in a week and then have to
start all over again the next, which must be grueling for
her. Not to mention the cooking and laundry.

Well, there was going to be much more work starting
tomorrow. I wondered if Augusta had thought of that.
If she'd even told Mary.

I walked down the hall to the library at a steady
pace, slowly accustoming myself to the formerly familiar surroundings. Perhaps it was only my imagination,
but the house *felt* different.

The doors into the drawing room and dining room
were closed, which made the hallway excessively dark.
Of course the wainscoting and the doorframes were of
dark wood, but the walls were cream plaster, and if
those doors had been open the hallway would have
been brighter, more welcoming. But that was not it entirely; there was a darkness here that had nothing to do
with mere absence of light. Or with the fact that I could
be virtually certain Augusta had taken no pains to cre-
ate a welcoming atmosphere, because she did not wish
to welcome me.

As Mary and I passed the tall-case clock in mid-hall I
noticed it stood silent; I hoped it was not broken, but
had been left unwound. I loved that clock, its face with
the Roman numerals and pastel-painted faces of the sun
and moon. What kind of person does not bother to
wind a clock?

Aha, I might know the answer to that: a very nervous person, whose nerves are aggravated by the constant ticking and by the pendulum's unrelenting swing;
a person for whom the passage of time somehow has
more import than merely the counting of the hours.
Was this more imaginative speculation? Perhaps; on the

other hand it could be my detective's brain working—a part of myself that had always stood me in good stead.

One door remained on our left. It was open; light and warmth poured out. Mary stopped in her tracks right in front of me, so abruptly that had I been walking more quickly I would have bumped into her. She turned around, an appalled expression on her face, and whispered, "I'm so sorry, miss! I forgot that other name you told me."

"Fremont," I whispered back, "Fremont Jones." I felt like saying not to worry, she would do fine, but somehow it didn't seem my place to be giving encouragement. Instead I paid attention to my own posture, stretching my spine tall and straight, shoulders well back, lifting my chin.

Mary went through the library door. She stood properly to one side and announced, "Miss Fremont Jones to see you, Mrs. Jones."

Augusta Simmons Jones received me from her seat in a chair by the fire. She did rise to greet me. She did not so much as extend her hand.

So this was how it would be: I'd get no respect as the daughter of this house, not unless my father were present looking on. From the corner of my eye I saw little Mary flee and I couldn't blame her.

Augusta looked me up and down, her head tilted a bit to one side as if I were an item being appraised, and she was dubious about the purchase. Abruptly she said:

"So you're insisting on that, are you? Fremont Jones. Well, I suppose it suits you better than Caroline, which after all is a very feminine name."

Not hello, how are you, how nice to know you survived that terrible experience, and oh yes, I'm so glad you came all the way across the country to see your father, that's a fine thing for a daughter to do. None of that, oh no.

With such a beginning, I certainly wouldn't wait to be invited to sit. I chose the wing chair on the other side of the fireplace, where I too could enjoy the warmth.

She hadn't greeted me properly, so I did not greet her at all. Nor did I look at her as I walked over and sat down, automatically careful of the Turkish prayer rug in front of the hearth, as it was inclined to slip.

When I felt entirely settled and ready I topped Augusta's ungracious remark with one of my own, couched in the polite tones of casual conversation:

"This has been my favorite room in the house since Mother died."

"It's your father's favorite," Augusta responded. "It's more Leonard's room than any other in the house, which is why I spend so much time here. I feel closest to him in this room."

Touché.

She had not changed the library much; I was glad of that. Of course it is rather hard to change a room whose walls are all books, and whose chairs are made of leather. Its principal floor covering was the same large, gently worn, rose-colored Persian rug patterned with thousands of fantastical, faded flowers and vines I used to trace with a finger, back when I was little enough to get away with sitting on the floor.

"Sherry?" Augusta asked.

"Please."

She did not have to get up from her chair to pour. She had the decanter and glasses on the leather-topped drum table by her elbow. Also on the drum table was an item that was new, quite lovely, and I imagined had been expensive: one of Tiffany's lamps. The shade looked as if it had been made of giant, translucent moths' wings.

Here, in spite of Augusta's presence, there was less of the oppressive atmosphere I'd felt in the hall. I relaxed a bit but did not let down my guard; in the months before Father's marriage to her I'd learned it was never a good idea to let down one's guard with Augusta. She was quite a different woman when Father was not around— something I'd once tried to tell him, but of course he would not listen to me, and how can such a thing be proved?

She handed me a small crystal glass of sherry. Our eyes met, and she was the one who first looked away.

I tried to see her through Michael's eyes, both because he was bound to be more objective, and because he is a man and so is Father. In four years Augusta Simmons, as was, had if anything grown younger-looking and more sure of herself. She was fashionably full-figured, wasp-waisted, well corseted, and not too tall. She wore her white-streaked brown hair up in a fashionable pouf, and her gray dress, with its many pleats and tucks and lace collar, was of better quality than the dresses she used to wear. For some people these things come with having money; however it is perfectly true that for some other people having money does not impart better looks or taste, so I supposed Augusta deserved credit there. She had turned herself into a wife Father could, at least outwardly, be proud of.

All right, but she still had mean eyes. Hard eyes, no depth to them, like brown pebbles. I made a mental note to ask Michael to look into Augusta's eyes and tell me what he saw there.

"I suppose you aren't going to forgive me for keeping those telegrams from your father," Augusta said, getting right to the heart of the matter.

I gave her credit for that, too. When I returned to the hotel I wanted to be able to tell Michael I'd been fair. Whether he believed me or not.

"An explanation would help," I said, thinking of the explanation she'd given William Barrett.

She gave the same one to me, but in a longer version: "Leonard believed you had died in that train wreck. We didn't know any different, regardless what that man of yours—Archer, Kossoff, whatever his name is—regardless what he said, on account of he didn't know anything for certain either, he was just whistling in the wind. It was weeks later when your first telegram came, and by then Leonard was in real bad shape, not in his right mind most of the time. It seemed best just to let him keep on thinking you were dead. Didn't seem like he could possibly live long enough to get to see you again, anyway. So why get his hopes up?" Augusta tipped up her sherry glass and almost drained it with one sip.

Perhaps she was more nervous than I'd thought. Perhaps even more nervous than I; I felt quite calm now, as I often do once some process I have dreaded is underway at last. I would always rather be doing something, even if it is unpleasant or dangerous, than to sit around thinking about it.

"Some people might say one reason to get his hopes up is that with reason to hope, sometimes a sick person gets well. A dying person lives longer."

"Hah. Not likely. It's more likely to mean a cruel disappointment." She tossed off the remainder of the sherry in her glass. Her veneer of gentility was cracking. I had always seemed to have that effect on her.

"I'm here now and the truth has been made known by my own devices. Father has not been disappointed," I pointed out, "you were wrong."

"You weren't here *then,* you didn't see what he was like. You ran off and broke his heart, young lady. Now you think you can come back and everything's fine, just like that?"

Snap. Augusta snapped her fingers, the sound sharp and startling.

I didn't flinch or blink or move a muscle. "I could not stay here and be married off, especially to your nephew. You need not pretend, Augusta, that you were sorry to have me out of the way."

"Oh, you'd have been out of the way anyhow, only it would've been *my way.* And at least you'd have been respectably married instead of . . . of whatever that is you think you're doing with some man twice your age. Oh, I heard all about it from your indulgent father, you can be sure."

She nodded her head a bit too vigorously and in her

rising temper the woman I thought of as the real Augusta—the one I knew but Father did not—began to come out.

"My personal life is none of your concern."

"It is if you're going to be living under my roof."

"I find it difficult to think of this"—I glanced quickly up toward the ceiling—"as *your* roof, when in total number of years I have lived in this house far longer than you. Longer indeed than you have even known Father."

Her temper was rising still; bright red blotches appeared on her cheeks. She put down the empty sherry glass and dug her fingernails into the upholstery of the chair's arms like claws—as if to stop herself from leaping up and clawing at me.

Which in fact, knowing Augusta, she might actually be doing. Stopping herself, that is; more than once, in regard to my refusal to consider marrying her nephew and other matters of my unorthodox conduct, she had raised a hand to "slap some sense" into me. But she had never done it—I think because I would immediately have gone to Father, and if my skin had borne the mark of her hand, neither she nor I knew what steps he would have taken.

I sipped sherry and decided it might be best to defuse this situation. "If I may change the subject: What has happened to the tall-case clock in the hall? Is it broken?"

"No!" She realized she'd spoken too loudly and lowered her voice. "No. I stopped the pendulum. I do not like loudly ticking clocks, I find the noise irritating."

"Father finds it soothing, and so do I." It was as if I could not help myself; the words that would most irritate Augusta slipped out before my mind could stop my tongue.

I would do well to finish with the things that must be said and leave as quickly as possible, even if that meant I had to stand outside in the cold and wait out the rest of the hour for my cab to return.

Augusta said, "I'll start the clock before he comes home tomorrow."

"We need to talk about that."

"I don't see why. You got what you wanted, didn't you, Fremont? First you got friends of yours to take your poor father to that hospital, where they couldn't save him anyway, and now you've got yourself and that man of yours moving right into my house, right under my feet. And as if that wasn't enough you've got Searles Cosgrove insisting we have a nurse right here in the house, not just one nurse but two of them so's they can take turns. It's a waste of money, invasion of privacy, it's—it's—"

"It's what Father wants," I broke in, my words sounding firm even though as to the last point, the nurses, I had no idea what Father really wanted.

"He also wants you to marry that man, that Kossoff," Augusta said in an evilly insinuating tone. "Leonard told me so himself, just tonight when I was there to keep him company at his supper. So, Miss Independence, Miss I-Will-Never-Marry, if you're so anxious to see your father have exactly what he wants, what do you plan to do about that?"

She had at last hit her mark. My face grew hot. "As I said before, my personal life is not your concern."

"And I'm telling you, it is. We're all tangled up in this together, you and me, whether we like it or not."

I supposed that was true. "For Father's sake," I said.

"You can bet your life on it."

As Father once bet his on this woman, and was now losing the bet, I thought. But once more I heard words come out of my mouth before my mind had a chance to examine and possibly suppress them: "Father will have everything, everything to encourage him to live and be well, no matter how many have died of this illness before him. Michael and I are to be married here in Boston. You may offer me your felicitations, Augusta, since you are the first to know."

NINE

—◆◆◆—

AS IT HAPPENED, Michael did not move into the house on Beacon Street after all. We decided in concert (remarkably enough, which no doubt bodes well for the future) to observe an appearance of impeccable propriety in the weeks before our wedding. Therefore, Michael remained at the Parker House, from which he planned to seek out a suitable apartment for short-term rental where we both might live for our remaining time in Boston, once the Deed—i.e., the marriage—Was Done.

I gave Father and Augusta and the nurses a day to get settled before I joined them. During that day—which Michael and I spent alone together, exploring the Common and the Public Garden in the morning and in the afternoon doing other things that generally are not mentioned in polite society—we also went to the jeweler Shreve, Crump & Low. There he bought for me an item I never thought to possess: a ring to signify our engagement.

In the store Michael asked me to choose my own ring, but I could not; in fact, I said customs like engagement and wedding rings seemed to me not too far a step away from being branded, and one does not expect the cow to participate in the heating of the brand. However, he is used to my quibbles, not to mention my foibles, and so he paid me no mind and picked the ring himself.

It is quite the loveliest piece of jewelry I have ever owned: a square-cut emerald, rather large, a clear medium green in color. To match my eyes, Michael said, but he is wrong about that, because my eyes are a lighter green tinged with gray. The gemstone is set down into a bezel of chased gold, rather than up on prongs with an openwork gallery beneath, as is currently the fashion for so many gems, especially diamonds. Those tall rings are forever catching on things, which can be irritating. My emerald is both elegant and practical because it is fairly flat, therefore I can enjoy wearing it all the time.

Having been lulled into a sense of security by Michael's excellent choice of an engagement ring, I threw caution to the winds and said I would trust him to choose my wedding band on his own; not only that, but I didn't even want to see it until the moment he put it on my finger. Which brought to mind the fact that we must set a date for the wedding.

We chose Saturday, the twenty-seventh of March, with the hope that in the intervening weeks Father might regain enough strength to join us for the ceremony. I thought this might provide an incentive for him. Certainly there is no more self-fulfilling prophecy than an attitude of despair, and my father had been subjected to quite enough of that already.

I did not want to make our wedding a public spectacle, but I did rather want Edna and Wish Stephenson to be there, and my friend Meiling Li. But if I invited them, then Father would think it peculiar if I did not invite some from my old circle of Boston friends as well, and then the first thing you know, their parents would have to be invited, and so on and so on, and the spectacle I did not want would be upon us. So Michael and I decided, once again with remarkably little discussion and no disagreement, to have a quiet wedding with only Father and Augusta as witnesses.

As to where and by whom we would be married, that was to be discussed with Father. I wanted him to decide both the place and the person to marry us; this was surely best, since I knew nothing of ministers and churches—not to mention that I was doing this for him. Always in the back of my mind there was the thought that, if need be, if Father's health took another downward turn, Michael and I could always be married on short notice in the parlor at Beacon Street.

Of course, I would never tell Michael I was marrying him only to make my father happy—and sometimes, in the heat of this or that moment of excitement, I forgot it myself.

AUGUSTA SHOWED SOME SENSE and hired a cook. Otherwise Mary Fowey had to manage on her own, because Augusta did no work around the house that I could see. What she did all day I had no idea; I stayed out of her way and she stayed out of mine. We encountered each other occasionally in Father's room, where we seemed to have worked out an unspoken agreement that whichever one of us was present would leave when the other arrived. Generally Augusta and I had to be together only in the dining room for the evening meal, which was tolerable because Michael would be there too, and in his presence she was invariably at her most charming.

All in all, living under the same roof as Augusta was working out better than I'd expected. She had not made major changes to the furnishings of the house, only in minor things such as a new china pattern, and an unfortunate tendency to clutter up the tops of things with insipid porcelain figurines of Germanic origin.

Because I found myself rather often at loose ends, I helped Mary Fowey in her work when I thought I could get away with it. She'd been so shocked at first that I'd had to persuade her I was only following the example of my own mother, which was true. Mother had liked to (using her own quaint expression) "turn a hand at housework" now and again. She'd been especially fond of trying new recipes, then teaching them to Myra, who probably would have preferred she stay out of the kitchen in the first place.

While I'd inherited none of my mother's culinary talents, I was far from helpless around the house; and in San Francisco I had not had help, so I was accustomed to doing things myself. Here at Beacon Street, regardless of what my habits might have been when I was the daughter of the house, I now made my own bed daily, took care of my clothes, and took a turn at dusting—once I'd found where Mary kept the dusting cloths. And I might casually wander back to the drying room just at the time when there was laundry to be taken down and folded, and so on, as various occasions presented themselves. Once she saw that I was really working too, not just trying to catch her in a mistake, Mary and I became friendly. At least, probably as friendly as it was possible to be with her, since Mary was by nature both shy and reticent.

It would have been nice if I'd been able to find a way to be friendly with Father's nurses, but I could not. Their names were Martha Henderson, who worked in the daylight hours, and Sarah Kirk, who came at night. These two paragons of rectitude and strict routine had been chosen by Searles Cosgrove's Nurse Bates—chosen for their nursing skills, which were considerable, not their social skills, which were none.

Augusta had been bound to hate the nurses no matter what, but in a way, after dealing with them myself I could hardly blame her. A nurse was always in the room when one went to see Father, day or night. After a while one came to regard her as a piece of the furniture—a strangely shaped chair with book-holding attachment, perhaps, or a floor lamp in the configuration of a woman reading a book—for both these women, when they were not fussing over Father, were constantly reading. They did not converse at all with any of us, and very little with their patient that I ever heard.

Nevertheless Father thrived in their care, and that was what was most important. In fact it was rather dramatic how much he improved. His color went from that unhealthy yellowish shade to something much nearer a normal flesh tone, though still with a slight yellow tinge; the whites of his eyes became clearer; his appetite improved, and he began to put on weight.

By way of explanation for this upturn, Searles Cosgrove said the human liver has an ability to heal itself. Although he'd thought Father's illness too far advanced for that, and had believed Father's organs were failing in a way that is always fatal, perhaps (the doctor modestly conceded) he had been wrong. Perhaps (he said) the liver was beginning to do its job, which is somehow regulatory.

I confess I did not entirely understand. This was not due to any willful ignorance on my part, but rather to Dr. Cosgrove's inability to explain the function of the liver in general or the exact nature of my father's illness in particular.

At any rate the most important point was that by the third week after returning to Beacon Street from the hospital, my father had made so much positive progress that no one was thinking he'd come home to die. Rather we had firm plans for my wedding on March 27 at King's Chapel. The ceremony was to be performed by a Unitarian minister of my father's acquaintance, whom I had not yet met. I kept putting it off; the thought of meeting the minister made me curiously uneasy.

I did, however, meet with the dressmaker for my wedding dress. I chose a two-piece pattern, a suit of very simple lines, with a long fitted jacket over a moderately full skirt with a bit of a train. The fabric was ivory brocade. In the matter of a veil I demurred, and on a hat too—though eventually I would have to decide on one or the other. I rather dreaded it, as I have an aversion to all manner of head coverings.

The one and only fly in the ointment, so to speak, was that Michael had not yet found a suitable apartment available for a three months' rental—which was the maximum length of time we could stay in Boston after the wedding, given our ongoing business obligations in San Francisco. Meanwhile he was indulging his fascination with the Vendome on Commonwealth Avenue, and had moved from the Parker House to a suite there.

I was teasing him about this one evening. We had just left Father's room and were on our way downstairs for dinner. Michael had tucked my left arm tightly beneath his, in a particular way that places his arm equally tight against my breast; I think he thinks I don't notice, which is rather endearing, but of course I do. This sort of surreptitious physical contact is one of life's little thrills. That evening I regarded it as a small reward for my recent graduation to the use of only one cane when I am indoors. When outdoors I still use two.

I said, "I wonder if the Vendome is a nest of spies. It has that still-elegant-yet-past-its-prime sort of European look, as befits a place of espionage. Is that the attraction? Do you feel at home there?"

Michael chuckled. "Clever woman. You've found me out."

"No, really, what is it that attracts you?"

He lowered his head and nuzzled my temple. "You do," he said in a voice so low and thrilling only I could hear him.

"And you me," I replied, feeling it all the way to my toes, "but still I really would like to know what it is about the Vendome. The place is not at all fashionable these days."

"Really, it is something like that. You are not so far off the mark. And besides, neither of us is a slave to fashion."

We descended the stairs very slowly, Michael carefully matching his steps to mine and taking part of my weight on his arm.

I frowned, thinking of Michael's determination to get out of the spying game. The problem with his extricating himself has been that neither country, Russia nor the United States, wants to let him go. In a way the United States is more problematic about this, because our country *says* he is no longer under any obligation, yet *still* they'll call him back "just one more time." The Czar of Russia has been much more straightforward, simply saying, "No, you have a hereditary title in this country and an obligation that goes with it, and that is that"—or words to that effect. At least in the Russian way one knows where one stands.

So I said, "Please stop being so cagey and tell me straight out what you mean."

"It's nostalgia, that's all, nothing important. That building reminds me of a place I lived in in St. Petersburg for a winter, long ago. I'm indulging myself—shall we say—in a last fling of bachelorish memories."

"*Katya*?" I whispered.

Michael squeezed my arm in a way that was meant to be reassuring but almost pulled me off balance. "Yes, in part I've been thinking of her. But it's more just what I said, simple nostalgia for the past. The snow, the cold air, the Vendome's ambience both inside and out—these are all things we don't have anywhere on the West Coast, and I'm enjoying the difference. It reminds me of Russia. That's all."

We reached the bottom of the stairs and Michael released my arm. He took my hand instead.

"That makes a certain amount of sense," I said. "If you find it is not entirely unsuitable, I suppose we could both live there after the wedding. As you said, neither of us is a slave to fashion. Certainly the location is convenient."

"Yes, and Back Bay is crowded. Rental properties are scarce, the landlords are taking full advantage."

I had told Michael I preferred Back Bay if there were nothing on Beacon Hill. As we reached the door to the drawing room I simply nodded my recognition of what he'd said.

Augusta was already seated on a sofa at right angles to the door, talking animatedly to someone I couldn't see. I hadn't known we were expecting anyone; in fact, I'd been somewhat dismayed by the fact that none of our old family friends had come to the house to visit—though of course I had not remarked on this to her. I was trying my best to keep peace, but I did wonder.

Tonight Augusta had almost outdone herself—she looked extremely fetching in a rose-colored dress with a wide collar of white lace. A three-strand choker of pearls clasped her neck, and her hair had been artfully arranged so that a couple of curls fell just so, down her nape, accentuating both the gleam of pearls and the line of her throat.

I glanced at Michael and caught the beginning of a smile on his face. Yes, there was no question Augusta knew how to handle men. I supposed if I wanted to learn a trick or two I should pay more attention to her. I might as well. One never knows when free lessons will come in handy.

I tapped my cane against the side of the door as if I had bumped it, my intention being to warn her of our approach. I wanted to see if she would stop her conversation abruptly or keep on talking while we entered the room, as most people would.

She heard me. She stopped talking immediately, turned her head, saw Michael, and not only smiled but popped up and came quickly toward us. The rose-colored dress rustled softly as she moved; at closer range its material proved to be silk faille. Very nice. I would not have minded owning such a dress myself.

"I'm so glad you've come down at last," Augusta said effusively, taking Michael's arm, which had the effect of separating him from me. Then with only the smallest hesitation, she stretched up on tiptoes—I am two or three inches taller—to place her cheek next to mine in familial fashion. That was something she had never done before, so I guessed it was for the benefit of the person watching, on whom I still had not laid eyes. She was standing in the way.

"There's someone here I've been so anxious for you to meet," she said, pulling Michael farther along and leaving me to follow.

This person Augusta was anxious for us to meet proved to be a young man, in his early twenties I guessed. As we approached he slowly, as if acquiescing to an inconvenience, obeyed the demands of good manners and stood. He was not long enough out of adolescence to have gained the easy command of his body more mature men possess. Yet he did not have the look of a college boy, either. In the main he simply appeared . . . unfinished. Without much presence or character.

"Fremont Jones, Michael Kossoff," Augusta said, her face glowing, "may I present my son, Lawrence Bingham."

Son! How could I have forgotten about the son?

"How do you do, Lawrence," I said with a nod, not offering my hand, as for a woman it is not required, and I did not feel so inclined.

All at once I recalled what Father had told me about Augusta's son during his visit to San Francisco the year before: "the boy's a ne'er-do-well," and "he has been a plague upon us."

Bingham? I speculated on this, wondering if Augusta could have borne her son out of wedlock? Perhaps that was the reason she had concealed his existence from Father until they'd been married for over a year. Not that it would have mattered to Father; he was not the type of man to change his mind for such a reason.

While I had been occupied with these thoughts, Michael was shaking hands with Lawrence, and Augusta was explaining to her son about our upcoming marriage. Then it was time for seating maneuvers, in which Augusta returned to the sofa, Michael went with

her, and I took a chair near the one in which Lawrence
had been sitting. He looked for a moment as if he
would have preferred to find another place, but then,
with a shrug he didn't quite manage to check, he sat
down again where he had been.

I was in a wickedly light mood. I felt as if I could
take on all comers, and so I said to Lawrence, "From
something my father said some months ago, I had the
impression you were living here at Beacon Street, with
him and Augusta. So where have you been? Off to
school perhaps?"

He hunched his shoulders and looked at me from the
corners of his eyes, then looked to his mother as if for
permission to speak.

In the meantime she answered for him: "Larry is a
journalist, isn't that so, son?" Of course she didn't give
him time to respond but went right on: "He has been
working in New York City, but now that Leonard is
better, well, I wanted my boy back at home with us. I'm
sure you can understand how that is."

"Of course," Michael said.

I was certain Father would not feel the same, but I
would take that up with him later.

"How fascinating," I said to Lawrence. "I should
think journalism would be an interesting profession
to follow. For what newspaper did you work in New
York, Lawrence?"

"Larry, my byline's Larry Bingham. Wrote for the
Daily News. Nothing much under my belt yet, so to
speak, you unnerstand," he said, his voice trailing away
in a mumble. Then he rubbed at the corner of his
mouth, which had the apparently miraculous effect of
restoring his speech. "I was a—whatchacallit—an ap-
prentice."

I raised my eyebrows; politely, I hoped, if skeptically.
At least I did not openly question the young man, who
had most likely had a tendency to be less than truthful
passed on in his mother's milk. So far as I knew, junior
journalists were not called apprentices. The only ap-

prentices at a newspaper worked with those huge presses, doing the typesetting. But then, I could be wrong—it was not something I had ever looked into thoroughly.

Michael was kinder than I. He sought to put Augusta's son at ease by mentioning a certain Manhattan crime that had been so much in the news at Christmastime that even the San Francisco papers had picked up on it. Larry claimed insider knowledge—due to his job at the newspaper—and discussed the case with an eagerness that might have seemed to me merely pathetic, had my father not already predisposed me to be on my guard with the young man.

Perhaps because I was thus predisposed, I saw instead in Larry a degree of fascination with evil that bordered on the morbid. When speaking of these matters the young man's unfinished features acquired a look of cunning, and a vivid alertness that both attracted and repelled. I believe Michael saw the same, even without Father to predispose his observations, for Michael steered the conversation back in a similar direction again and again throughout the evening.

In the crime at Christmas—to which I hadn't paid that much attention at the time—a man had been fatally stabbed on the steps of a church and left there to bleed to death, at an hour not long before people began to arrive for the traditional midnight services. No one had been arrested yet. The police had not found a single witness to the stabbing. Larry claimed to have much more information than the police had allowed the newspaper to report, and he proceeded to tell us all about it.

I observed quietly, my former teasing mood forgotten. I became impressed all over again, or perhaps it was more than ever before, by my partner's skill in drawing out the young man, providing him opportunities to say more and more and more. There was no question in my mind that Larry Bingham was building himself a cage of lies from which there would be no escape—had we any reason to trap him in it, but we did not.

But then, after a while, I saw something else, something that did at last make me feel sorry for the young man: Larry was performing for his mother. She believed every word. She was proud of him. Augusta was the reason for all these lies.

I AWOKE SUDDENLY and came wide awake in an instant, the way one does when something has happened that is out of the ordinary, even if one does not yet know what that something may be.

I groped at the bedstead and found the pull cord for the ceiling light. By my watch on the bedside table it was 3:10 A.M., and the house felt cold as only a house in New England can be cold when there is snow outside and all the fires have been out for hours. My bed was warm but my arm, the only part of my body that I had yet allowed out from beneath the goose-down comforter, was freezing. So, I realized, was the tip of my nose. My ears were all right due to an unattractive but serviceable flannel nightcap with a ruffle—an object that had made me smile when I put it on because it reminded me of my first landlady in San Francisco, Mrs. O'Leary.

I pulled my arm back under the comforter and lay still as a stone, listening. What had awakened me?

Augusta had given me the third bedroom on the second floor of the house. My own old bedroom had been on the third floor at the front, directly over Father's room, but because climbing stairs is not so easy for me at present, Augusta had put me in this guest room, which is near the back stairs. I supposed Larry Bingham probably had my old room now, and for a moment I felt a ridiculous juvenile flash of jealousy, but it quickly passed.

There were three bedrooms on each floor, each separated by smaller rooms that could be used as sitting or dressing rooms, and one of these on each floor had been fitted out as a bathroom.

The room I was in, at the back, was the one on this floor that had given up its extra room for the bath. Augusta's bedroom came next in order, moving from back to front of the house; whether she used her extra room as a sitting room or not I didn't know. My mother had called that little chamber adjacent to the middle bedroom her "quiet room," and when she was in it no one had been allowed to intrude, not even Father, and certainly not I.

Mother had not slept in the room Augusta used now. My parents had been an exception to the general fashion for married people of the times: They had not kept separate bedrooms. Rather they'd slept together in a big bed in the front room where my father now lay. In the single most touching thing my father had done before he married Augusta, he had moved that bed he'd shared with Mother up to attic storage, and had a new bed put into the big front room.

Interesting, and sad, I thought, that he now lay in that new bed alone. I wondered if Augusta had ever shared it with him all through the night . . . and then I wished I had not, and so chased off the thought by returning to the principal matter at hand: What had awakened me?

Listening hard once more, I did not hear anything beyond the ordinary, except for the wind pushing against the windows as if it would like to come inside. And inside, all was quiet.

This house was more solidly built than any of the houses I'd lived in in San Francisco. Sounds did not carry through these walls. When one was inside a room with the door and windows closed, most little disturbances remained outside, unheard and unnoticed. If I wanted to know what had awakened me I would have to get up; there was simply no other way.

I hated the thought of getting up. It would be far more pleasant to snuggle back beneath the warm covers and try to forget that something had awakened me. More pleasant, yes, but not easier. In fact it would be impossible. My curiosity would torture me to pieces, even if there were nothing whatever out of the ordinary to find.

With a sigh I flung back the bedcovers all at once. If I were going to do this thing I might as well get it over with. As I bundled myself into a woolen bathrobe and threw a shawl across my shoulders for extra warmth, I began to speculate. Most likely while still asleep I'd heard the night nurse, Sarah Kirk, going down to the kitchen by the back stairs to fix a cup of tea. She claimed she never left her patient's bedside, but I didn't really believe anyone could be that faithful.

The slippers into which I thrust my bare feet were so cold I almost yelped. Suddenly I thought about Mary Fowey in her little room up top where Augusta had banished her, getting up in the dark at five o'clock to light fires in the fireplaces all through the house, all by herself. I shivered. It wasn't right; Mary should have had one of the Porters' old rooms.

Since I was going out into the hall, I had to light a candle. There were no electric lights in the upstairs hallways, only in the main hall on the first floor, and a ceiling fixture in each room. My banker father with his idiosyncratic ideas about money had had some interesting places of drawing lines on expenditures. I got the candle lit and replaced its glass chimney, then took the candleholder in my left hand by its curving handle and my cane in my right.

At the door I paused before tucking the cane under my arm long enough to turn the doorknob. If there was any danger outside my door, as more than once had been the case when I'd awakened suddenly in the night, I supposed I could throw the candle in the miscreant's face. I might bash him with my cane, but I rather doubted I could manage that because my legs were weak. Much of one's fighting strength and balance comes from the thighs—I doubted I could get the firm leverage to strike a good blow. Finally I ignored these distressing thoughts and pulled back the door, which opened inward.

The hallway was black as pitch, save for the strip of light in which I stood, light that cast my shadow before me as if I were a giantess. I advanced a few steps with my candle held high. Such a puny flame. How strange to think that for centuries upon centuries such small lights were all we had against the night.

In mid-hall, outside Augusta's room, I stopped. Had I seen a sliver of light around her doorframe? No, probably not. I listened intently; all I heard was the tall-case clock downstairs—tock, tock, tock, tock; true to her word Augusta had wound it before Father came home. Once more that old clock, which had come from England such a long time ago, was marking time for the Pembrokes and the Joneses.

I told myself I would go a few more steps to Father's room, I'd push open the door, and there would be Sarah Kirk with a steaming cup of tea. She'd raise a finger to her lips and mouth the words "Don't wake your father!" My own breath was coming like steam from my nose and mouth, it was that cold inside; in San Francisco it hardly ever got this cold outside, much less in.

I opened Father's door. Sarah sat in her usual place beneath a reading lamp, and her book was open, as usual. She'd had a cup of tea but it was not steaming; she'd already drunk it and the cup was empty. Sarah was asleep with her book resting on her small bosom, moving gently up and down with the rhythm of her breathing.

Well, who could blame her? Not I.

It was so very, very quiet in this room.

I walked across to Father's bed, the one he'd bought to share with Augusta Simmons: a large bed of dark mahogany with solid panels at the head and foot, not a four-poster, no canopy, no fancy carving, just good craftsmanship and good wood.

I think I knew before I got there what I would find.

Something, some quality of absence within these four walls had already told me.

Father's chest did not go up and down beneath the covers the way the nurse's bosom did beneath her book. His head was turned away from me but his eyes were open. His mouth hung open too.

"Daddy?" I whispered. I hadn't called him Daddy in a long, long time. "Daddy?"

TEN

SOME PEOPLE FALL apart in a crisis, they dissolve into tearful babble and pointless actions. Others are rendered speechless and paralyzed. Still others are able to perform well, with almost preternatural calm. Women are generally supposed to fall into one of the first two categories, but that is not always the case; nor is it fair to men to expect them always to conform to the third. It is impossible to know, until one finds oneself in more than one real crisis, what one's own pattern will be.

I'd had no crises in my life until I moved to California, and so I was somewhat surprised to find that I was one of those who perform well, with that preternatural calm. I might fall apart later, but while the crisis was in force I always somehow knew what to do and had some confidence I would be able to do it.

But there are limits for everyone—and by its very definition, one cannot find where the limit lies until one reaches it. My father's death was the limit for me. And I went over it, into the frightening unknown beyond.

"Daddy?" I called for the third time. I heard my own voice as if from very far away, sounding small and pitiful and painfully young.

I put the candle down on the bedside table carefully,

the way I'd been taught, because candles can start fires. I propped against the wall a stick I found in my other hand—I couldn't think what it was for. Then I walked around the bed, holding on tight because my legs were all wobbly. I felt the mahogany footboard cool and slick with wax under my fingers. I needed to look into my father's eyes, but he wouldn't turn over, so I had to go to the other side of the bed.

A part of me knew he was dead, but another part of me kept shaking her head and insisting he was only asleep with his eyes open. It was very, very important, yes, yes it was, to look into his eyes because the eyes are the windows of the soul, and so I had to look in and see if my daddy's soul was still in there.

But it wasn't. I looked in his eyes and nobody looked back. His soul wasn't there. I couldn't find my daddy anywhere, he was gone. Gone away. Flown away. Too soon, no warning, not fair, he'd been getting better. But he was . . . just . . . gone.

I crawled into the big bed to lie with my dead father, because I didn't know where else to go, what to do. Maybe I had some dim hope he might come back again. But he didn't come, and after a while I fell asleep right there in the big bed.

Dr. Cosgrove came but I wouldn't open my eyes because I didn't like Dr. Cosgrove. He talked and talked at me—his voice was so annoying, like the buzzing of a horsefly; and just like those flies, he wouldn't go away no matter how hard you shooed him. He made me drink something that tasted nasty, and after that I didn't hear anything at all, or see anything at all. I went off somewhere inside my head. Which was what my daddy had done, he went off somewhere too, didn't he? Only he didn't come back . . .

MY MOUTH felt like a sandpit—I needed water in the worst way. I forced my eyes open. Sick, I must be sick.

"Fremont."

I knew that voice. "Michael?"

He was there, bending over the bed, his arm going behind my head and helping me to sit up.

"Water," I said, "please." My head felt very odd. Aside from being dry as the desert, there was an unidentifiable, bitter taste in my mouth.

Michael poured water into a glass from a pitcher on the bedside table. He held the glass to my lips and helped me drink, but soon I had the glass in my own hand and was swallowing gratefully on my own.

"It's too dark in here," I said. "What time is it? Have I been sick?"

"Apparently you are unusually sensitive to laudanum, or he gave you a greater dose than he claimed he did. It's almost eight P.M. You were given the laudanum by Searles Cosgrove sometime early this morning, before anyone called me. You've been asleep for more than twelve hours."

"Oh. Laudanum? Well, no wonder. I don't know how I react to that stuff; I never had it before."

"Do you remember what happened?"

I rubbed my forehead because my head hurt, and although one knows intellectually that rubbing it is not likely to make a headache go away, or to make remembering easier, still one does it. And I suppose it did feel good. However, overall I felt so bad that it would take much more than forehead-rubbing to make an improvement.

"I remember Dr. Cosgrove," I said slowly, "he—he was very annoying, he kept talking at me and wouldn't leave me alone. I wanted to swat him like a fly."

Michael smiled. He took the glass from my hand, sat down on the side of my bed, and bent me forward a little so that he could rub my back.

"And he did make me drink something that tasted horrible. I suppose it was the laudanum. But why would he do that?"

"Ah, Fremont." Michael's arms went around me and he pressed my head to his shoulder. Then he began to rock me gently, back and forth, back and forth.

And I began to remember.

Tears leaked from my eyes. I didn't cry, didn't sob, didn't have the cathartic experience that real crying can produce. I just leaked tears.

"Father died. Didn't he, Michael?"

Michael continued to rock me. "Yes, Fremont, your father is dead."

IT WAS MORNING when I awoke the second time. I felt more clearheaded. Weak, but in control of myself. And I remembered everything. Not in great detail, but enough: Father died and for a while I'd been like a child again, wanting him back, not knowing what to do . . . and then the damn doctor had drugged me out of my mind.

That made me angry, and the anger gave me strength. I sat up, ready to go on with the day, and with my life. There was much to be done.

Michael sprawled in an uncomfortable position half on and half off the fainting couch that was a part of this guest room's furnishings—a more useless article of furniture I cannot imagine, as it is too big for sitting and too small for lying. How he could sleep like that I did not know.

I smiled, remembering how kind he had been to me last night.

There is one thing about being in love with a spy: they are very easy to wake up. Michael will wake if you look at him for more than a second or two, and he did.

"I am perfectly certain you should not be in here with the door closed," I said.

"Convention be damned," he growled. Then he gathered himself into a sitting position, stretched, and said, "Hmm. You must be feeling better. Your dubious sense of humor has returned."

I sighed. "I wasn't trying to be funny. I really meant it, you know. This is Boston and we aren't married yet. We should observe the proprieties. By noon today, according to the usual way of things, Augusta or that young man she calls her son will have told anyone who'll listen that you spent the night in my room with the door closed."

"I don't give a fig."

Michael came over to the bed and kissed me, at first tentatively and then rather well, after which he took my chin in one hand and searched my face. "You sound like your usual self. You kiss like your usual self. Are you really all right now?"

"I think so."

"Can you tell me what happened?"

"I know Father died and I, I did some odd things. That part is like a dream—in the dream I'm a little girl, walking around his bed, looking at him, knowing he's dead but not wanting to believe it. I didn't know what to do and so I just lay down next to him. Then the doctor came and made me drink nasty stuff.

"I won't forgive him for that, by the way. Now I'd like to wash and dress and then have some breakfast. Will you stay and help me? I have a feeling I may be a little unsteady on my feet when I first get out of bed."

"WHERE ARE THEY?" I asked later, meaning Augusta and Larry. We were having breakfast in the dining room: scrambled eggs and bacon that had been left in warming pans on the sideboard. The house seemed empty. Someone had once more stopped the tall-case clock, which made it seem emptier still.

"I don't know," Michael acknowledged.

"And Father's body?"

"Taken to the mortuary yesterday."

"Oh."

The door at the back of the dining room opened and Mary Fowey came in with a plate of toast. "I heard you get up, miss. And Mr. Kossoff. So I made toast. Cook's gone to market."

"Thank you, Mary." She put the toast on the table and for a moment looked straight into my eyes, an unusual thing for Mary to do.

"I'm sorry for your loss, Miss Fremont," she said.

"Thank you," I repeated, and because something more seemed called for, I added, "I only hope Father is at peace."

Mary nodded, averted her eyes, and moved back from the table.

"Will there be anything else you're needin'?" she asked.

"Fresh coffee, if you can manage it."

"Yes, miss. I can do that."

"Oh, and Mary: Where are the others?"

"Mrs. Jones and her boy, they went out. Didn't say where, didn't say how long. If anyone comes to the door, I'm to say we're not receiving callers and they're not to leave their card, those were my instructions."

I looked at Michael to see if he thought there was anything odd about that. Certainly it seemed odd to me. But I could learn nothing from Michael's face, which was a cipher, as it so often is.

"Not even to leave a card?" I couldn't help sounding incredulous.

"That's what she said. It's been the same since your poor father got so sick. Mrs. Jones don't want no callers nor no calling cards neither."

Well, that explained a few things I'd wondered about—such as where Father's friends had gone, and why. I said:

"As long as I'm in the house, Mary, if anyone comes calling you're to have that person wait in the hall and bring his or her card to me. Most likely I'll be happy to receive anyone. If I'm not here, I'd like you to take the card and say, 'Miss Caroline Fremont Jones will want to know you've called.' Then give any cards to me when I return. Can you do that?"

Mary smiled and did her quick little dip. "Yes. It'll be better, too, won't it, having people come to the house, like at most folks' houses. 'Specially when there's a grief in the house, you want your friends around, anybody would."

A remarkably long speech from her.

"You're quite right," I agreed.

Mary blushed, and fled in the direction of the kitchen. I hoped she wouldn't forget to make the coffee.

"I hope you know what you're doing," Michael commented when we were alone again.

"I do." I continued to eat my breakfast quite calmly. Food had been what I needed, and when I'd had at least two cups of good, hot coffee I expected I should be quite restored to my former self. Already I was beginning to remember details of finding Father, details that were important, things I'd observed before the child in me had taken over.

"Augusta isn't going to like you giving orders to her maid in her house."

"It doesn't matter." I broke a piece of toast in two and buttered it. Simple toast—and it tasted simply delicious.

"What do you mean, Fremont?"

"This is not her house anymore."

"Not her house."

"Father left the house to me, Michael. He left everything to me except enough of a legacy to provide Augusta with a living for the rest of her life—as long as she doesn't live extravagantly."

Michael let out a long, slow whistle and reared back from the table, as if he suddenly needed to distance himself from me. "How long have you known this? Does Augusta know?"

"Since last April when he came to see me; and no, I don't believe she knows. Certainly she wouldn't have liked it, and Father would have wanted to avoid unpleasantness—that was his way. He had a new will drawn up shortly before he came out to San Francisco, and I rather doubt he told anyone other than me. The bank is executor, and the document is stored in a safe-deposit box there. He used one of the bank's lawyers. At the moment I do not recall the lawyer's name but I have it written down."

"You are speaking of your father's bank where he used to work, Great Centennial."

"Yes."

Mary returned with a pot of steaming coffee, and I gave her my most effusive thanks.

"I don't understand why he would do such a thing," Michael said, "cut his wife out like that."

"He didn't tell me. I don't know either." I shrugged. Every moment I was feeling better, stronger. The coffee tasted fine and was working its magic.

"You must have asked," Michael said, narrowing his eyes at me and bringing those dark eyebrows together until he looked a bit like a bird of prey. "You're of too curious a nature, you can't stand not knowing things."

I buttered more toast. I had already eaten all my eggs and bacon. "In general, yes, that's true. But Father was a private man, and one did not question him. I inherited my, ah, rather uncharacteristic nature from my mother's side of the family."

"Fremont, sometimes you are the most extraordinary person!"

"Thank you," I said, inclining my head with a small smile.

"I'm not sure I meant that as a compliment."

"I'm sure you won't mind if I take it as one."

"You never told me you were for all intents and purposes your father's sole heir."

"What does it matter, Michael? You know I don't care that much about the money. And while I acknowledge that this is a much finer house than I ever really understood when I was living here, it will only be a burden. I'll have to figure out what to do with it. However—" I broke off to drink more coffee, as a new thought had just occurred to me. "However, I expect the house had a great deal to do with it."

"With your father's virtually cutting Augusta out of the will?"

"Yes. I expect he wanted to keep the house in the family. And I shouldn't have been a bit surprised if Mr. Larry Bingham didn't have quite a lot to do with that decision. Father didn't like him. He told me so."

"Mm-hm."

A silence fell between us at the table while we each thought our own thoughts. Then Michael said:

"I expect Augusta and Larry have gone to make arrangements for the funeral."

"Then in that case," I said, putting my napkin properly draped on the table, "you and I should be on our way."

"Where are we going? I expect I should go back to the Vendome and change clothes, since I've slept in these, before I go anywhere else."

"We are going to Father's doctor, Searles Cosgrove, to request an autopsy."

"An autopsy?"

"Well, you needn't look so shocked. I want to know the exact cause of Father's death. Cosgrove will have filed a death certificate, I expect. I do not know exactly how these things are done in Massachusetts, but surely it cannot be too difficult to find out."

ELEVEN

AT MY SUGGESTION we walked through the Public Garden and then up Commonwealth Avenue to Searles Cosgrove's office. I did not call ahead to announce that we were coming, because I did not want to give him the benefit of prior warning. I was still more than a little angry with the good doctor for having drugged me without my permission. It is one thing to offer painkilling or sleep-producing nostrums to a patient in discomfort, but quite another to force the same on someone temporarily unable to refuse.

I wanted to walk because I felt the exercise and the fresh air would serve to clear away what few cobwebs remained in my head. I'd chosen a good day for it: As often happens in New England at this time of year, the cold wind that ruled the weather a couple of days ago had served to clear the skies and make room for a balmy day. There was a hint of spring in the air, blue sky reflected in the puddles formed by melting snow, and I saw a robin hopping in a soggy brown patch that would soon be green with grass.

There was no spring in my heart, however, nor was I inclined to ooh and aah over the tiny tips of crocuses pushing up through the snow, as some other strolling couples would stop to do now and again. Rather I was filled with a sense of all-consuming purpose—and the anger that I knew was justified, yet amplified by the loss of my father.

Michael noticed, of course; he does not miss much. Sometimes I am glad of this and other times I am not. Today I supposed I did not particularly care one way or another when he said, "You're very angry, aren't you, Fremont? I'm assuming this anger has nothing to do with me, but is related to your father's death."

It was not really a question, so I didn't answer.

"When someone dies, anger is a common response, Fremont. I've felt it myself in such a situation."

Still I did not answer; I thought it unlikely that Michael, although both his mother and his father were dead, had ever been in my precise "situation." And I thought it best not to say so.

"Are you going to tell me before we get to Cosgrove's office why you want an autopsy to be performed on your father, or do I have to wait and hear it with him?"

This time I responded with a question of my own: "What did he say was the cause of Father's death?"

"Heart failure. He called it 'cardiac arrest.' "

"That will be what he wrote on the death certificate, then."

I'd had some experience of death certificates and coroners and such a couple of years ago, when I'd been a temporary lighthouse keeper and had spotted a woman's dead body rolling over and over in the waves breaking on the rocks along the shoreline of Monterey Bay.

After thinking for a few moments I went on: "And did Cosgrove tell you that himself, or did you hear it from Augusta?"

Michael glanced down at me. This day might be clear and sunny, but his blue eyes, which can change like the weather, were gray and foreboding. By that storm in his eyes I anticipated I would not like what he had to say in reply, and I was right. He said:

"Actually it was neither. Larry Bingham called me at the hotel and asked me to come to the house because you weren't well. It was Larry who met me at the door and told me what had happened."

"What time was this, Michael?"

"Midmorning. Ten or ten-thirty, I should say. Cosgrove was no longer there, he'd left. And Augusta was in her room with the door closed. I didn't see her until later, around noon, when Mary came to your room and told me luncheon had been set out as a buffet in the dining room. When I went down, Augusta was there and we talked. She confirmed what Larry had said, that your father died of heart failure."

"They waited a long time to call you," I said. "What else did Augusta say?"

Michael's hand came out to cup my elbow as we stopped at the curb, waiting to cross Arlington Street. The wheels of passing carriages and autos spewed muddy water from the melting ice, but I daresay no one minded much. Muddy hems are a small price to pay for a day that has broken the grip of winter.

"Ah," he said, "let me think. She said Leonard died sometime during the night, and his death had put you in such a state that Dr. Cosgrove thought it best to dose you with laudanum."

"What about the nurse, was she there?"

"Not that I saw. Of course, by the time I arrived there would have been no need for her. Augusta had already called the funeral home and they came for your father's body while I was sitting in your room with you in the late morning."

"Hmm," I said, although that was usually Michael's line.

"You still haven't said why you want this autopsy. You must have a very serious reason."

"Yes, Michael, I do," I said grimly. "You may be certain I would not have some pathologist cut open my father's body without good reason. Aren't you the slightest bit curious yourself to know why, with no warning whatever, Father suddenly had a heart attack when up to then he'd been getting better? Not to mention that his problems were with his stomach and digestive tract, not with his heart."

"And his liver," Michael added. "Watch your step."

"That too," I said as we crossed Clarendon Street.

Just when I thought he wasn't going to say any more, Michael caught me by surprise: "To tell you the truth, Fremont, I was not so much taken aback to hear that your father had died as I was to have been told about it by someone other than you. Why didn't you call me immediately? You know I would have come right away. You have the telephone number at the Vendome."

"Oh, Michael. When I found Father dead, it was the middle of the night."

"Fremont, the Vendome has a desk clerk on duty. I'm sure he would have summoned me no matter what the hour."

We'd reached Searles Cosgrove's house and office in the middle of the block. I stopped at the foot of the steps, grasped Michael's arm, and pulled him around to face me. "Dearest Michael, I don't know why. The horrible truth is, I didn't think at all. I wasn't able to think—I wasn't really myself. I'm sorry."

There was more, of course, and I'd tell him the rest soon; but not until after I'd confronted Cosgrove. If I said more now, particularly if I told him everything that was going through my mind, Michael might very well think he should talk me out of what I intended to do. I couldn't let him do that. I didn't have enough energy to deal with Cosgrove and Michael both.

Michael's eyes searched mine, and softened. He touched my cheek briefly but tenderly with the back of his hand, and I knew if we had not been standing on the street he would have bent his head and kissed me. He said gruffly, though in a soft voice:

"It's just that sometimes you're too damn independent. With you I never know when I'm going to be left on the outside."

I might have said the same was true of him, with me, but I didn't.

I said instead, "Be patient," which is another thing he always says to me—impatience being just one more trait we have in common; and then I began to climb the steps.

Michael stayed with me until Nurse Bates had grudgingly agreed I could sit in the waiting room until the doctor had time to see me, then Michael went on to his room at the Vendome to change his clothes. As the Vendome was just half a block away at the corner of Commonwealth and Dartmouth streets, he should be back shortly.

The cross streets in Back Bay run along in alphabetical fashion, from A for Arlington through H for Hereford. After that comes the tail end of the long sweep of Massachusetts Avenue, which originates on the other side of the Charles River and crosses it by means of a bridge by the same name. Beyond Massachusetts Avenue lie the Fens, which are all that is left of the swamp that once was Back Bay. I sat thinking of these streets and of how I'd planned to show Michael more of the Boston I'd loved as a girl. Not quite, of course, in the same way I'd fallen in love with San Francisco—but still there was so much here I'd wanted to do with Michael. I'd thought there would be time after our wedding. Before the wedding I'd wanted to be with Father, to keep encouraging him to get better, and . . .

And to watch over him, said that inner voice of mine that compels and protects me, even from myself.

"Doctor will see you now," Nurse Bates said, startling me from my reverie, though she was not speaking to me. A man who was the only other occupant of the waiting room hauled himself out of his chair with difficulty and went off with the nurse.

Alone now, I returned to my thoughts and to the comment of my inner voice. Yes, I'd wanted to watch over Father; and perhaps some of my unhappiness, my discomfort, came from the nagging possibility that I might not have been vigilant enough. But the two private nurses had been doing such an excellent job. Who would've believed the scrupulous night nurse, Sarah Kirk, would fall asleep and let Father die?

She wouldn't have, my inner voice said.

Yet in my mind's eye I could see her asleep in the chair where she always sat, beneath the reading lamp, her book open on her chest, rising and falling almost imperceptibly with each breath.

"Oh, my God!" The words came out of me involuntarily, and I clapped my hand over my mouth as if to put them back in. But of course the horse was already out of the barn, so to speak.

Nurse Bates had just returned from escorting the man she'd summoned, and was shutting the door that led to the examining rooms and to Cosgrove's private office. She looked at me sharply and said, "I beg your pardon?"

"Nothing," I replied, too quickly perhaps, with the first thing that came to mind. I could only hope I didn't sound as flustered as I felt. "It's just something I forgot. To do, I mean. At home."

She gave me one more keen glance, then shrugged and sat back down at her desk. She returned to her task of writing notes in the patients' charts.

At home. The words echoed, running round and round inside my head . . .

I hadn't called the Beacon Street house my home for years, but ever so subtly, the ties of birth and ancestry had asserted themselves. Now Beacon Street felt like home again. Now the house *was* mine. I felt the stirring of some urgency for the necessary legal proceedings to confirm this—but, one thing at a time.

A different man came out of the door to the examining rooms. He tipped his hat wordlessly both to Bates and to me, walked through the waiting room, and left. The doctor's previous patient, I presumed. Interesting they'd both been men, similar in age and appearance to one another, though the one who'd just left had more of

a jauntiness to his walk. Where were Cosgrove's female
patients? I could not recall ever having been in a doctor's waiting room without at least one other female patient present.

I worried over this a bit to no avail, and ended by de-
ciding I must just have been in a suspicious mood.

"Are you all right, Miss Jones?" Bates asked.

"Yes, I am. Perhaps not quite my old self yet, but I'm
all right."

"I expect it will take some time," the nurse said.

It was the first reference she'd made to my father's
death. She went on to be more specific, "If I didn't say
so before, my condolences on the loss of your father."

"Thank you."

"He was a fine man."

"Yes. Yes, he was."

Nurse Bates cocked her head to one side, as if considering, and then said something more: "Sometimes
when men get older they make poor choices. Even fine
men. Guess you can't blame them." She narrowed her
eyes for a moment, pressed her lips into a firm line, and
returned to her work. She'd said her piece, that was it.

And I understood. You could have tipped me over
with a feather I was so surprised, but I understood. And
I knew she knew I'd understood.

Bostonians, all Yankees in fact, will do that. They'll
go around with their lips tight shut for weeks, months,
years even, minding their own business and keeping
their opinions to themselves, but then one day they'll
bluntly state a truth as they see it. Bam, there, just like
that—and then those lips close tight again. Nurse Bates
had just now given an excellent demonstration of this
Yankee trait.

No comment was required from me; the proper response to one of these verbal offerings is a curt nod of
the head, or some nonverbal vocalization such as
"mrmph." So I nodded, whether with her head lowered
to her work she could see me or not.

But I had an idea. I waited; I paged through an almost new copy of *Collier's* magazine without reading a word, barely even looking at the pictures. When I dared not wait any longer, for no one else had arrived to see the doctor and the man who'd gone ahead of me had been in there for some time, I said, "Nurse Bates, I wonder if I might ask you something?"

"Hm?" She looked up, rather severely, but I fancied there was a softness in her eyes. I was beginning to like this woman, who was more than she had seemed on the occasion of my first visit to this office.

"About the night nurse you arranged to look after my father, Sarah Kirk. She's an excellent nurse, wouldn't you say? The other one too, Martha Henderson, they were both very good, but Sarah was especially kind to me. And, I think, to Father too."

"Yes, Sarah's good. A conscientious woman. Has two children, one sick all the time with something chronic. Costs a bundle to take care of that sick child, so Sarah works at night when her husband's there to take a turn at looking after the children. Anything else you want to know?"

"Yes, there is, and what you've just told me about Sarah makes it all the more important: I wonder if you'd be so kind as to give me her address. I'd like to write and thank her myself for taking such good care of Father and for her particular kindness to me the night he died. And of course I'll enclose a little something in the way of extra appreciation—if you take my meaning."

Bates smiled. "That'd be a fine thing to do, Miss Jones. Here, I'll write it down for you."

"Thank you. I can't tell you how much I appreciate this. While you're writing, if it's not too much trouble, please put Martha Henderson's address too—because of course I'll also want to send her a note of thanks."

I HAD BEEN in Searles Cosgrove's office not five minutes when there was a tapping at the door and Nurse Bates looked in.

"This Mr. Kossoff says he's to join you. Is that right?"

Cosgrove looked at me, although I'd already told him I expected Michael to be along. I nodded, then the doctor said, motioning with his hand, "It's all right, come on, come on, we don't have a lot of time."

After shaking hands across the desk with Cosgrove, Michael took a chair and brought it up next to mine. As he settled in the chair I could smell the faintest whiff of Pears soap, and a vision of Michael in the bath flitted through my mind—all that dark hair, soap suds . . .

Yes, I was glad to see him; I was also somewhat concerned at the way my mind was wandering—more than wandering, jumping—all over the place this morning. I resolved to focus, to get and maintain control.

"Now where were we?" Cosgrove asked crossly.

He wasn't going out of his way to be sympathetic, that was for certain. If he was like this now, I hated to think how hostile he was likely to become before I'd finished with him.

"You were saying how Father's death was probably a blessing in disguise, et cetera, et cetera," I said, "and I'm afraid I don't want to leave it at that. I have questions."

I did not intend to come right out and demand an autopsy. I wanted to lead up to it. To wear away at him for a bit first, as it were, so that when I mentioned the word "autopsy" he would be inclined to think if he agreed to the autopsy it would silence me, and that would be a good thing. Therefore I had to be a bit of a nuisance first.

I must say, I quite relished the role of nuisance.

"What's he here for?" Cosgrove rather rudely waved his hand in Michael's direction. It was a dismissive gesture, and I bristled.

Placing a hand on my arm, Michael answered for himself. "May I remind you, I am Miss Jones's business partner. Now I am also, as I expect someone in the family has told you if Fremont herself has not, her fiancé. I am here in a supportive role, as I'm sure you'll agree is perfectly proper."

"Yes, yes, of course." Dr. Cosgrove rubbed his forehead, closing his eyes for a moment as if immeasurably weary. "Well then let's get on with it. What do you want to know?"

"I've been told," I said, "that you attributed Father's death to heart failure. Is that right?"

"Cardiac arrest. Yes. Same thing. Means his heart stopped."

"I know what it means."

"Eh? How'd you know medical terms, then?"

"I have studied Latin in school, Dr. Cosgrove, and most medical terminology is derived from Latin. It is not so difficult, but that is beside the point. The point is: *Why* did Father's heart stop?"

"Could be any one of a lot of reasons. The man had been very sick for a very long time. His heart just gave out. It stopped beating. That's all."

Yes, that had been all, quite literally, for Father.

I persisted: "But he had been getting better. Every day he seemed stronger and more alert. He was beginning to talk of getting out of bed, getting some exercise by walking up and down the hall inside the house, and then going outside when the weather improved. We were planning to get one of those special chairs for him, the sort that would allow him to wheel himself, as well as to be pushed by others. Surely Augusta discussed all this with you? Father had not taken any downturn. So how could this have happened?"

"Young lady, we don't know how the heart decides when it's worn out. But when it's ready to stop, it just stops."

"You don't know, you say. But after death if you look at that heart, you can tell if it was really worn out, or if something else caused that person to die. Can't you?"

"Well yes. Maybe I couldn't, but a cardiac specialist could, or a pathologist. That's—"

"I know what a pathologist is, Dr. Cosgrove. I have a friend who is a pathologist in California. Not only that, he is the coroner for Monterey County."

"Is that so?" Searles Cosgrove stared at me, then repeated the stare at Michael.

I'd stretched the facts a little—the pathologist was an acquaintance, not a friend. But I needn't have worried, though, because Michael took this opportunity to become a part of the conversation by answering Cosgrove's challenge.

Michael said, "Yes, it's so. Fremont Jones is no ordinary woman. Those of you who know her only from the days of her youth here in Boston may soon be in for a surprise."

"Is that so?" Cosgrove asked again, turning to me and sweeping his eyes up and down.

As the doctor's eyes swept over me I suddenly had a creepy, dirty feeling, and thought of all the things that could be done to a person rendered insensible by laudanum.

I shuddered, repressed that unpleasantness, and held to my original thought.

"We can come back to pathologists and so on in a minute," I said, firmly taking hold and banishing everything from my mind except my own foremost purpose. "Now let me ask you something else: Who called you to report that my father had died, and at what time did that person call?"

"Mrs. Jones, Augusta, telephoned. It was just after seven o'clock in the morning. I arrived at the Beacon Street house to pronounce death at seven-thirty."

"What about the nurse, Sarah Kirk?"

"What do you mean, what about her?"

"Weren't you surprised that the nurse wasn't the one to call you? Shouldn't that have been a part of her duty?"

"Well, no, I wasn't surprised. Perhaps I should have been, but I didn't think about it. She wasn't there, she'd gone off home, I suppose."

"I see."

I didn't want to pursue this with the doctor at the moment, I'd only wanted him to confirm what time he'd arrived and what the situation had been on his arrival. I intended to take these things up in much greater detail at a later time, with Sarah herself.

"I might add," Searles Cosgrove said, looking very stern, "that you, young lady, were hysterical when I arrived."

"I doubt that." My chin came up. "You may have found me stubborn and uncooperative," I admitted as a dim recollection of my behavior came to mind, "but not hysterical."

"You refused to get off the bed. Your father's bed with him in it, stone dead. I call that hysterical."

Michael turned his head toward me a bit too sharply. This was the first he'd heard of that part of this whole thing. To his credit Michael kept quiet, but I saw the knuckles of his left hand go white where he gripped the chair's arm.

"I was upset, yes," I said, "but I had good reason. Further, I am an adult, and I don't recall that I gave permission for you to administer laudanum to me. Certainly I never asked for it! Are you aware, Dr. Cosgrove, that the dose you forced me to take was so heavy I slept around the clock? A full twenty-four hours?" Of course I wasn't counting the one time I had awakened, but I didn't think I needed to. I couldn't have stayed awake then for more than a few minutes if my life had depended on it. Which I suppose I was quite lucky it did not.

I held up my hand palm out, as if to stay any comments from Dr. Cosgrove, who had clamped his lips shut and wasn't about to say anything anyway.

"Nevertheless," I went on with a deliberately exaggerated air of generosity, "I won't hold you responsible for overdosing me, nor will I ask again what caused Father's heart to stop."

I paused, and in that pause I fancied the tight line of

Cosgrove's lips relaxed a bit. But my pause was only a brief one, and then I let him have it:

"Dr. Cosgrove, I want you to arrange for an autopsy to be performed on my father, Leonard Pembroke Jones. I want to know *exactly* why my father died."

Searles Cosgrove made his fingers into fists and did that annoying business of bumping them together at the knuckles. He opened his mouth as if to speak, but licked his lips nervously instead.

Then he got up from his chair and, turning his back on me and Michael, walked over to his big double windows that looked out over Commonwealth Avenue. He stared out while I became ever more impatient.

The more impatient I became, the straighter I sat; I stretched my spine until it would stretch no higher . . . until my tension became such that I feared my spine might shatter.

Finally Cosgrove turned around and put his hands behind his back. Standing with the light from the windows behind him, he said two words: "You can't."

Michael mumbled something under his breath.

I said: "I don't understand what you mean."

Now Cosgrove walked toward us, rubbing his hands together in a motion that in a different situation might indicate glee. He said:

"You can't order an autopsy, Miss Jones. You are not legally responsible!"

TWELVE

———◆———

I'D LIKE TO know just exactly what you mean by that statement, Cosgrove," Michael said, in a voice as close to a growl as it is possible for a human being to utter and, at the same time, form words.

Meanwhile I was no longer seated, but standing, ready to leave without further ado and take my business elsewhere. Along with an accusation or two, perhaps. My cheeks were burning, I expected with a high color to match my high temper, but I did not care.

"There is no point trying to communicate any further with Dr. Cosgrove, Michael," I said, "since he has made it clear he does not wish to help, or indeed to do anything further in my father's interest other than to see him buried."

"You misunderstand me," the doctor said mildly, coming back to his desk and leaning against it, casually crossing one ankle over the other and stuffing his hands deep into the pockets of one of those white coats doctors always wear. To intimidate normal human beings, it seems to me.

"I don't believe so," I said, "since you've just said I'm not responsible, which indicates you think me of unsound mind, and that certainly is not true."

Michael too was standing now, but he was staring

intently at Searles Cosgrove as if the man were a puzzle to solve. I took up my cane, wanting nothing so much as to whack him with it; but instead I put it to the floor and turned toward the door.

"Miss Jones, Mr. Kossoff, you misunderstand my intention," Cosgrove said, "in much the same way you've obviously misunderstood my high standards of caring for my patients. If you will be seated again, I'll explain."

I turned back to Cosgrove. Standing, I was taller than he; I had no intention whatever of sitting down again.

"You can tell us as we are, or not at all, they are both the same to me," I said.

Michael said nothing, but moved to stand at my side, and he placed one hand at the small of my back as if to steady me. Perhaps I needed steadying; nevertheless, at that particular moment I did not want to be touched. I would have shaken off his hand if it were possible to do so without making a fuss. It was not, so I clenched my teeth, raised my chin, and endured.

"When I said you, Caroline Jones—Fremont Jones as you prefer to be called these days—are not legally responsible, what I meant was that you are not the person responsible for making such a decision. You cannot do so because you are not your father's surviving next of kin."

"I am his daughter, his closest living blood relation. Of course I am his next of kin!"

Cosgrove shook his head slowly from one side to the other. "By legal definition, a wife precedes a child. Leonard Pembroke Jones has a living wife, who has survived him. In other words, Augusta Simmons Jones is his legal next of kin, the only person who can order an autopsy performed."

I was stunned. For just a moment I wished I had been sitting down. Then I felt Michael's hand press more firmly at my back . . . but rather than the reassurance and support he no doubt intended, his touch sent my anger soaring. Immediately I thought he had known this was coming, that must have been why he'd placed himself just so, why he'd set himself up like that with his hand at my back, he'd anticipated a need to steady me; and if he'd known, why hadn't he warned me before we'd come to this infernal doctor's office? Why hadn't Michael told me himself?

Tension and anger had set my ears roaring. Over the roar, or perhaps under it, my inner voice counseled me: *Listen, he's saying something important!*

Searles Cosgrove, after observing the effect his words had on me, was continuing to speak:

"Of course, if the death were from anything other than natural causes—that is to say, any sudden, unexpected death, or a death under suspicious circumstances such as murder, or if I as the physician in whose care the patient died had questions as to the cause of death—then it would be different. In the first two instances, the police would automatically ask for an autopsy. In the third instance I could do it, even overriding the wishes of the next of kin if I were callous enough to do so."

Michael glanced at me. Seeing my jaws clamped together like iron, he correctly concluded I had no intention of speaking. So Michael took it upon himself:

"I should think it would be in your best interests, Cosgrove, to have the autopsy done. My fiancée's points are well taken, don't you think? Her father's health had improved dramatically. His abnormal pallor had all but disappeared—you saw it for yourself, man! We'd set the date for our wedding and he was greatly looking forward to it. Leonard had many reasons to live, and a passionate desire to do so. Only the day before yesterday he and I had talked about how, with the aid of a wheeled chair, he could not only be present at the wedding ceremony but could do the double duty of escorting Fremont down the aisle and handing me the wedding ring."

I had not known that, about their having talked, or that Michael had in effect asked my father to be his

"best man." My anger deflated like a pricked balloon
and tears came into the corners of my eyes. I blinked
them away determinedly—this was most definitely neither the time nor the place to cry.

My inner voice, which often remembers things I've
learned the hard way even though the rest of me may
forget them, cautioned me with something I'd heard
from the nurses after the San Francisco earthquake:
*First too angry, then too sad—these are extreme mood
swings due to having been under too much stress. Time
to rest. Time to be alone for a while.*

By way of reply, the doctor challenged Michael:
"Why can't you two feel the same way Augusta feels?
She is glad Leonard died in his sleep after having had a
few happy days. Glad he died at home with his family
around him. The last thing on this earth that poor
woman wants is to have some stranger cut open her
husband's body."

Cosgrove hunched his shoulders, his eyes wide in either disbelief of or dismay at us; then he took his hands
out of his pockets, folded his arms across his chest, and
fixed his stare on me.

"Fremont, if you're so callous—or perhaps jealous is
a better word?—as to be determined to cause Augusta
more grief, then by all means try to persuade her to request the autopsy. But you'll have to go through the
police, or straight to the medical examiner yourself, because I'll have no part of it. I trust I have made myself
clear."

"Perfectly," I said.

I signaled Michael with a darting glance and he
opened the office door. I wished I'd been wearing a
longer skirt, one of those with a small train, so that I
could have flipped it behind me disdainfully as I turned
away; those long skirts are good for that, if not for
much else. But my skirts just covered my ankles, as was
better for walking, and so there was nothing I could do
but make a dignified exit with my head held high.

Dr. Searles Cosgrove meanwhile, cool as you please,

went around his desk, sat down, and started to read through some papers there.

Neither Michael nor I said goodbye; and certainly we did not thank him for his time.

"YOU SHOULD REST for a while," Michael said as soon as we were again out on Commonwealth Avenue. "I suggest you come with me to the Vendome, since it's only half a block from here. You can rest in my bedroom in complete privacy—I have a suite. Or I can try to find a cab and take you back to Beacon Street."

"I don't think it would be a good idea for me to be seen going up to your room with you, suite or no suite. Nor do I feel like standing here and waiting for a cab to come by. Let us walk."

Michael was disturbed, I could sense all sorts of things rumbling around inside him like thunder. Well, I was disturbed myself.

"When did you turn so prudish?" he asked. "The Vendome is closer, you and I are hardly strangers, and besides I've never known you to care so much about appearances."

"That was in California. Things are different here, especially now. I have to care."

I walked doggedly on, fueled by my angry energy, knowing perfectly well that I did need to withdraw for a while and be quiet, even to rest if I could make myself do it. But I didn't like Michael telling me what to do, any more than I'd liked his hand in my back during Searles Cosgrove's horrible speech.

"*You* certainly are different here," he said.

"What do you mean by that?" I hurled the question sideways at him, then stepped off the curb without waiting for him to accompany me. I'd stepped a little too close on the heels—or rather the wheels—of a passing horse cart and so I got mud sprayed on my skirt, but I scarcely noticed.

"Nothing," Michael grumbled, catching up easily

with his long legs. "I'm having a bit of trouble keeping up with you, Fremont, in more ways than one."

"I don't think so," I said hotly. "Far from having trouble keeping up, I think you were *ahead* of me back there in Cosgrove's office. I think you already knew he was going to tell me I don't have the right to require an autopsy to be done on Father. You knew, and you didn't tell me!"

"What makes you say that?"

"Never mind, I have my reasons. So tell me. I'm right, aren't I? You did know!"

"Goddammit, Fremont!" Michael's hand jerked upward in the beginning of a gesture that's habitual when he is frustrated or angry—but because he was wearing a hat he could not thrust his fingers viciously through his hair, and so he settled for punching his fist at the air instead.

I continued to walk at the most rapid pace possible. I suppose if I'd been in any mood to notice such things, I would have noticed that forgetting to be cautious greatly improved my walking ability. I hardly limped at all, and with the cane I stepped out almost as briskly as I'd done in the days when I'd kept a special walking stick for self-defense rather than physical assistance. I did not break stride or even look at Michael, nor did I care very much how he responded. I didn't trust him now, not on this.

I didn't care, didn't trust, because he lies when it suits him, I know he does. His whole adult life Michael has been a spy and spies are experts in duplicity. It becomes second nature to them, and so perhaps he cannot help it. But still—

My thoughts slowed down a bit and I admitted: I hadn't thought he would lie to me, not anymore, not since the agreement we'd made to establish our partnership. Perhaps I was wrong . . .

"All right," Michael admitted, "I did think Cosgrove would probably say something about Augusta's wishes in this matter having precedence over yours. The same would be true for the wife in most of the United States, and I believe in most other countries as well."

"Hah! I knew it!" So much for thinking I might have been wrong.

"Will you please let me finish, Fremont?"

"I beg your pardon," I said somewhat sarcastically.

"And so you should, because I was about to say that I don't underestimate your powers of persuasion. There was always a chance you could convince Cosgrove to override Augusta. To get him on your side."

"Hah!" I said again, this time bitterly.

"Indeed. Far from having won him over to your side, you seemed to have put the man into a hostile mood even before I arrived at his office. What did you do?"

"I didn't have to do anything. He was like that from the moment I went in and sat down. Obviously, no matter how courteous he seemed to be before, he wants nothing more to do with me now. Searles Cosgrove is just one more male of the species besotted with Augusta."

"Nonsense. You must have said something to rile him, made one of your, er—"

"Unwise accusations?" I supplied. "Never mind that they are only unwise in your estimation whereas in mine they are well founded."

We approached the corner of Commonwealth Avenue and Berkeley Street. Michael saw an autotaxi coming our way, so he stepped out into the street, saw that it held no passengers, and hailed it down.

I picked my way through the slush—wet feet are more irritating than mud on one's skirts—and got in. None too soon; I was tired but the walk had been exhilarating. My sense of purpose was exhilarating too, even though the anger behind it was troubling.

Michael gave the Beacon Street address and instructed the driver to go the long way, around the Common. I didn't mind, as I expected he'd done so in order to assure the cabbie a better fare, and I could use the extra time to compose myself.

"At any rate," Michael said as if picking up where we'd left off, "though Cosgrove's manner was rather offensive—leaving aside the question of whether or not he was provoked—"

I shot him a look but kept quiet. My mind was made up. I knew what I was going to do, I accepted that I would have to do it by myself, and I didn't care what Michael or anyone else thought or said or did.

"—really, Fremont, my dear, you must admit the doctor was right in at least most of what he said."

"I admit no such thing!"

"Won't you agree that it's better for your father—for *anyone*—to die happy and at peace? To die at home with his family around him?"

After a long silence during which I examined Michael's bearded face minutely, as if I had never seen him before, or perhaps on the other hand as if I would never see him again, I very carefully said, "I think it is always better to live than to die. As for choosing one way of death to be preferable over another, I will leave that to the gods and to murderers, as only they have control over life and death."

I LET MYSELF into my house and went straight back to the kitchen. The cook was puttering about in the pantry closet, where I could hear but not see her; Mary, however, was rinsing something in the sink. I asked her to bring a bowl of soup and some oyster crackers to my room in an hour, or a sandwich if Cook had no soup available, and to wake me if I were sleeping. In her taciturn manner she assured me she would do as I'd asked. Then I went up the back stairs.

"Oh, Miss Fremont!" Mary called out when I'd gone up about three steps.

I stopped and turned in the narrow stairway, which was dark enough to be unpleasant. I thought I should have to do something soon about better lighting for these stairs and halls.

"I'm sorry, I almost forgot. There was a caller," Mary said, "a gentleman that's been here before, but like I told you, I was supposed to send everybody away and say no visitors. I mean that was before, 'til you said different this morning. If you take my meaning, miss."

"I understand, Mary. Go on."

"Well, this gentleman, he asked for Mrs. Augusta Jones and for you, too, the both of you, so I told him like you said. And he give me his card. Here 'tis."

"Thank you, Mary."

"But I didn't say nothing to Mrs. Jones. I hope that's right."

"Yes, quite right—she is the one who doesn't want visitors, not I, and so it's best that we not trouble her. You've done well."

"I hope so. Have a good rest, miss. I'll keep a careful watch on the clock, you can be sure of it."

"I know you will."

I smiled at her choice of words, "watch on the clock." I liked Mary. It would be so easy to forget that it was Augusta who'd hired her, and, therefore, Augusta who most likely had Mary's loyalty.

I continued on up the stairs, squinting at the calling card as I went, but it was too dark to read on the staircase. I wasn't able to see the name on the card until I came out into the hall, where daylight streamed through the windows at both ends: William Reginald Barrett.

Hmm, I thought. I hadn't known his middle name was Reginald. Musing, tapping the card against the palm of my hand, I went on to my temporary quarters in the guest room.

Immediately questions presented themselves: Could William have learned of Father's death already? Or had he been coming by regularly since Father's return from the hospital? Was this just one more visit I'd never known about? Or might Augusta have gone to the bank when she supposedly went out with her son this morning to make arrangements for Father's funeral?

Oh how that galled me: She had taken her son, not Father's daughter, to make plans for his funeral. She had not had the decency, or the consideration, to inquire as to my wishes—what words should be said, what songs sung, when my dead father's body was laid into the ground.

Tears pricked at my eyes again. For a moment my most fervent wish was that the animosity between the two of us, Augusta and myself, could end. I wished that we could bury my father in peace, then each of us go her own way and there would be an end to it.

I sighed, tossed my cane upon the bed, and sat down upon the mattress. Bury Father in peace: Michael would like that alternative. Then peace also could be restored between him and me . . . and surely that would be a fine thing.

Peace, yes—

But peace at such a price that I would never rest again a day on this earth! I blinked back the tears and with the back of my hand dashed away a few that had strayed down my cheeks. Unable to stay still, I popped up and began to pace back and forth. As I paced I continued to think, for there was plenty to think about. Such as:

If Augusta had already gone to the bank this morning, and if on that trip to the bank she had seen William, then I expected she would also have stopped in to speak to one of the two lawyers in the bank building who handled all Great Centennial's legal matters. They had handled my father's legal matters as well, and would know of the new will waiting in its safe-deposit box. *But*—

Reaching the corner of the rug, whose border I was following as I paced, I turned sharply and started back the other way.

But neither of the lawyers would say a word to Augusta until they'd contacted me, because I was the principal heir and would have to be notified first. Surely that was the way it worked.

Oh, God! What if I were wrong, what if they'd already told her?

I would have to go to the bank myself this afternoon. I must make certain Augusta did not learn about the new will until after the funeral.

Make peace with her? Not likely! Once she'd been told the terms of that will, anything like an amicable co-existence between myself and Augusta as was Simmons would no longer be possible. She was going to be very, very angry.

In fact—I stopped short, gripped by a new and horrible thought: If Augusta had already been to the bank, and if she'd been told that the bulk of the family money and property had passed to me, I could be in danger.

And here I was with no way to protect myself. My weapon of choice, a somewhat old-fashioned type of gun called a Marlin, had gone the way of everything else I'd lost in that same disaster that caused my broken legs. Since I could hardly handle a gun and a cane at the same time, and didn't like guns anyway, I hadn't even begun to think of getting another—

The cane! Good heavens. I'd been pacing the room without it!

My cane still lay on top of the bedspread where I'd tossed it. I stared at it for a moment, looked down at my two feet sticking out from beneath my mud-splattered skirt, and laughed aloud.

But I laughed for only a brief moment, because the sound of laughter echoing off the walls of this house seemed wrong. The house at Beacon Street was a house of mourning.

I TOOK OFF my skirt and lay down in my bodice and petticoats, pulling an afghan over me. I tried to sleep for the time that remained before Mary came to wake me.

Surprisingly enough, I was able to quiet my mind and I did doze off. But I awoke before Mary's knock, went to the window, and looked out.

This window on the back side of the house looked down into the little walled garden, which seemed forlorn and abandoned. I supposed it had always looked like that in the wintertime. I tried to see it as it had been in my mother's time, and as I'd tried to keep it after—with flowers growing in large pots all about, changing with the seasons. I wondered if there were still the big stone planters of daffodil and tulip bulbs down in the basement where they used to wait all winter until, when it was warm enough, Mother would have Ralph Porter bring them up and put them out against the garden walls. Later there would be pansies in pots, and petunias, and impatiens; and still later the spicy-smelling, brightly colored blooms of midsummer, the zinnias and the marigolds.

I doubted the flowers were brought into the walled garden anymore if Ralph were not there to help with the doing of it. The planters and pots were heavy when filled with dirt, too heavy for a woman. I could not see Mary's thin arms equal to the task of moving them about; nor could I picture Augusta with dirt on her hands.

Not the good honest dirt of the earth, anyway.

I left the window and rummaged through the dresser drawers until I found a stiff wire clothes brush, then set about brushing the dried mud from my skirt. As I brushed I decided I would try to find Ralph and Myra Porter. I wanted to know if they'd left of their own accord, or been dismissed. I wanted to know anything they could tell me.

The changes Augusta had made in this house were subtle. They didn't show on the surface, yet they had a lasting effect—even if that effect were only symbolic of something deeper. Symbolic: such as the stopping of the tall-case clock, which just happened to have been Father's favorite clock, a legacy from the family as old as the house itself. Practical: such as no longer having a manservant to do the tasks that had been Ralph Porter's responsibility, for example looking after the horse and carriage this house no longer had.

All right, one might argue—as Michael certainly would if I were to discuss this with him—that carriages were fast going out of date and automobiles were the coming thing. One might argue that in a city like Boston, where there are plenty of carriages for hire, and autotaxis, and even a subway train that runs underground, one does not need one's own horse and carriage.

However—I gave my skirt a last whack, the final bit of dried mud dropped away, and I pronounced it clean enough—*however*, I did not believe any of those things had anything to do with why the carriage house out back was locked up tight, probably empty and certainly dusty. I believed that like Ralph and Myra's being gone, like the failure to replace Ralph with another manservant, getting rid of the horse and carriage had been just one more step toward my father's isolation. Augusta had achieved it so subtly, so slowly, that most likely he had never even noticed.

I didn't doubt there were other things she'd done to isolate him, other steps she'd taken . . . and I wanted to know them all. I wanted to know everything.

THIRTEEN

———◆———

I HAD TOLD Michael I'd be resting all afternoon, when I had no intention of doing so. Therefore I thought it advisable to find Mary before I left the house and ask her to say to Mr. Kossoff, if he should happen to stop by or to call on the telephone before I returned, that I was resting and had asked not to be disturbed.

Augusta was apparently resting too; I hadn't seen her all day. And while this state of affairs could not last forever, for the moment it suited me. I was not to escape unscathed, however: Larry Bingham strolled into the hallway from the library just as I went walking purposefully down the hall toward the front door. While I didn't think he'd been lying in wait for me, he did have a rather predatory appearance about him. Perhaps it was only my eagerness to be on my way that gave him that appearance, but I didn't think so.

"Going out all on your own?" he asked. Without giving me a chance to reply to that he immediately offered, "Want a companion? Somebody to walk between you and the street to keep the mud off you from the passing vehicles and all that, y'know?"

"Yes, I'm going out, and no, thank you, I do not

want companionship. I have a few things to do that are better done alone."

"Oh, well. I thought ladies wasn't supposed to go out alone. That's what Ma says." He winked.

"An outmoded view, surely," I conceded, slowing.

The expression on his face, along with the wink, was so out of the ordinary that I could not help being intrigued. That wink had been knowing yet not salacious or in any way offensive; it simply suggested he knew something I didn't, as if he had an inside track on something, perhaps many things.

The facial expression somehow went with that. He reminded me of a junior gangster, one of those young men who hang around South of the Slot in San Francisco—South of Market Street, that is—pretending to be much tougher than they really are. They must keep up this pretense for their own protection; otherwise men who are older and tougher, some of them true criminals, will do the young ones in.

What could it hurt if I were to stop long enough to exchange a few words with him? After all, Larry must know Augusta better than anyone else in Boston could. At least he'd certainly known her longer, if only by virtue of being her child. Perhaps if I cultivated him a bit I might learn a thing or two.

A primary rule for an investigator: Talk to everyone and forget nothing you have heard from any source.

I said, "I thought you already went out with your mother this morning. Surely that should be enough of older women's companionship for one day."

Larry flicked his gaze up and down my body, neither insolently nor expertly but in a novice sort of way, as if he were just practicing. I almost smiled but at the last minute that didn't seem a good idea.

"You're not exactly all that much of an older woman, are you?" he asked.

"I suppose not. But then I also suppose I'm older than you. I should think you'd want to be out with your friends, not with me or your mother. I understand you lived here for quite a while—you must have friends here from before you went to New York. How long was it you lived in Boston? And were you in school then?"

"So how old are you anyway, Fremont?" Larry persisted, completely ignoring my conversational gambit, "and what kind of name is that for a girl?"

Oh, very bold, I thought. I rather admired him for that. Nevertheless I gave the conventional answer: "A woman doesn't tell her age. You know better than to ask. I, on the other hand, can ask with impunity: How old are you?"

"Old enough. Turned twenty-one a few weeks ago. December 28's my birthday. I reckon you couldn't be too much older'n me."

He was more correct than I cared to admit.

"So what about that name, Fremont?"

"It is my middle name, and my mother's maiden name. I am not fond of my given name, Caroline."

"And what d'you want hooking yourself up with a fella as old as that Kossoff?"

This young fellow was incorrigible! I gave him a long look while considering my reply.

Larry was leaning with one shoulder propped against the doorjamb of the library door, and he'd crossed his arms, as if settling in for a long talk. He was more relaxed than I felt, and he seemed both more mature and more attractive—many times more so—than he had on my first meeting with him, when he'd felt obliged to perform for his mother.

"I think you will make a good reporter," I said, aware of the non sequitur, unbothered by it, as I expected he would be. He was not the type to have difficulty following.

"Why's that?" he asked, picking right up.

"Because you're good with questions. You're genuinely inquisitive. And," I added, recalling something that had seemed distinctly unpleasant at the time but which now, looked at in another context, made some sense, "you appear to be interested in the types of things that make for sensational headlines."

He looked puzzled, so I added:

"I refer not to our present conversation but to our previous one about the man who was found stabbed on the church steps before Midnight Mass."

"Oh yeah." His face cleared of its puzzlement. He was not a bad-looking young man, really. A few more years would put character into that face, but right now it was simply unmarked and therefore unremarkable, with light brown eyes and rounded contours to cheeks and chin. He had his mother's fair hair and no shadow of beard whatever, as if he might not even shave yet—though surely that could not be the case.

"Back in San Francisco," I said, deliberately dangling bait I thought he would find irresistible, "there are any number of people who would accuse me of the same thing."

"How's that?"

"I mean, they'd accuse me of being interested in things of a rather sensational nature. Didn't your mother tell you?"

"Tell me what?"

"Michael and I run a detective agency. I am a trained private detective. My first big case got quite a lot of newspaper coverage. It was very good for our business." As I said this last I began to walk away, adding, "I'm sorry, I'd like to talk more but I really must be going now."

Larry Bingham followed hot on my heels to the front door.

As I passed the clock I noticed it had been stopped at 8:30. And I vowed to start it up again as soon as I could without causing a deliberate provocation. I wondered if tall-case clocks were sometimes called grandfather clocks because so often they'd belonged to one's grandfather.

"Change your mind, why don't you," Larry was saying as we hurried along. "Let me come and you can tell me more on the way."

"Certainly not, because I must go shopping for clothes. I need black dresses and a black coat."

This was true, though, as usual, having the right clothes had been down at the bottom of my priorities. Nor was I anxious to wear anything designed to remind me I was in mourning.

Larry looked unconvinced, so I added, "It would be extremely boring for you."

"I could carry your packages. I want to hear about the detective agency."

I had hooked this fish, all right!

I smiled at him. "We will do it another time under more conducive circumstances, I promise. For today if your mother does not need you, I suggest you go look up those old friends we were talking about earlier."

My suggestion did not go down well. In fact it produced a truly unpleasant expression from him, almost a sneer—which he hid by turning abruptly away and stalking back up the hall.

An odd young man, I thought as I closed the door. He had left it standing wide open. He had not said goodbye, either.

Oh, well. I'd learned a few things about Larry Bingham in a short time, among them the fact that he was unpredictable, almost mercurial. And that he was unlikely to go out of his way to please anyone . . . except his mother.

GREAT CENTENNIAL BANK is on Tremont Street. In all but the worst weather one would simply walk across the Common to get there; this was indeed the route Father had taken every day of his life, except perhaps in the teeth of a New England blizzard—and maybe even then.

This afternoon, however, I knew I'd best have help getting to the bank, as the exertions of the morning had worn me down a bit. So I had telephoned ahead to engage a horse and buggy for the afternoon. With a driver, of course. All three were waiting in front of the house on Beacon Street when I emerged.

I had my cane with me in case I needed it, though through the morning's turmoil I'd learned a valuable lesson: I didn't need it as much as I'd believed. To think that I, Fremont Jones, namesake and blood kin of that intrepid explorer of the Old West John Charles Frémont, had become physically timid! How awful.

I assured myself that was not a state of affairs I would allow to continue any longer. Surely, I thought as I allowed the driver to assist me up the one folding step into his high, enclosed carriage, it must be possible to achieve a balance between wisdom and adventurousness? Otherwise, as one grew older and suffered the vicissitudes of life, one would have to become unendurably boring.

I gave the name of the bank and its address to the driver and we were on our way.

To my embarrassment, I had not been able to remember the names of the bank's two lawyers; therefore, I hadn't called ahead for an appointment. I did, however, recall the location of the legal department—it was in a corner of the large, impressive main lobby, near the stairs that go down to the vault and to the safe-deposit boxes.

Great Centennial had opened in its impressive new building, as one might guess from its name, on our country's one hundredth birthday. Father was at the bank from its beginning. The building was designed in the days when banks were Temples of Commerce—and that is what it looks like, a Greek temple, inside and out, if one ignores the tellers' cages, that is. Nor have I seen any of the bank's officers sacrificing birds or sheep and reading entrails, but perhaps they do these things in some secret chamber behind closed doors. Who knows how officers of banks choose to watch over our money.

Entering by the front door, I walked swiftly across the marble floor toward my intended goal in the corner, my cane barely tapping. In the interests of decorum, particularly considering I didn't yet have the proper mourning clothes, I had worn the black Russian sable hat and scarf and carried over one hand a large muff, also of the same black fur. The muff was wonderfully warm, a further incentive to be done with canes forever.

I did not expect this bank to have changed in the slightest in the four years I'd been away, as it had not changed a whit in twenty-two years previous, nor had it. Given the open floor plan of this templelike building the private offices are set against the outer walls, enclosed by wood and glass but of necessity open at the top, as the bank's ceilings soar to a height of twenty-five, perhaps thirty feet.

These offices are back behind a deep railing such as one might find on a jury box at court, and the railing is guarded at intervals by a secretary or a clerk who sits alertly at a desk. The clerks are usually, but not always, male. I approached the man guarding the office enclosures of the two lawyers, whose names were inscribed upon their doors just as I'd thought they would be: James Palmer and Elwood Sefton. The latter, I now recalled, was the name my father had mentioned in connection with his new will.

"Good afternoon," I said, "my name is Caroline Fremont Jones. I'm the daughter of Leonard Pembroke Jones and have come to see Mr. Sefton. I'm sorry to say I do not have an appointment, but the matter is somewhat urgent."

The clerk was new enough at the bank never to have met me, but my father's name caused him to come to attention extremely fast. In less than five minutes I was behind that wide wooden railing and being ushered into the lawyer's office cubicle.

"Miss Jones. This is an unexpected pleasure. How long have you been in town?"

Elwood Sefton was one of those long-boned, lean New Englanders who seem old even when they are young, so that it is difficult to guess at their age. However, if one might judge from the sparseness of his hair and the whiteness of the little that remained, then likely he was older than Father.

For a moment the grim nature of my task here caused a hole to open up in the pit of my stomach, and I all but fell through it. I thrust both my hands into the muff, where they could not be seen, and clasped my fingers together as hard as I could, for courage.

"I've been here for a little over three weeks, Mr. Sefton. I admit I've rather lost track of time, as something—distressing—has happened. Are you aware that my father has been ill?"

He nodded his long head gravely. Lean though he was, the looseness of the skin at his neck gave him jowls when he bent his head, rather like a bloodhound. "Yes, I knew he had not been well. I take it, then, he is no better."

"No indeed, Mr. Sefton. My father died yesterday."

"Oh! Oh, my dear young lady, I am so very sorry! But should you be here? Are you quite all right? Shall I have young Franklin bring you something, water, tea, coffee?"

"I am fine, and I need to be here—as I hope you'll understand shortly. However, if Franklin is able to bring coffee without too much trouble, I would like that very much."

The coffee, when it came, was blessedly fortifying. In the interim I told the lawyer how my father had fared in the hospital and upon his return home, and how suddenly he had died.

Finally, braced by a couple of sips of the strong coffee, I came to the matter at hand:

"I know Father made a new will last year and placed it here in a safe-deposit box, I believe you wrote out the will for him, the bank is Father's executor, and you have the key to the box that contains the will. Am I correct in these assumptions?"

Sefton nodded. "You are correct on all counts." He averted his eyes, fiddled with a paper clip, using it to draw a line on his desk blotter, then looked at me again

and said, "You are familiar with the terms of the new
will, then?"

"Yes. I suppose, since you and Mr. Palmer handled
all Father's legal affairs—he can't have had many—
you'd know he has already given me half my inheritance."

Now Sefton's eyes glanced up toward the ceiling, as
he did rapid calculations in his head. "If you do not include the value of the Beacon Street house, then that
would be correct. And of course I did know. I assisted
with the, ah, liquidation of certain assets in order to
handle the transaction between our bank and your
bank in California."

"Is it too much to hope that Father might have told
you *why* he made these changes?"

Sefton looked toward the glass-topped door of his
cubicle to be sure it was closed all the way before he
answered. "He did not say a word against Augusta
Simmons, if that is what concerns you; but he did say
she has a number of relatives he had not known about
when he married her, that he felt these relatives were ra-
pacious and were not to be trusted. He most specifically
did not want the Beacon Street house to pass out of the
immediate family, and that is why it comes to you, and
any children you may have after you."

"I see," I said, though so far the only one of Augusta's
relatives I'd seen was Larry, and he hardly seemed rapa-
cious.

"If you do not wish to live in the house yourself,"
Sefton continued, "then it is to be maintained for your
children."

Oh Lord, I thought, children.

I couldn't stop myself from asking the question:
"What if I do not have children?"

"Hm. I can't recall. Shall we go downstairs and re-
trieve Leonard's last will and testament from the box
where it is stored? I have the key here in my desk."

"Let me ask you a question first: I know there is seldom something so formal as a reading of the will, with

all the heirs gathered in one room. But once you've shared the contents of the will with me, aren't you then obliged to inform everyone else who is mentioned for bequests?"

"Within a reasonable amount of time, yes."

"And what would be reasonable?"

"In the case of everyone concerned living in the same general proximity, I should say a night and a day. If some heirs have to be located, then it would vary."

"Do you recall if there was a bequest to Ralph and Myra Porter? They are a couple who worked for my family for many years. I was distressed to find they are no longer employed at the house, but I never said anything to Father about it because I didn't want to upset him."

"I'm sorry, I can't say that I recall. But let me get the key—"

He pushed his chair back and bent down to open a drawer near the bottom of his desk.

I interrupted his rummaging. "No, please, don't do that. Not right now. I would much prefer to leave this matter until after the funeral."

Sefton returned to his upright position with key in hand. "As you wish. However, since you're here—"

"I'm thinking of Augusta. She will more than likely be upset to find most of the . . ." I hesitated over the unfamiliar word, "estate will go to me."

"Hm. She might, yes. She might. I do see your point. Well then, when is the funeral to be?"

"I don't know. She went out to make arrangements this morning, but she hasn't told me what they are specifically. I know Father has a plot in Mount Auburn Cemetery next to Mother, and I know he would not have wanted very much in the way of a religious ceremony, because he wasn't a religious man. He felt we are all a part of Nature, and at the end of our lives our bodies will go back to the earth, and that is as it should be—"

"Oh!" One hand flew involuntarily to my mouth. "I wonder if Augusta knows about the wooden coffin?"

Sefton frowned. "I'm not following you."

"When Mother died, Father had her buried in a coffin made of wood, even though it's no longer the . . . the usual thing. I recall the undertaker's being quite upset about it, shaking his head, much mumbling in the library and so on. Father chose wood because of his belief that for our bodies to decay after death and mix with the soil is the natural way of things."

"You've just jarred my memory, Miss Jones. I'm afraid your wish to wait until after the funeral to begin dealing with these legal matters won't do. Leonard put his wishes for his own funeral into writing, and included them as part of the will. As soon as I'd heard of his death, I should have had to contact both you and Augusta Simmons. Indeed I'm somewhat surprised she hasn't already been in. But in any event, the usual thing is for a death announcement to be placed in the newspaper. When I read that, I'd have called right away. It's only that you got here before I received notice, don't you see."

"Oh dear," I sighed.

"In fact, I don't understand why she hasn't been in contact with the bank already."

"I expect Augusta is assuming some earlier copy of the will is still in effect. It will be your unfortunate duty to tell her otherwise, Mr. Sefton."

"Unfortunate, yes. But necessary. Now"—he once more held up the key to the safety-deposit box—"shall we go down?"

FOURTEEN

───◆───

ON MY WAY out of the bank I stopped to thank
William Barrett for having called at the house.
His clerk, another of the guardians at the rail,
told me William was in a meeting; I left a message.

Actually I felt fortunate that William was unavail-
able, because the whole business with Elwood Sefton
had taken longer than I'd thought it would. He had insisted on going over every paragraph of Father's will
with me. There had been no surprises, but I'm sure it
was something that had to be done and therefore it was
just as well to have it behind me. Nevertheless, it had
taken a long while and had been more than a little
draining.

On exit I raised my arm to catch my carriage driver's
eye. While waiting for him to disentangle himself from
his carriage post and get the horse in gear, as it were, I
reached into the pocket of my long coat and found the
slip of paper upon which Nurse Bates had written the
address of the nurse, Sarah Kirk. The name of her street
was unfamiliar to me, but the driver knew it well
enough, for he nodded and, as soon as he had assisted
me inside, got us underway without a word. No questions, no comment. He did not even cluck at his horse.

I wondered if I were being hypersensitive due to—well, really, due to more things than I cared to think about; or if I were correct in my observation that the inhabitants of Boston did not, in general, converse as openly and casually as do the inhabitants of San Francisco. This carriage driver provided a good example: I knew if I were to ask him a direct question he would reply, but otherwise he would have no more to say to me on our way to Sarah Kirk's house than he'd said on the way to the bank, which amounted to sum zero. How was it that I, a native Bostonian, had never before noticed how much people kept to themselves?

And further, was this self-containment a good thing, a desirable trait? Were San Franciscans by contrast boisterous and even boorish? Or simply friendly and more relaxed? For a moment I wished Michael were with me. I would have liked his opinion.

However, it was a short moment, for in truth I could not have Michael with me on this visit to Sarah Kirk. This, and probably more, I must do on my own. Lamentably, uneasily on my own.

Michael did not share my suspicions of Augusta. He had outright accused me of having an unreasoning dislike for her. While I could not quite defend myself against that statement, I could say that my dislike was not unreasoning, but reasonable in the circumstances. Yet even that much he would not acknowledge.

His attitude wounded me. I did not want to—no, more than that—I *could* not hear anything more from Michael right now. I was so afraid he, or I, or the both of us, would say something that would then stand between us forever, would be impossible for us later to forgive and forget. We had come dangerously close to that point already.

The carriage rumbled on, into a poorer section of town. Streets grew narrower, dirtier, and bumpier; I had not seen an automobile for blocks. I had a sense that we were working our way gradually toward Boston Harbor, but due to the density of structures leaning close in over the street I could barely see the sky, much less a patch of water.

On reflection, considering these surroundings, I was glad to be taking this trip in a hired carriage. That did not mean, however, I'd be wrong to consider the purchase of my own automobile.

I mulled over this idea, glad it had come to mind. Given my inheritance, I could well afford my own car, and having one would greatly increase my ability to get around without having to depend on Michael or on anyone. That was an exceedingly attractive thought. On the unattractive side was the idea of spending so much money on any one thing. For most of the past four years I'd had very little money—the year after the earthquake, desperately little—and that experience had changed my attitude toward money forever.

In case I should need to return to this neighborhood again without someone else to drive me, I began to pay closer attention to the route. I recalled having passed Fanueil Hall some time back, after which the carriage had made a sharp turn to the right. Since then the driver had been moving forward in a sort of zigzagging progression, like tacking a sailboat—that image may have come to mind because I could smell salt water, but it was nevertheless apt. Not to mention confusing.

Hmm. Chances were slim to none that I would ever find my way alone through this warren of streets. There must be another way to go about it, if only one had a map. And if only all these streets were on the map. Sometimes streets, whole towns even, were left off maps; that was something I had learned last year in Utah.

Just when I was beginning to feel so hopelessly lost as to become a tad uneasy, the carriage emerged onto Hanover Street, which I recognized, and then I knew we were in the North End. Soon I saw the spire of Old North Church upon its hill. Then, with a jerk that almost upset the carriage, the driver made an abrupt turn into a street so narrow we were barely able to pass.

It was dark and noisy, full of the smells that build up when too many people have lived too close together for too long. Dogs barked and babies cried. A cat streaked across our path. Curious heads leaned out of windows—the carriage was a novelty and a disruption.

Slower and slower the carriage wheels turned. I had the presence of mind to snatch the fur hat off my head, likewise the scarf from around my neck, and to stash them and the fur muff too under the lap robe.

"Do not let anyone into the carriage while I am gone," I admonished the driver, "not even curious children." It wasn't that I minded if these things were stolen, but rather that I did not want to be any more set apart from the people of this neighborhood than I had been already, just by arriving in a hired carriage.

The driver allowed as how he wouldn't think of it, then in a surprising outburst of garrulity added, pointing, "There's the house you're wanting, miss. If anybody comes along and makes me move the carriage, don't you worry, I'll go round the block and come on back. But I don't think that'll happen. It's mostly foot traffic in these parts."

I thanked the man, gathered my skirt close in to my body with one hand, and with the cane in the other approached the door the driver had indicated. Along the way I stepped over some potato peelings and other assorted debris that was probably best left unidentified.

These houses were very old, and had never been the least bit grand even when they were new. Now they seemed to be doing all that could be expected of them if their four walls simply did not fall down. The stoop was a cracked, irregularly shaped piece of stone. I stepped up onto it and rapped on a door so old the wood had turned almost black. In some places it had cracked clear through and I could see light from the other side.

Light and movement: With what felt like a hundred curious eyes on my back, I stood waiting as the door opened and there stood Sarah Kirk.

"Sarah, forgive the intrusion," I said, "but I must speak with you."

Her eyes were huge and frightened in her gaunt face. She bit her lips bloodless and said nothing.

"Surely you do recognize me?"

She nodded. A whimper came from somewhere in the dimly lit room behind her and she cast a quick glance over her shoulder.

"May I please come in?" I asked, and God forgive me, I did not wait for her invitation. I put my cane on through the door and followed it one foot at a time.

Sarah backed up as I came through but still she said nothing, and she left it for me to close the door behind me. In truth the little room was so stuffy I would have preferred to leave it open, but that would have meant all those eyes continuing to stare. And no doubt a hundred ears would have been overhearing us as well.

Another whimper, and Sarah turned and left me.

She is going to her sick child, I thought.

Oh, but I'd had no idea how sick he was . . . I had no idea such a creature could be human and continue to live.

Sarah came back with her child—I supposed it was a boy—wrapped around her. If he were able to stand, he would likely have been as tall as she, for Sarah Kirk was a small woman both in stature and of limb. But one doubted he could stand; his arms and legs were white as mushrooms that have grown in a cellar without ever knowing light, and they were thin as the bones beneath that too pale skin. His hugely misshapen head lolled against her shoulder, his almost white hair was wispy and thin as a baby's, his blue eyes were vague and unfocused, and his protruding tongue leaked drool down her dress.

"You see how it is, Miss Jones," she said.

"How—how old?" My own problems, whatever they might have been, had shrunk to nothing and temporarily fled my mind. I could not even begin to frame the words I wanted to say, nor were the words I'd come in here intent on saying necessarily the right ones, the words that most needed to be said.

"Thirteen years. But he won't last much longer. Can't. His lungs don't half work anymore."

As if to demonstrate, the creature in her arms sucked in a heaving breath, so heavily congested it sounded as if he were breathing underwater.

"Can we—" I began, then backed off what I'd originally intended and tried again. "Ah, that is, he must be heavy for you. Perhaps we might sit down?"

Sarah stiffened. "I have nothing to say to you, miss."

The words sounded as if she had rehearsed them. As if she'd expected eventually to see me here, or to be questioned by me at some time and place. Ah, but had she rehearsed them all on her own or had someone else required it, even chosen what she was to say?

With the purpose of my visit thus forcefully recalled to me, I made a quick decision. I knew it might prove disastrous, might backfire, but still I went ahead on pure instinct.

Quietly but forcefully I said, "Whatever amount any other person has paid or offered to pay you, I will pay you double. I don't mean to offend you, Sarah—I can see you truly need money for the boy. But the thing is, I must talk to you, and have some answers from you. I think you know why."

The boy groaned and his head lolled dangerously. He had very little control over his musculature, and as he moved, Sarah's hand came up automatically to protect that huge head, as one does a baby's. A glistening thread of saliva stretched between his head and her upraised arm like a piece of spider's web.

Sarah's eyes lost some of their fear and gazed at me questioningly instead. Finally she jerked her head toward the dim recesses behind her and said, "All right, we can sit over here, if you think you can stand it."

Her remark and the tone in which she said it made me thank God I had not come in here dripping Russian sable. I followed her farther into the room, which was small and therefore crowded, rather dark owing to its having only one narrow window, but perfectly clean.

I felt so keenly the unjust disparity between Sarah Kirk's situation and my own that if I could have run out and immediately sold the things I'd left on the carriage seat beneath that lap robe, I would have done it, and given her all the money . . . for nothing. I'd have done it just because she needed the money far more than I needed furs; far more indeed than any human being needed such frivolity as furs, except perhaps in Russia, where furs may not be so frivolous, as without them the Russians might freeze to death. At any rate, I would have given Sarah the proceeds from such a sale gladly, whether she gave me information or not.

But that was a fantasy, and here and now the reality must be dealt with. I watched the nurse arrange her deformed and probably mentally defective son on a pallet atop a wooden platform at waist height. Nearby a very large wicker basket held soiled bedding. There was a slight stench, but not much. I surmised the boy must have no control over any bodily functions, that she changed the bedding frequently, most likely washing the boy each time she changed it, and the bedding once a day. A formidable amount of work, especially considering she also had her nursing jobs at night.

I stood looking over her shoulder, so interested in the diligent way she cared for her son that I could not feel repelled. Sarah glanced at me and said, "You can sit over there, miss."

"Please call me Fremont," I said absently, "I do not hold with formality. Did someone build this platform for you especially? It's an interesting arrangement, well thought out so that you do not have to bend down so far to pick him up as you would if he were in the usual sort of bed."

"Yes, that is so." Sarah seemed surprised. "You know something of nursing then? How is that, a lady like you?"

I smiled. "Those who know me in this city might

disagree with you about my being a lady. You see, Sarah, I did a shocking thing a few years ago: I left home in order to work for a living, to have my own business. I went all the way to San Francisco in order to be sure of that freedom. But then, as luck would have it, the very next year we had a huge earthquake out there, and most people lost everything. Including me."

"I heard about that." She nodded. "Edwin will be all right for a while now, so whyn't we sit down. I could make tea if you like."

Edwin—what a noble name for a boy whose life turned out to have only the most pathetic prospects.

"No, thank you," I said. "I had coffee not long ago, and I don't plan to intrude upon you for very long. You asked if I knew anything of nursing—what I know, I learned after that earthquake. I worked for quite a while with the nurses of the Red Cross, though I never had formal nurse's training myself. Disaster relief, it was called—we did a lot of everything. I admire women in the nursing profession tremendously. You're obviously doing a fine job of taking care of your son, Sarah."

Sarah bit her lips again.

I added, "I am sure you did an equally fine job taking care of my father. But still, we must talk about that."

Sarah wore a white apron over a checked flannel dress—the apron's material was thin yet not fine like handkerchief linen; rather it had been washed and ironed countless times to near-transparency. She unconsciously took up a corner of the apron and rolled it against her knee.

I drew in a deep breath and got on with it. "Am I correct in surmising that Edwin cannot understand what we say?"

She nodded. "He's an idiot."

In spite of the seeming harshness of the word, especially when applied to her own son, I understood that Sarah was speaking as a trained nurse to whom the word "idiot" was a medical classification. Meaning he lacked the mental capacity to learn and to think and behave like a normal human being.

"Very well," I said. "To get straight to the point: Night before last, the night my father died, I came into his room at about three o'clock in the morning. Something, I don't know what, had awakened me. You were sound asleep in the reading chair."

"I—"

I held up my hand to stop her before she wasted valuable time defending herself. I overrode her words with my own: "I'm not taking you to task for sleeping, or even blaming you for it. In fact, I do not think it was your fault that you were asleep. I think your sleeping at that particular time and in that particular circumstance was beyond your control."

Now Sarah's expression was both puzzled and wary. "I don't understand you."

"I believe you will understand shortly. Now, at what time did you wake up?"

She bit her lips again. Any harder, I thought, and she'll draw blood.

I decided to try another tack. "All right. Why don't you tell me then, in your own words, what happened on the night of my father's death. Everything, just as you remember it. Starting from whenever it was that the house grew quiet and you were left alone with your patient."

"He . . . he was sick, and he died, and that's all there was," Sarah said in a strained voice. "I don't know what you remember, Miss Jones, Miss Fremont, but the truth is, when he died you went all hysterical. Mrs. Jones, Mrs. Augusta, she came and saw how it was, and then she went and called the doctor. Dr. Cosgrove, that is. I work private duty for a lot of Dr. Cosgrove's patients. By the time he came you were, well, you weren't yourself. I wouldn't expect you to be able to make sense of anything, on account of being out of your senses for a while. That was why the doctor gave you the medicine, to let you rest until your senses could return to normal."

I was too stunned by this recital to say anything at all.

Sarah looked at me steadily. "I'm glad to see you're feeling so much better now, and I appreciate your coming by."

I turned my head away. The impulse to simply give up and leave was very strong, but I fought it down. When I had control of myself and had regained a measure of determination, I looked at her again and said:

"I believe either Augusta or Searles Cosgrove paid you to tell me that story, and perhaps to tell it to the police or anyone else who might ask, as well. I say to you again that I will pay you double, if you will tell me the truth. And I will protect you too. I can do this because I, not Augusta, am Father's heir. No one will say you neglected your patient."

I took in another deep breath, and with it that faint stench of soiled bedclothes from the basket by the bed with its human burden. "So, Sarah, shall we begin again?"

Sarah stood up, tall as she could, which was not very. She folded her hands very properly and said, "Miss Fremont, there is no need to say any of that again. I won't tell them you offered me money. I've already told you what happened, and now I think you'd best go."

FIFTEEN

———◆———

THERE WERE FOUR of us around the dinner table at Beacon Street that night: Augusta, Larry, Michael, and I. Augusta was very properly dressed in unrelieved black, not even pearls or a cameo in sight; her jewelry was jet. This was the first I'd seen of her since Dr. Cosgrove had rendered me insensible with laudanum.

It was chilly in the dining room in more ways than one.

Michael looked grim. I wondered if I were the cause, or just this whole unhappy situation.

He has his black moods from time to time; generally when he has them he goes off alone somewhere, sometimes without notice. Would he do that now? Would Michael completely, physically desert me? I felt he had already deserted me in a significant way, because he did not believe in the legitimacy of my concerns about Father's illness and death. I felt doubly wounded, as if not only had I lost Father but now Michael was drifting away from me too.

My inner voice, which had not had much to say to me for a while—or perhaps I had not been listening— made a comment. It seemed to come from so far away that I had to strain to hear it: *You could be overreacting, Fremont.*

I replied to the inner voice with a silent snort: *If I'm overreacting, then why isn't he helping me to find out what really happened to Father?*

Because he too had fallen under Augusta's spell, that was why. I was sure of it. Why, even now he was smiling at something she had said. Some inconsequential frivolity I had missed.

Hah! This was hardly a time for inconsequential frivolities. I felt an awful urge to jab him with the toe of my shoe, and I probably would have except that he was sitting on the other side of the table, where my foot could not reach. Augusta had seated Michael at her right hand.

I decided to leave him to flirt with her—if he dared do such a thing right on the heels of her husband's dying—and I turned to try my wiles on Larry.

Two could play at the flirting game, and in my case it was more excusable because I had loftier intentions. Michael was only acting like a man, and of course all men are beasts . . . at least, from time to time. They have been only barely civilized by women down through the centuries, I am convinced of it.

"I hope you had a pleasant afternoon," I said to Larry. "Did you go out in search of old acquaintances as I suggested?"

He looked up from his soup, which he had been taking from the spoon with a slight slurp. "I'd thought I might, but then right in the middle of the afternoon, when I was about to leave, Ma got a call from the bank."

Oh dear, I thought. So Augusta had heard about the will already.

"I had to go down there with her. To keep her company, you know. She's upset still at losing Leonard."

I could not tell if I were imagining it, for we were dining by the uncertain light of candles flickering in two candelabra, but I thought Larry Bingham was regarding me speculatively.

"Of course she is," I said. "So am I."

Larry looked as if he expected me to say more, but I resumed eating my soup instead.

Augusta's visit to the bank and what she likely learned there was not a subject I could pursue, nor could I encourage her son to do so. Augusta would have to broach it herself if it were to be discussed at all—and I rather hoped it would not. Not tonight, I did not want to deal with all that tonight. Money, property, who would get what—surely it was unseemly to talk of these things before Father's body was even laid in the ground!

I heartily wished Elwood Sefton had not been so insistent upon it—especially since the only items in the will having to do with the funeral itself had been the mention of the plot in Mount Auburn Cemetery and the proviso that Father's coffin be made of wood. I had already known both those things, and would most certainly have told Augusta, so really it had been unnecessary for Sefton to get into Father's will now.

On the other hand, said my inner voice, *when you know something is bound to be unpleasant, perhaps it is best just to get on with it. Do you really believe revenge is a dish best served cold?*

Revenge. Was that what I was embarking upon, a course of revenge? I did not think of it as revenge, but rather as a search for the truth, and for justice, for my father's sake.

Tears pricked at my eyes, and I covered them with my hand. If only I were not so very tired—it was hard to keep myself in control.

To my great surprise, Larry, who was seated at my left, sensed my disturbance and reacted with sensitivity. He reached out and put his hand over my other hand, which remained in my lap. Too intimate a gesture, perhaps, for one of such short acquaintance. Yet I appreciated it, because at that moment I was in need of a human touch.

"I'm sorry," he said. "I know you must be at least as unhappy about losing your father as my mother is about losing her husband. It's not like she's the only one has a right to be upset, I know."

He'd spoken so quietly I doubted if Michael had heard. But Augusta did, and her head snapped up as she shot me a keen glance.

I had no idea what she and Michael had been talking about; I'd been distracted by my own thoughts. Whatever it might have been, she abandoned it and directed all her attention to me.

"Fremont," she said in a disapproving tone, "I heard you went out today."

Why should I not go out, and what concern should she have over my comings and goings? The tip of my tongue itched to snap back at her, but I did not wish to be unnecessarily provocative, and so I said nothing.

Augusta regarded me with what could only be called a withering glare. "I hope you have done something to obtain the proper wardrobe. Was that where you went, if I may inquire?"

"I beg your pardon?" I asked, blinking in disbelief. Proper wardrobe? She wants to talk, to make a fuss, about *clothes*?

Ah, said my inner voice, *but you are supposed to be in mourning.* And Augusta's next words confirmed that my inner voice was right.

"I would offer you something more appropriate myself, but you are so much taller than I am—"

Not to mention too thin for fashion, my feet are too long, my hair is straight as a stick, blah-blah-blah. Oh really, the triviality of this whole subject made me want to tear out what hair I had, straight or not!

Once again I sensed I was on the edge of my control, and so I reined myself in and tried to pay attention to the topic. There had been a death. Mourning was appropriate.

For dining alone with family, even in the circumstances, I'd thought I was properly enough dressed. Since Mary had informed me we would all be eating together in the dining room tonight, I had changed my day dress for a gown of midnight-blue silk, with a high neck and long sleeves and a full, floor-length skirt. I showed not even the hint of an ankle. What could be more proper than that?

Actually I knew the answer to that question, and loath though I might be to talk of clothes, I gave it: "I know I am not wearing black, Augusta. I'm not fond of black and so I own nothing of that color. This means I must provide myself with an entire new wardrobe, which takes time. I am taking all the necessary steps to see to it; you need not be concerned."

There. That should satisfy her. And I thought too that I had rather neatly sidestepped the matter of my going out, not mentioning where I'd been. I couldn't tell them about my visit to Nurse Kirk, not even Michael; nor did I want to have to make up a tale to account for half my afternoon's whereabouts.

"These steps," Augusta said, "had better not take too much time. Leonard will be buried day after tomorrow. The death announcement will appear in tomorrow's newspaper with all the details."

I nodded. Surely at R. H. Stearns I would be able to find something ready-made that I could wear with only a quick alteration to the bodice. I always needed a quick alteration to the bodice; and I always had to deal with both the saleswoman and the fitting woman fussing at me for not wearing a corset. No wonder I hated buying clothes.

But Augusta was not done with me yet, not by a long shot. She said, "You really should not have gone out today in that coat of yours—some shade of red, isn't it? Highly inappropriate!"

"The coat is burgundy," I said, "and it is the only one I have. At the moment. I will have another tomorrow, I assure you."

"But you went to the bank this afternoon, your father's bank, wearing a red coat. Didn't you, Fremont?

Red, burgundy, they are much the same. Of course, everyone knows you have a reputation for being unconventional, but that is too much."

Larry Bingham had tucked his head down so far, if he lowered it any farther he'd be beneath the table. Michael, however, gazed intently at me through a thicket of candles in the tall candelabra. Even in this light—perhaps especially in this light—I could see that his eyes had gone dark and cold as sapphires. This is something that happens only when Michael is gripped with some intensity of feeling. His eyes look like that in orgasm; but they also look like that in rage.

"My trip to the bank was necessary." My chin came up; it was time for me to defend myself, even if I intended to do so with half-truths and a few outright lies. I continued:

"If you had consulted me before making Father's funeral arrangements, my trip to the bank today could have been avoided, Augusta. But you went ahead with those arrangements on your own, without doing me that courtesy. This was unfortunate, because I knew there were certain aspects of the burial that he was likely to have wanted a certain way. Father felt so strongly that I expected he would have included these wishes in his last will and testament. That document is, as I knew, being kept at the bank by Mr. Sefton, and so of course I had to go there to see him. Would you expect me, Augusta, to allow you to bypass me entirely in such a crucial matter? Especially when to do so might have meant that Father would be buried in some way other than he most wanted? His wishes were spelled out in the will, by the way. I was correct."

"I know," Augusta said, with a most peculiar intonation to her voice. "I saw Sefton myself. Now I know everything. Don't worry," she threw her napkin down on the table suddenly, "he'll get his wooden box, and everything else he wanted, just exactly as he wanted it. Now if you will all excuse me, I have a headache and am going up to my room."

Michael stood politely, and mutely.

Larry jumped up, forgetting to push his chair back first, banging his legs against the underside of the table and jostling the plates and crystal. "Want me to come up with you, Ma?"

"Certainly not," Augusta said, turning in the doorway with an expression on her face that was almost a sneer. "You stay here with your new friend."

By "new friend" I did not think she meant Michael.

When his mother had left the dining room, Larry collapsed back into his chair like a deflated balloon. This time he caught the edge of the tablecloth on his way down, and I reached over to rescue his water glass just before it fell.

It was on the tip of my tongue to say I was sorry, but I'd be damned if I'd do that. What did I have to be sorry for? That woman had killed my father, I was certain even if I couldn't prove it, and for all I knew her son had helped.

But as I looked closely at him, I could not believe he'd had any part in it. He seemed altogether too young, too ... well, *incompetent* to be a murderer, or even an accomplice to murder.

"Errh-um," Michael said.

My thoughts were still on Larry: He did get excited about criminal acts, that was true ...

"Fremont?"

... but no, I didn't think his was the kind of excitement that would carry him into the doing of criminal things himself. He liked to read about them, and he would have liked to write about them if he had the chance. That was all.

I felt sorry for Larry; I remembered how hard he had tried to please Augusta that first night, had worked himself up practically into a fever. Now he seemed somewhat desperate since his mother had gone from the room. Remembering his recent sensitivity to me, I reached out and patted his shoulder in what I hoped was an encouraging manner.

"Fremont?"

"What?" I asked Michael sharply.

"Would you mind telling me what just went on here, since you and Larry Bingham both seem to know? I would like to be let in on the secret."

I hesitated, and into my hesitation, Larry blurted:

"She's upset because she didn't get the money!"

I placed my hand on his arm again, and this time I left it there. To calm him was my intention.

Addressing Michael, I said, "As I told Augusta just now, I expected Father would want to be buried in a certain way—"

Larry interrupted: "She should've waited till you could go with her to talk to them about the funeral and all. I mean, he was your dad same as she's my ma—I never had a dad, and I guess you were a long time without a ma either, and I reckon I know how that feels. I wanted to make her wait but I couldn't, she never listens to me, she never lets me tell her anything!"

"That's hardly an unusual state of affairs between mothers and sons," Michael said dryly.

I hastened with my explanation, sensing something here I didn't like any more than I understood it: an atmosphere of tension in the room that had not dissipated, as I thought it should have, with Augusta's departure. I explained how I had recalled my mother's burial in a wooden coffin, how this had prompted my own trip to the bank, and so on.

With a nervous glance at Larry, who seemed now thoroughly miserable and therefore at least five years younger than his real age, I touched on the major points of Father's will. For Larry's sake I emphasized the security of the fund Father had set up to provide for Augusta the rest of her life. I concluded:

"It is only unfortunate, I think, that this could not have waited until after the funeral."

Michael nodded. His eyes had stopped glittering, which was a relief to me.

"I don't know," Larry said, throwing his own napkin

on the table in an exact if unconscious copy of his mother's gesture not long before, "maybe it's better for me this way."

He got up from the table, but this time he remembered to push his chair back first. With one hand he slicked back his hair at the sides of his head, first one and then the other, as if in this way he might also restore order to his troubled mind.

"What do you mean," I asked, after having darted a glance toward Michael and seeing that he wasn't going to, "better for you?"

"I had a pretty good job down there in New York. They didn't want me to leave, and if I go right back maybe I can get there before they hire somebody else to take my place. I'm not staying for the funeral. He wasn't my daddy—" Larry stared at me for a minute with a challenging look in his eyes. "In fact, the old guy didn't even like me very much. I bet he'd rather I wasn't here."

I had the feeling he wanted me to ask him to stay. But my voice stuck in my throat, and I didn't ask, and the moment passed.

"Your mother wants you here," Michael pointed out.

Larry made a face, as if he'd swallowed something that had left a nasty taste in his mouth. "She nags me. And she embarrasses me all the time. Like tonight. I've had enough," he said.

And then he left the dining room.

Just as Larry went out the door to the hall, Mary Fowey came in from the kitchen with a platter of roast chicken, the main course. I believe we had all forgotten there was to be anything more to this meal.

"What's this, then? Only two of you left?" she asked.

SIXTEEN

"I CAN SEE you're on the edge of exhaustion," Michael said, "but you and I have to talk as soon as you feel you can."

He had his hat in hand already; I'd walked him to the front door to say good night. Our dinner unexpectedly *à deux* had been almost silent by mutual agreement, I'd thought. I had appreciated the respite.

I nodded. "I feel better since eating, although I thought I wasn't hungry," I said. "And I agree, we do have to talk. But not here, where, as they say, the walls have ears. Tomorrow morning?"

Michael bent his head, bringing his face close to mine, close but not touching, respectful and perhaps wary of the distance that had grown between us of late. Across that distance, which was somehow so much farther than mere inches, I felt him draw me like a magnet. I felt irresistibly attracted, yearning to touch the rough silk of his beard, to taste the sweet salt of his skin.

I lifted my face, wanting him, wanting *us* to be as we had been together in the best of times, and he kissed me. There in the hall, in the hush of my ancestral house, Michael kissed me. It was like kissing a stranger; but it was also like coming home.

In this kiss I felt something I had never felt before, not like this. I felt how strongly this man and I were bonded together, like two trees whose roots have intertwined belowground, although aboveground they seemingly stand separate and apart.

In this kiss I found the knowledge that he would not desert me. My inner voice had been right: the stresses of this day, the day before, and many days before that, all had led me temporarily astray, made me doubt and overreact.

"I love you," Michael said solemnly as his lips left mine.

"I love you too," I replied, equally solemn. Such simple words, yet are there any others?

"Tomorrow morning I will come for you early. We'll go over to the Parker House and have a fine breakfast, with some of their famous rolls. Then if the day is fair we'll walk and talk—in the park where we won't be overheard."

"That park is not a park, it's the Common. I know: You can walk me up Tremont Street to the department store, since I must go there anyway."

"Eventually," he promised. His eyes were dark with concern and the tone of his voice was grave. "You were right, you know. There are far more important things going on here than the need for mourning clothes."

"Thank you."

Could I hope he was beginning to believe me, to see things my way? I cared so much, wanted so much for him to believe, that I didn't dare ask.

Michael touched my cheek with his gloved fingertips, then turned to open the front door. We were still alone in the hall, with the house a huge, hovering presence at my back.

"Good night, sleep well," I said.

I ached at seeing him go. I would have given much to sleep in Michael's arms tonight . . . even if I had to wake and find on the morrow that he did not believe me after all. All of a sudden I understood how it is with those silly creatures in fairy tales who do things like trade a kingdom for one night with their beloved.

THE HOUSE was too quiet. Eerily quiet.

I lay in bed in the guest room, which I hoped would not be my room much longer, and listened to the silence. I tried to analyze what there was about the particular quality of the quiet in my old house that bothered me so much.

It was almost a hundred years old; generations had lived here. Maybe there were ghosts. Maybe the ghosts were real; certainly I knew enough people who thought such things were real. But I did not. Anyway, ghosts would have been too easy an answer for this problem.

I sighed.

Too, too quiet.

I wished I had Hiram, my black cat, here to amuse and comfort me. His soft paws would make a circle in my lap two or three times, then he'd curl himself into a ball with the tip of his tail over his nose, close his eyes, and purr until he'd purred himself to sleep. Hiram could purr me close to contentment too; he'd done that many a time.

I sighed again.

Earlier I had brought in the reading lamp from Father's room because there was no good lamp in this room to read by; wasteful as it was of electricity, after Michael left I'd kept that lamp burning through the remainder of the evening and into the hours past midnight. I had dozed from time to time with a book open on my chest, just as Sarah Kirk had done on the night my father died.

Her denial had not fooled me for a minute. Well, to be truthful, not for much more than a minute. When things are dire, one may rather easily be persuaded to doubt oneself. And things were certainly dire.

I was waiting until I could be sure both Larry and

Augusta were sleeping soundly; Mary Fowey was of no concern. If she were to walk in on me, I'd just enlist her help. I truly did not think Mary would give me away, especially since Augusta would not be mistress of this house much longer. Mary's job here was secure, though Mary herself might not know it yet.

Once again, as on the night Father died, it was between 2 and 3 A.M. when I opened the door from my room into the hall and listened with all the intensity at my command. Still only the silence.

It was then that I realized what was so strange about the quality of this silence: I missed the ticking of the big clock, and its chiming of the half hour and the hour. In this house that clock had always been a constant in the background, in much the same way my father had constantly been in the background of my entire life . . . until now.

I could, and would, restore the clock to its rightful place in the working order, but not yet. Father, alas, could not be restored, but he could be avenged—only not yet. For many other things, too, the bywords were "not yet." Now there was much I must do to see to it that Augusta moved out of Beacon Street and into the place she rightfully belonged—wherever that place might be.

I hadn't bothered to try to persuade her to ask for an autopsy on Father's body. Trying persuasion on Augusta would have been a complete waste of time; Dr. Cosgrove, who apparently was far from always right about everything, had been right about that at least. She would never agree to an autopsy, though not for the reason he thought. Or professed to think. If she'd had an accomplice, Cosgrove would make a fair candidate for that position. The doctor would be a more appropriate partner in crime than her strange and strangely affecting son.

I comforted myself with the thought that all criminals make mistakes. If I were diligent, I might uncover Augusta's. I lit the candle I needed for a light down the hall, closed my own bedroom door as if I were still reading, and stood outside Augusta's door for a couple of minutes. As my eyes adjusted to the near-total darkness, I did not see around her door the thin line of light I could see even at a distance around mine. Nor did I hear any sound coming from within; but, as I had noted earlier, this house was so solidly built that sound did not pass easily through the walls.

Ah well, that would work to my advantage once I was in Father's rooms.

Borrowing the lamp earlier had taken away some of the element of shock I felt at being in Father's bedroom again. Still, I had an uneasiness in the pit of my stomach as I shut the door and closed myself in. I took a good, deep breath, turned on the electric light, blew out the candle, and began methodically, as I'd been taught in my training as a private investigator, to search.

Everything was clean and tidy, and appeared to be exactly as it was the night Father died, and all the other days and nights before it, since his coming home from the hospital. This was as unsurprising as it was unhelpful.

If only I'd been able to keep my wits about me when I found Father dead, how differently things might have gone that night, and the day after! I cursed myself for those hours of childish regression until I found my hands were shaking so much that I could hardly proceed.

"What's done is done, Fremont," I said aloud to myself. There was no point blaming myself any more than I had already, it would be a waste of time and self-destructive. Nor should I doubt the little bit of memory I did retain, of how the nurse sat sleeping, the position in which Father lay.

I reconstructed the scene in my mind but it did no good. No new ideas sprang to mind, no new observation leaped out at me.

I conducted the most diligent search of which I was capable throughout the bedroom, and found nothing other than the things one would expect to find.

In the dressing room it was another story.

At first I thought that, like the bedroom, this one held nothing worth noting. Yet some instinct nagged and nagged at me all through my search of drawers and shelves, in pockets of jackets and trousers and shirts and inside shoes, even in the secret recess at the back of the carved base of the washstand, where I'd liked to hide things when I was a child. Nothing! Nothing, nothing, nothing, and yet nag, nag, nag.

"*What*?" I asked aloud in exasperation.

Then I knew: the dressing room was too neat, neat in a way that was not Father's way. Not that he was messy, but he had not been one of those people who square up corners and make sure everything is spaced out equally along an invisible line. Someone, most likely Augusta, had been through *everything* here, down to the very back of the very bottom drawer. She had restored order, all right, but in an excessively orderly fashion that told its own tale.

I did not know what she'd been looking for, or what she'd found, but one thing she had removed I did know: pictures of Mother. Every single informal photograph of my mother was gone from the places in his drawers where Father had sentimentally and randomly kept them, so that—as he had told me—he might stumble over Mother from time to time. It made a nice surprise, he'd said.

Augusta'd had that whole day when I was drugged with the laudanum, I thought—a whole day to do this wholesale clean-out job. Damnation!

But, all right. If she had gone over this dressing room so meticulously, she'd done it because she was looking for something, hiding the evidence, effecting a cover-up. That was evidence of a kind in itself. It was enough to keep me going.

And besides, I knew Father, and I knew all the secrets of this house.

I had been here in his two rooms too long anyway; it was time to go downstairs.

First I went into the kitchen, where I found a tin of graham crackers and put some on a plate—not because I was hungry but because the crackers would provide an excuse for being in the library: I could say, if challenged, that I'd been unable to sleep and had come downstairs for a snack and to look for a book. It might have been nice to have a cup of coffee to go with the graham crackers; but making it would take too long, so I settled for sweet cider from a stoneware crock. Then I took my small-hours-of-the-night repast into the library, which had been my destination all along.

I did need to sit down; my legs were growing tired. I'd conducted this entire search without the aid of my cane. Not by design—I'd just forgotten and left my room without it.

I sat behind Father's desk and turned on his banker's lamp with its green shade—he had electrified this lamp with a cord running up the brass part and a lightbulb where the wick for the kerosene used to be. I sat in Father's chair until I felt its leather cushions, so soft from years of bearing his weight, forget the contours of Augusta's recent brief occupation and shape themselves to my body. I ate graham crackers, spilling a few crumbs as I would have if I were eight years old and being allowed to sit at this desk; and as I would have at eight, I brushed them into the palm of my hand and dumped them on the plate. Then I drank a little cider, and all the while my eyes roamed over the desk and around the room.

I was operating on a strong hunch: If Father had hidden something in his dressing room—or even if he'd just kept this thing, whatever it was, in a safe place there—if it were truly important, he'd likely have had a duplicate. That duplicate he would have put away here in the library.

I was excited. What if Father himself had come to suspect, as I did, that his long, slow illness was caused by some kind of poison? Oh, I doubt he'd have thought Augusta was the one poisoning him, but this did not matter since he was no longer around to be asked. Nevertheless, if he had suspected *someone,* and if he'd found any kind of proof, he would have hidden it away. And Augusta would have looked for it the first chance she got.

Father's desk is an antique from the eighteenth century. Actually it is not a true desk but rather a library table. Like many items of furniture from that period, it has cunningly hidden compartments; due to the shape of the table these are long and shallow, most of them concealed behind a flange that disguises the depth of the tabletop, and some are tiny recesses—big enough only for something like a key—hollowed out of the table legs, hidden by a detail of carving.

I found a treasure trove of photographs of my mother, most faded to shades of brown, in the secret shallow drawers. I also found something else: a bottle. Not whiskey, but it did contain alcohol, according to the label. Some of the liquid remained.

Eventually, after going through all of the secret drawers and in addition searching behind certain books on the shelves where I knew Father had sometimes hidden things, I found three of these bottles. I took one and left the other two. Michael had to see this. He would confirm if the liquid in the bottle was meant for what I thought, and he would know too how we could find out if this stuff had slowly killed my father.

SEVENTEEN

———◆———

M Y FATHER'S OBITUARY, black-bordered in the traditional manner, was printed in the newspaper the next morning. Along with the rest of Boston, I read of his various accomplishments, and finally that a graveside service for Leonard Pembroke Jones would be conducted in Mount Auburn Cemetery at eleven o'clock, Friday morning March 26, 1909. This was the first I'd known of the exact time and place, as Augusta had not seen fit to inform me, nor had I been willing to ask her.

A graveside service at this time of year could be rather uncomfortable for the attendees, I thought, but Father would not have minded. Grudgingly I admitted that Augusta had made the right choice: it made sense not to have a church service for a man who so seldom went to church.

Mother would want flowers to go with him into the grave, I thought; she'd been very fond of flowers, especially lilies and roses. White lilies, pink roses (if there were hothouse roses to be had), in one of those long arrangements for the top of the wooden coffin, that was what she would have chosen. And so I would choose them for her, for us both.

Flowers: Dimly from childhood I remembered early mornings tagging along behind Mother or Myra Porter to the Haymarket, which was full of wholesale vendors of flowers and vegetables, all those mingled fragrances and colors under skies that were always gray in recollection. Mother always said, for the best and the freshest of these perishables, one must go early. And so, although the hour was still early, I knew those who dealt in flowers would already be abroad, and I telephoned a Back Bay florist and placed my order.

I had no sooner hung up the telephone and put on my coat than the front doorbell rang, and Mary Fowey, pale-faced but alert and neat as a pin, scurried to answer the door.

I expected Michael, but it was William Barrett who came inside.

Mary was saying, to the accompaniment of an even smaller version of her dip than she used for most people, "Begging pardon, sir, but was that Mrs. or Miss Jones you was asking for?"

I distinctly heard William reply, "Mrs. Jones."

I thought: Hmmm. Then I revealed my presence by stepping out of the telephone alcove.

"Never mind, Mary," I said, "I'll speak to Mr. Barrett in the parlor. When Mr. Kossoff arrives, show him in there if you will."

"Yes, miss," she said politely, but she lingered and I turned to her. "Will you be in to breakfast, miss?" she asked.

"No, but I have time to speak to Mr. Barrett. Thank you, Mary."

"Welcome, miss, I'm sure." But still she didn't scurry off and so I looked at her again, my eyebrows raised this time. "Coats, miss? I thought as how you and the gentleman might like me to take your coats if you'll be in the parlor."

Well, of course she would think that—she was a well-trained maid and William Barrett and I were both dressed for the out-of-doors, he because he had just come in and I because I was about to leave. But the house was chilly, there was no fire in the parlor, and I did not intend William should feel too welcome lest he settle in.

So I said, "No, thank you. I don't expect we'll be here long."

This time Mary took my hint and returned to the back of the house without making her next offer, which would have been to light the parlor fire.

"Caroline," William said, unbuttoning his long black overcoat, "I can't believe I haven't seen you since . . . When was the last time?"

"It was at the hospital, I believe, and do, if you please, call me Fremont."

I preceded him into the parlor and perched on the edge of one of the wing chairs flanking the stone-cold fireplace, then said further, "I was leaving one day when you were on your way in to see Father, about a week before he was discharged and we brought him home."

"Ah yes, I remember now. In any event, my condolences on your loss." The expected words. As if to be completely consistent, William perched in the expected place: on the other wing chair, though somewhat farther back from the edge of the seat than I had done.

"Thank you," I said. "On my part, I must apologize for having been unable to stop by your office when I was at the bank yesterday. My business with Mr. Sefton took more time than I'd thought it would."

"I understand. Legal matters can be time-consuming." William had removed his hat, and his surprisingly stubby, pale fingers were turning it around and around by the brim.

"The maid said you've often been here to the house. I had no idea, until after Father, ah, after he was gone, that Mary had been instructed never to receive callers or even to allow cards to be left. I'm afraid that may have created some misunderstandings, not only with you but with others among my father's friends."

William flushed slightly and for a moment could not meet my eyes.

I wondered why.

Then he cleared his throat, tucked his chin down, and said, "I expect people will understand. Most know that for the past couple of years nobody but Augusta's favorites has been welcome here."

"How . . . interesting." I placed my cane (which I was being careful to take with me today whether I needed it or not) squarely in front of me and then folded my hands on top of it, left hand over right. It is an old woman's gesture that gives one a feeling of authority; small compensation for the infirmity that causes one to need the cane, but be that as it may. "Perhaps you can enlighten me, William. Who would those favorites be?"

"Oh, well"—he glanced away, his eyes darting rapidly from the parlor door to something behind me to the carpet—"nobody at the bank."

"And?"

"Well, Cosgrove, I suppose—"

"Cosgrove? I thought you said Dr. Cosgrove was surprised to hear of my father's condition when you contacted him, and you didn't do that until I wrote to you, which was not much more than two months ago."

"Since then, I mean," William said hastily, "just since then he's been here a lot. But you're here too, so surely you knew how much he was here?"

Maybe not to the extent William seemed to imply, I hadn't; but more importantly, how did *he*, William, know?

I shook my head. "I hadn't paid attention," I said, a rather large fib that I intended to be disarming.

Then I proceeded to tell an even larger one: "But then, Dr. Cosgrove is not of much interest to me, other than his having taken such good care of Father. If he was here often, well, he had good reason. I suppose that would be why I didn't particularly notice."

William simply nodded and continued to look uncomfortable.

I decided to increase his discomfort: "You came to see Augusta this morning, I heard you say. I'm sorry, but I myself have not yet seen her this morning; I believe she has not been downstairs at all. She's been keeping much to her room since Father died. Grief-stricken, I'm sure. I'd be surprised if she's even dressed. May I give her a message for you later on, when I next see her?"

"Is her son still here?"

Now, how did he know about that?

"Larry Bingham?" I asked, giving myself a bit of extra time to think.

"I know the young man as Lawrence, but I expect we mean the same person."

"Augusta has other sons, I'm told," I said without precisely answering the question. I was setting out on a tangent, a kind of fishing expedition. William Barrett had not been truthful with me. He knew more of the doings of this household, and of Augusta in particular, than he had ever let on. I do not take it very kindly, I must say, when I am misled or, worse, outright lied to.

He said, "I've heard, too, that she might have other children, but I haven't met them myself."

This was getting more and more interesting. From the early days of Augusta's tenure, when she'd been known as "the Widow Simmons," I knew she had a nephew. Indeed, she had almost persuaded Father to marry me off to this nephew, who had sounded sufficiently loathsome that I had not bothered to meet him. But as for other relatives, including any putative sons, I had only Father's vague mention of "her many relatives" in one of his letters.

William asked, "Will they be here for the funeral, do you think, her other children?"

"I don't know," I replied. "I've not heard. As for Larry, he had to go back to New York. Something about a job on a newspaper that couldn't wait. He said that he and Father were not overfond of one another in any event, so I am not offended that he didn't stay."

The doorbell rang. Mary came scurrying again, this time to admit Michael.

As she was opening the front door, William said hurriedly, "Your stepmother will need someone at her side for the funeral. It is most unfortunate her son cannot accompany her. Augusta is not the sort of woman to do well through something like this alone."

How eager William Barrett was to volunteer!

This was an interesting wrinkle. Had Augusta charmed him, as she did so many, in these few weeks of William's knowing her? Or had he really known her for much longer than he had led me to believe? And why would he do that?

One thing I knew for certain, from my father's experience: Augusta was a woman who did not improve the longer one knew her. Rather the opposite.

Who knew if it was mischief or compassion that caused me to do what I did next? As Michael came into the parlor and I prepared to leave the house with him, I took pity on William and said, "You're quite right. If you don't mind waiting an hour or so, I'll have Mary go upstairs and inform Mrs. Jones that you are here."

"I don't mind at all," William responded. Which was exactly what I'd thought he would say. Poor man.

I GLANCED UNEASILY at the sky when Michael and I came out of the Parker House after breakfast. The clouds were high, thick, and not so much gray as white—a snow-laden sky.

"Father's funeral may have to be postponed," I said.

"Hm?"

"I think it's going to snow, and the services are to be graveside only. I suppose it's a good thing we had that little thaw yesterday—even so I wonder that they can dig the grave."

"In Russia, where the ground freezes as solid as a rock, the bodies of those who die in winter are buried in banks of snow where they also freeze until spring thaw.

But it is possible here, where it is not quite so cold, to break ground that is frozen only near the surface. If they could not dig the grave, someone would have said so, Fremont."

"I suppose," I conceded rather glumly.

I hadn't wanted to enter the Common by the path that leads around the Old Granary Burial Ground—there being entirely enough of burying and graves in my life already—so we walked up Tremont Street, past Park Street Church with its elegant white steeple. Though I do not know the facts about my own house, it seems I've always known this steeple is over two hundred feet high. I looked up at it soaring over us as we turned right just past the church and entered the Common.

A few dauntless mothers walked their babies, who were all wrapped up like little bundles inside their carriages, but otherwise very few people were abroad. Winters here are capricious; they tease you into a visceral recollection of spring, only to bring the cold down upon your head again with a vengeance.

Yet for my purpose fewer people were better than many and I was glad at last I could get to something I had not quite dared to do in the dining room of the Parker House.

"I have something to show you," I said, and withdrew the flat dark brown bottle from where I'd been keeping it, inside my fur muff.

"What's this?" Michael took the bottle and turned it over once in his hand. Then he read the label, which said:

Dr. Zahray's
HERCULES TONIC
Exclusively for
MALES

An erectile Performance enhancer

Active Ingredient: Fresh Testicle
Also Contains: Alcohol, Water, Strychnine, and Glycerol

"Hmm," Michael said, which was precisely what I'd thought he'd say.

"Is that what I think it is?" I asked.

He arched one black eyebrow, in a way he does better than anyone else I have ever known. "That depends, my dear Sherlock, on what you think it is."

Then, immediately his tone changed and the eyebrow came back down where it belonged. "I apologize if you think I was making light of something that concerns your father's death. That was not my intention. It was . . . merely habit, I suppose. Please forgive me."

"There's nothing to forgive, think nothing of it."

Over breakfast Michael had encouraged me to tell him all my suspicions, and my grounds for them; he had also acknowledged that my hunches were usually right—with, however, the caveat that sometimes where one's nearest and dearest are concerned, hunches can go wrong or be harder to interpret. With this last I could not find fault.

So I said further, "We've agreed you and I will work on this matter as if we were investigating it together for J&K, and so we shall . . . Watson."

I dared to grin at him.

"Do you know," Michael stopped in his tracks, and stopped me too, "that's the first smile I've seen on your face in a very long time."

I was still smiling, though perhaps not as broadly as was my usual wont.

"Michael," I said, "your willingness either to believe me about Augusta or at least to suspend your disbelief long enough to help me with this investigation is the first thing I've had to smile about in a very long time. So now tell me: Is that bottle what I think it is, a patent medicine designed to, uh, take care of that problem you told me about when sometimes *it* just doesn't work?"

Michael nodded.

A squirrel running across the path in front of us dropped a huge acorn it had dug out of hiding. Michael bent and picked up the acorn, then threw it after the squirrel.

"It's not too surprising that your father would have this . . . concoction," Michael said, "considering what Cosgrove told us about his medical history. But, Fremont, I hardly think Augusta would poison your father just because he couldn't, if you don't mind my saying so, give her sexual satisfaction."

"But the bottle says strychnine. That's a poison!"

"It also says 'fresh testicle.' Now maybe that's not a poison, but I for one would have to be pretty desperate to drink it!"

"That's the point, Michael. Apparently Father was pretty desperate. Come now, you know a thing or two about poisons, I know you do."

"How do you know that?" He shot me a suspicious glance.

Oh, dear! I had almost let an old cat out of the bag.

Fortunately, at that moment we passed a tree, beneath which I spied something that might have been a clump of new-sprung crocuses; to hide my sudden dilemma I bent to inspect them. My face was burning: the truth was, I'd never told Michael about the time four years ago when I hid under his bed and discovered his journal about poisons. Especially mushrooms, but there had been other poisons—organic poisons, now that I thought of it—in that book too.

"I'm sure you were bragging to me at one time or another about your expertise," I said, straightening up, then pointing. "Look, Michael, crocuses. Let's hope it doesn't snow too hard, so that they will survive."

I do not think my diversion had fooled him, judging by the expression on his face, but he let it go. We had now walked as far as the Frog Pond, and by unspoken agreement we turned and began to walk slowly back.

I leaned on my cane a little, more tired than I cared to admit, and I heartily wished I did not now have to go try on dresses and coats and such. But I did. We would go next to R. H. Stearns Department Store, and after that I could go back to Beacon Street for a most welcome nap.

"Come now," I urged, "don't be coy. Tell me about

this so-called tonic in light of what you know about poisons."

Michael rubbed thoughtfully at the white streaks in his beard. "Well," he said, "strychnine is very bitter in taste. Small doses are considered to be therapeutic, the theory being that in a tiny dose the poison may go to whatever is poisoning the larger organism. The person, the host, is presumably large enough to remain unaffected by such a small amount of poison. Many herbal medicines work that way."

"So it is supposed to work on the principle of 'what doesn't kill you will heal you,' is that correct?"

"Something like that."

"But if Augusta, or someone else—I still think it almost has to have been Augusta—were to add *more* strychnine to this tonic, who would know? I mean it would be bitter already, yes?"

"I don't know, Fremont. It seems far-fetched."

Michael remained quiet for a while, thinking. Then he continued:

"I agree with you that the fact that your father's dressing room had been searched right down to the farthest corners is suspicious. But a man would've had to be taking this tonic in very large quantities for it to be an effective way to deliver enough poison to sicken, and eventually to kill him. Even if she—or someone—did increase the amount of strychnine."

"I think he *was* taking it in large quantities," I said grimly, hating the mental picture that fact brought to my mind.

"I do not believe, though, that Leonard's symptoms were at all consistent with strychnine poisoning. I shall have to go to the library and do some research."

"I wondered what you've been doing with your days," I commented.

"Yes," Michael said with a smile, "I've been spending some time in your excellent Boston Public Library."

"It's nice to know you're doing something constructive."

"I can also find a chemist to analyze the contents of the bottle," Michael offered, "and to tell us if there's anything there that should not be, or in quantities that should not be present. Shall I?"

"Yes," I said, "I want you to do that. And, Michael?"

"Yes?"

I stopped walking, waited until I had his full attention, and then lowered my voice to make certain no one could overhear: "I want you to buy me a gun. A revolver, the kind you wanted me to have before, when I refused and chose the Marlin instead."

He studied my face, and apparently was satisfied with what he saw, for all he said was, "If you're absolutely certain."

"I am. Absolutely."

EIGHTEEN

SNOW FELL OVERNIGHT, not in a storm but softly, like a late-winter blessing. In the morning sun, the streets, the hills, the bare-branched trees, the frozen river Charles, all were covered with a clean layer of white.

Our funeral cortege, by contrast, was all in black, even to the black plumes on the heads of the matched pair of black horses that pulled the carriage in which Augusta rode alone. Michael and I followed her in our own hired carriage, our one horse *sans* plumes; behind us were others. I did not know how many, but I knew they too were all in shades of black.

I, who detest hats, wore a hat with a brim and a heavy black veil and I was grateful to have it hide my face. Not that I really cared a whit to have my face all swollen and blotchy from crying, but I could not seem to stop and I did not want people watching me do it.

The previous night I'd kept vigil with Father's body at the mortuary. Michael was with me. That was when he gave me the gun I'd requested, a revolver small enough to hide inside my fur muff. And so I sat with my dead father and my hidden gun and let all the emotions I'd been holding back wash through me, the sorrow and the rage.

Some of the time Augusta had been there, accompanied by Dr. Searles Cosgrove. But most of the time she was not; I thought her visit was perfunctory, but for all I knew she had been at the mortuary before, whereas I had not. I felt some guilt over that, but I told myself Father would understand; more than that, he would approve of my attempt to discover the real cause of his death, and perhaps to bring a murderer to justice.

One hears that the police, in their attempts to find murderers, will attend the funeral services of the victim on the theory that the murderer may be present and may do something to give himself—or herself—away. If that were the case today I should never know it, because grief had become my whole world.

Mount Auburn Cemetery is a beautiful place; if one must lie in the ground to fulfill that grim prediction in the Bible—"dust thou art and to dust thou shalt return"—then I can think of no better place to do it. At least one is in good company here, with Mr. Longfellow and Mr. Justice Holmes, not to mention my mother. With the new snow over everything, it was particularly beautiful, everything so white and pure; here and there among the gentle curves of its hills one could see a tiny temple in the style of Greek Revival, and the mournfully graceful droop of a willow, no less weeping without its leaves.

Father's grave lay gaping and ready, undisturbed by the snowfall; I supposed the gravediggers, not wishing to have their hard work ruined, would have covered it overnight. There were many flowers, all in muted colors and white or cream. The wooden coffin when it was brought down from the wagon, which we had followed from the mortuary, was covered as I'd wished with a funeral spray of pink roses and white lilies. Standing at the head of the grave, where one day a marble marker would be, was a three-foot-tall arrangement of ivy and carnations twisted, tortured, and twined into the shape of a large heart. Augusta's ironic tribute, no doubt; the sight of it sent me into another paralyzing paroxysm of anger and tears.

The clergyman who said the words over Father, and over us all—for it was impossible to escape the grand resonance of his voice—seemed familiar to me somehow though I couldn't recall his name. At any rate he was a good choice for the task of laying Leonard Pembroke Jones in the ground, because he read little from Scripture and much from the Transcendentalists; later, at Beacon Street after the funeral, I met the man, whose name turned out to be Hawthorne—a fine old New England name, whether related to Nathaniel or not. He was a minister of the Universalist denomination, not from Boston but from Cambridge, and he claimed long friendship with Father—but this was rather curious, as I still had no specific memory of him.

The at-home after the funeral was a kind of necessary nightmare: necessary because one must do it; nightmare because one seemed trapped inside it, unable by force of will to make the misery come to an end. I could not, of course, wear my hat with the veil inside the house, and so I presented my naked, grief-ravaged face to all comers without much grace but also without shame. Michael provided some distraction, as over and over again I introduced him as my intended husband. He liked this a great deal; when I was able to come out of my own trouble from time to time, I could feel him quietly glowing by my side.

The light through the windows looking out on Beacon Street had the purpling cast of late afternoon by the time people began to leave. Only a handful of guests remained when Augusta made her shocking and vindictive move.

She came over toward me where I sat with Michael near those front windows, a cold and drafty place we'd chosen for its proximity to the door from the parlor into the hall, where we could most easily accept condolences and say our hellos and goodbyes.

I must say Augusta looked fine, considering the circumstances—even in my distraught and distracted state I could see that. She was, as I have said before, a handsome woman, with most excellent skin for a female her age, and a lot of only slightly graying, docile hair that would take a curl, stay in place, do whatever she wanted. Her clothes were always of good quality and becoming to her fashionably full but small-waisted figure. Further, she had a certain charm, which she displayed for men and on social occasions; this worked well for her since neither men nor society are particularly good at detecting superficiality.

All of Augusta's best qualities had been in evidence today, whereas I was at my weakest and worst. I knew, as I watched her approach, that I could not deal with her. I think she knew it too.

I believe she had planned this for days, lining up her witnesses and asking them to stay on when others left. Except for the minister, Hawthorne, who had stayed on to talk to me and Michael, they were all her allies: Dr. Searles Cosgrove, William Barrett, a man whose name I could not recall at the moment but who'd spent considerable time with her tête-à-tête, and the two silly Forrest sisters—relative newcomers to Mount Vernon Street who will social-climb anything and anyone on Beacon Hill. Mary Fowey was also present, no longer passing sandwiches but now picking up empty plates.

I suppose I smelled the scent of battle on Augusta. I was so ill prepared for it that the intelligent thing to do would have been to surrender and try for an escape later, but some instinct drove me to my tired feet when she was perhaps a yard away. Standing I have something of an advantage, for I am several inches taller than she.

Mr. Hawthorne, perhaps sensing a sort of current like an electrical charge between us in the air, stepped back out of the way. Michael remained seated where he was.

Augusta clasped her hands together and took her

own stand then, when she was still far enough away so that she did not have to look right up at me. She inclined her head slightly to the right and the man whose name I couldn't remember took that as a cue. He came up and stood beside her . . . and he was very tall indeed.

"Fremont, I don't believe you know James Carraway," she said.

"We met this afternoon for the first time. Thank you again for your condolences on this sad occasion, Mr. Carraway," I said. My manners were in place at least, and if I sounded rather stiff—well, it had been a long day.

He simply nodded his head. His expression was grave and he had the face for gravity: large ears with pendulous earlobes, a long nose that flared into large nostrils at the tip, loose skin covering a narrow jaw, a high forehead marred midway by a thick, unruly shock of stark white hair.

"Mr. Carraway is *my* lawyer," Augusta said, emphasizing the word "my."

She turned to include the others, her witnesses as I later would think of them, in her next statement even though she addressed it straight to me. "Caroline Fremont Jones, daughter and only child of Leonard Pembroke Jones, so-called businesswoman, bluestocking, and runaway whore, did you really think I would allow you to get away with your elaborate plan to pass off that so-called new will in which my dear Lenny left everything to *you*?"

"I beg your pardon," I said, my head reeling from her accusation and my ears burning from the word "whore," "but he did not leave me everything. Father left you a more than adequate settlement, enough to buy a house of your own where you may live in comfort for the rest of your life. And to suggest that Mr. Elwood Sefton, or anyone at Great Centennial Bank, would collude with me in the perpetration of such a trick is . . . is disgusting!"

"I beg your pardon," said Augusta, "but what is disgusting is taking care of an old man through long, long

months that turn into years of a nasty, messy illness,
only to have his whore of a daughter come interfering
at the last minute. Listen to me, you tall skinny bitch, I
earned that inheritance and I won't allow you to snatch
it right out from under me!"

I was stunned. Had Michael not shot to his feet and
put his arm around my waist to support me, I do believe I might have collapsed. I felt physically assaulted.

Now William Barrett, that sterling employee of
Great Centennial Bank, the very man my father had
hoped would succeed him, stepped up and said, "I am
willing to testify that Mr. Sefton is getting along in age
and his mind is not quite what it should be. He could be
easily manipulated by a clever person, even a woman.
Though his reputation has remained untarnished until
now, there is always a first time."

And here I'd thought this man, William Barrett, was
such a great friend not only to me but to Father. Of all
the people to whom I could have written, I had chosen
him. It seemed the poor judgment for which I'd been
noted before Michael took me in hand had returned to
plague me once again.

The Forrest sisters tittered. For lack of anything else
I could think of doing at the moment, I glared at them
and they stopped, just in time to hear Augusta's final
declaration:

"You are hereby put on notice in front of these witnesses, Caroline Fremont Jones: I intend to break that
will. In court. With James Carraway as my lawyer. Your
enormous inheritance will not stand!"

THERE IS AN EXPRESSION "to sleep like the dead,"
which well describes how I slept the night after Father's
funeral. Ordinarily I am not so heavy a sleeper, but I
suppose it came on me from sheer exhaustion and to
pay back a sort of deficit of sleep, since I'd not had
much for the past several nights.

Thus I did not hear Mary Fowey's knock at my bedroom door, and woke more because she had entered and was standing by the bed, than because she was calling "Miss! Miss!"—a form of address I scarcely recognize. People are not generally so formal in San Francisco, at least not in my circles, thank goodness.

To have someone in your bedroom unexpectedly is not a pleasant way to awaken, and so I came out of sleep with a most unpleasant jolt, and I expect I grumbled as I asked her what she wanted and what time it was.

"It's just after seven in the morning, miss, and there's a policeman downstairs. He said I was to say would you please get dressed and come down."

She was already at the wardrobe, opening its doors so that I might choose a dress, but I stopped her. "Mary, go back downstairs and tell him I'll be there directly. I can manage on my own."

"Yes, miss. If you're sure."

"I am." I swung my feet out from under the covers and put them on the cold floor, always an effective first step toward awakening. Thus jolted I called out:

"Oh, Mary, wait. Do you have the slightest idea what he wants? And are you sure he wants me, not Augusta?"

Her eyes seemed huge in her face. My addled brain finally realized the poor maid was afraid of something. "What is it, Mary?" I prompted.

"I'm sure I don't really know, but Jem next door told the cook on her way in just now, a few minutes before seven that was, somebody's dead in the park across the street. Begging your pardon, I mean the Public Garden. And Mrs. Augusta, she's not in her room. And that's all I know."

Before my "Thank you" was out of my mouth, Mary had slipped out and closed the door behind her.

Now, on any morning until I have had coffee, I am slow to put two and two together, and on this particular morning after having slept "like the dead" I was worse. I do not much like the police at the best of

times—perhaps an unreasoning prejudice due to a bad
experience I had, but still, there it is—and I do not like
being told what to do either, so I saw no reason to get
dressed just because some strange policeman downstairs had sent word that I should. I put on my perfectly
decent green wool robe and belted it tightly over a
nightgown which was already buttoned up to the neck,
and because the floor was cold I put on wool stockings
with my black kid house slippers. I took a couple of futile brush strokes at my straight, thick hair, gave it up as
a lost cause, and left it hanging down my back like a
slightly untidy curtain.

In the hall on my way to the head of the stairs I
passed Augusta's room. The door was open, which
meant the room was empty as Mary had said. When
Augusta was in that room she invariably closed the
door. I supposed she'd already heard about the body in
the "park" and had gone across to satisfy her morbid
curiosity.

I'd gone halfway down the stairs when my slowly
waking brain presented me with an interesting coincidence: Last night I had slept with my new gun under my
pillow, and this morning someone was found dead
nearby. Had I perhaps known, on some mysterious
level, there would be danger nearby in the night? An involuntary shudder passed through my body.

I was two steps up from the bottom of the stairs
when it occurred to me that I should have brought my
cane, or even both of them—eliciting the sympathy of
the police is never a bad idea. Mary was standing in the
hallway, darting nervous glances first toward me on the
stairs and then toward the smaller of the two parlors,
which was no doubt where she had put the policeman. I
sent her up to fetch both canes, and waited at the bottom of the stairs until she handed them to me.

As she did, I cautioned her: "Mary, don't make my
bed, just leave it. I expect I am going to want to sleep
again when this business is over. I can't imagine what
they want with me, but it couldn't possibly take long."

I had seldom been more wrong about anything in my life.

IN SPITE of the early hour, a small crowd had gathered just inside the iron fence surrounding the Public Garden. The bystanders were being held off by a number of uniformed policemen who had arranged themselves in a circle around the body, which I could not yet see through the crowd.

The officer who was my escort—name already forgotten—had been told by one of these bystanders that I would be able to identify the dead person; while I did not want to believe it, I was more than a little apprehensive as I approached, leaning by turns on each of my two canes as if I needed them far more than I did. I was afraid it might be Michael, because who else would I be called upon to identify?

So I was afraid, and because of the fear my body began to sweat beneath the new black cloak that was a part of my mourning raiment, and I wished I had dressed after all in warmer clothes. At least no one would know that beneath this cloak I wore only a nightgown and robe, for it was voluminous enough to hide the sins of the world and then some.

The police officer, who was quite tall, bent down and whispered apologetically, "It's not too bad as these things go. That is—"

I interrupted him: "Don't worry, I shall be fine. I am not the squeamish type."

It had been on the tip of my tongue to say I was not unaccustomed to death because of my profession; thank God I did not say it. The police are not favorably disposed toward most private detectives, and it does not do to alienate them without good reason.

My policeman escort made a path for us through the bystanders. We had entered the Garden by a small gate that is approximately halfway between Charles Street and Arlington Street, almost directly across Beacon from Pembroke Jones House. The body lay not far into the grounds. My first instinct was relief, because by its dress I could tell the dead person was a woman, therefore could not be Michael, and my major fear was relieved.

But my fear was relieved only to be immediately supplanted by an awesome sense of dread. This was wrong, very wrong. It was the last thing I would ever have thought could happen.

I didn't want to believe what my eyes told me, and so I circled the body twice, my canes poking holes in the crunchy snow and my feet, in spite of their thick socks, going cold through the soles of my thin slippers. Finally I bent down over the head that had leaked its red blood into the cold, frozen whiteness—not very much blood— she had died quickly after being shot. She, too, like me, was wearing her nightgown; but she had on nothing else, not even slippers. Her feet had turned blue.

Straightening up, I choked down that awful feeling of dread and said, "The dead woman is Augusta Simmons Jones, recently widowed by my father, Leonard Pembroke Jones. She was his second wife, and she was not my mother."

NINETEEN

—◆—

I HAVE OBSERVED that if one proceeds with an air of certainty in an uncertain situation, one will more often than not achieve one's goal.

Therefore, while the police were gazing about indecisively—waiting for a coroner or someone senior, I supposed—I took advantage of my certainty that I had things to do. I did not wait to be asked further questions or to be given leave to go, I simply left. I walked across the street, up the steps, and through my own front door, and no one called me back or hindered me.

They would be here presently, I was sure enough; and when they came again they would be asking me questions in their official capacity.

I went back to the kitchen and in a blunt manner imparted the facts to Mary Fowey and the cook, Mrs. Boynton. I put off their questions by pleading both upset and ignorance, took a cup of coffee with me, and went to telephone Michael's hotel. I did not have time to wait for him to be brought to the telephone, so I left a message to be delivered to his room: *You are needed as soon as possible at Beacon Street—Fremont.*

Every minute now was of the essence.

Back in my room I first checked under my pillow: the gun was still there. Not that I'd thought it could be anywhere else—how could anyone have stolen it right out from under my pillow, after all—but still the coincidence of my having obtained a gun from Michael only a few hours before Augusta had been shot was a little eerie. Almost as if I'd had a premonition that I didn't remember.

I couldn't keep it under my pillow, of course; nor was it going to do me much good to hide it away in some place so secret that even I, the hider, would forget where it was. That is only one of the problems with guns, one must figure out where to keep these bothersomely destructive things.

Not having much time to think over the matter, I put the gun inside the muff again, where I had carried it before. After a quick but uninspiring look around, I placed the muff in a dresser drawer. I would have preferred to leave it out for quick access, but if I did, that tidy soul Mary Fowey would only come along and put it away herself. Then no doubt the gun would come tumbling out of hiding and frighten her to death, after which she would probably quit her job, and *then* where would I be?

Rhetorical question, yes—but the answer immediately popped into my mind: I'd be alone in this very big house, that's where I'd be, and it did not strike me as a very good idea. In fact, the two of us, myself and Mary, alone in this house did not strike me as a very good idea either. One more thing to worry about later.

The matter of the gun taken care of, I went next door into Augusta's room.

It looked to me as if she had been sleeping, but not for long, when for some reason she'd left her bed. Either that, or she was a remarkably tidy sleeper, for the covers were scarcely mussed and there was one simple indentation in the feather pillow where her head had lain.

Now here was an interesting note: Her robe, a very attractive peach-colored garment of soft wool with satin lapels and satin cuffs, lay folded on top of the blanket chest at the foot of the bed. Matching slippers—of course Augusta would have matching slippers—were there too, lined up on the rug in front of the chest. So why had she not put them on?

A chill passed through me as I acknowledged the inevitable answer: She hadn't had time. Exactly *why* she hadn't had time was not something I wanted to think about at the moment.

I was less interested in who had killed Augusta Simmons Jones, and why, than I was in pursuing my own need to know if she had or had not deliberately poisoned my father. Let the police look for her killer—I would continue my own single-minded pursuit. And these few minutes might be the only time I would have in her room before the police insisted on coming in, causing havoc and who could know what else.

Two days ago I would have jumped at this opportunity to be let loose alone in Augusta's territory, but today I stood rooted to a spot in the middle of the rug, unable to proceed. Why?

This was exceedingly unlike me!

Perhaps it was only that so many bad things had happened, and a very large part of me simply wanted it all to go away. That part of me wanted only peace and quiet and time with Michael. I wanted to go someplace where we could be alone, where nobody could find us, and no one would kill or be killed or call anyone ugly names like "whore" and "bitch."

Ah, but that was not the real world, was it? Not the real world Michael and I knew, at any rate—and where the whole of me, not just a part of me, lived. In our real world people did far worse things than call each other bad names. And our job, Michael's and mine, was to see to it, in whatever way we could, that they didn't get away with it—including Augusta, even if she was dead. The truth must come out.

So, no more procrastinating or whining or feeling sorry for myself, but on with the job.

I didn't think I had time to do a general search to turn up any and everything that might be the least bit suspicious, so I searched for poisons, poisoning agents, anything that might be combined with something else to make a poison reaction, books on poisoning—or anything that resembled any of these.

After considerable work, for in her own space Augusta was revealed to be an even more remarkably acquisitive woman than she appeared on the surface, I'd found only one thing: a bottle of cleaning fluid that struck me as a bit suspicious. I took it.

I also took her address book. If the police noticed its absence and said anything to me about it, I could always claim I'd borrowed the address book to write thank-you notes to people who had extended their condolences.

I hadn't found a diary and spent extra time going through her desk again, but still no diary, no journal, and this was odd considering most women of a certain degree of education would have kept one. Could it be that Augusta was not an introspective enough person to do so? Or was she just too canny to reveal her inner thoughts on paper?

If the latter were the case I would have to plead guilty too. I do not keep a journal anymore because a few years of detecting, both amateur and professional, have made me wary of what can happen if a diary falls into the wrong hands.

I confess I did have a perfectly horrible, probably unforgivable thought as I was leaving the small room my mother had called her quiet room. Augusta had jammed that room full of enough clothing and personal ornaments to open a miniature women's department store, and I thought what a great pleasure it would be to give all those things to the poor. Assuming her son did not want them—but of course he wouldn't.

AUGUSTA'S SON came up again about forty-five minutes later, when I was ensconced with Michael in the dining room. I had washed and made myself presentable in a plain black dress of silk gabardine with a long, very full skirt, buttons down the front, in its way a classic—which is to say that with a hoop under it, this dress would have passed muster in the previous century. The police still had not arrived; I was counting my blessings minute by minute.

"There is an address in New York for Lawrence Bingham," I said to Michael, pointing to the address book, which was written in Augusta's somewhat irregular hand. "Do you suppose he might have gone back to the same place?"

"Very likely." Michael nodded.

He copied the address into the flat, narrow notebook he always carries in an inside pocket. Michael is one of the most organized human beings I have ever known, although he does leave his ties draped over the door of the armoire and his socks on the floor.

"These other Binghams," I said, pointing again, "must be some or all of the 'many relations' Father had discovered Augusta to have. I suppose they must be notified as well."

"I'll take care of it for you, if you like," Michael offered, continuing to write.

"Thank you, I'd like it very much if you would."

I'd told him of my determination to see through my own investigation into Father's death, even if it were no longer a matter of bringing Augusta to justice in any public way. He seemed to understand that I could not be at peace with myself otherwise.

"Michael, do you think Bingham could have been Augusta's maiden name? Or do you think she was married to a Mr. Bingham before Mr. Simmons?"

"The latter is more likely. She might have had one child out of wedlock and given him her own last name, but more than one? I don't think so."

"If she'd been married more than once before she met him, my father didn't know. It makes me wonder . . ." My voice trailed off as my thoughts leapt around in speculation.

"What?" Michael prompted.

"If she would lie about that, what else would she lie about?"

"Is that a serious question, Fremont?"

"Yes, it is."

"Well then I should have to say, there are degrees of liars, and as of yet, neither you nor I know enough about the woman to be able to tell in which level of degree she fell. I know you prefer to believe the worst of your stepmother—"

"Michael! Please don't call her that!"

"All right, the worst about Augusta—"

"—which would be that she lied all the time, about everything."

"Yes. But she might instead have been someone who would lie to reach a specific goal and then not again, unless and until a strong desire surfaced, which then became a new goal. Do you follow me?"

"Yes, I do. I see your point," I said grudgingly.

"I do not think Augusta was an indiscriminate liar. I think she was too clever for that, too calculating. I believe she was the kind who does not bother to lie unless it is to achieve a very specific purpose."

"Um-hm."

We were silent for a few moments, and then I spoke again:

"I am thinking Father died, and Mr. Simmons died—these are both indisputable facts. If there was a Mr. Bingham, then . . . ? Well, I expect you follow my line of thought. Don't you?"

Michael sighed. "Yes. What a mind you have, my dear! But you could very well be right, and I suppose it must be looked into."

"You would be just the one to do that, with your vast experience, your connections in many cities, and so on."

He sighed again. "You know, Fremont, I had just begun doing some riveting research into ancient Greek Orthodox ecclesiology at the library."

I rolled my eyes.

He finished: "And now you want me to stop my riveting research to find that rather pathetic young man, and—"

I didn't wait for him to finish, but leapt in to supply my own, as it were, happy ending: "—and quite possibly help me to expose a killer."

Michael, however, did not give up so easily. He must have really been getting much more of a kick out of his ancient Orthodox whatever than one would have thought such a thing could provide.

"Has it occurred to you," he persisted, "that the police will have to find Larry Bingham themselves, in order to notify him of her death?"

"Yes, but the police won't ask him the same questions you would. Nor will they find him if he isn't in the place where he is expected to be, whereas you will hunt him down. Once you've put your mind to it, that is."

"Granted. Still, may I point out, the San Francisco Library does not have quite the capacity that the Boston Public Library has, and when you consider also that the Widener at Harvard is just across the river—well, you're asking a lot, my dear."

I smiled. "You will be amply rewarded."

He smiled too. "Is that as in 'virtue is its own reward,' or did you have something more personal in mind?"

"Oh, more personal, definitely."

I was enjoying this, I admit. When Michael and I combine our forces and work together instead of against each other (which we have occasionally done), we are very good at this investigating business if I do say so.

"And besides," I added, "when we're married we'll have to live here at least part of the time anyway. You will have plenty of opportunities to do more research in Boston and Cambridge."

Michael took my left hand in his, interlaced his fingers

with mine, then turned the back of my hand up so that he could admire the emerald engagement ring.

He said, "I've been wondering how our living arrangements will work."

"So have I, and I'm not sure yet, but I have some ideas."

We both fell quiet, looking into each other's eyes, thinking the same things, probably. About marriage. How he'd avoided the institution for so many years for his reasons, and I had avoided it also for mine. Michael was afraid to love too much, because much love brings with it the possibility of so much pain. I was afraid of the social and legal consequences of marriage. For example, as soon as I marry Michael, everything that is mine becomes his. Including my body. My very name becomes the same as his; in the eyes of polite society I will no longer be Fremont Jones, I will be Mrs. Michael Archer Kossoff. And if I have his children—

Well, I wouldn't think about that part right now. I looked away, withdrew my hand, and took a deep breath. We still had work to do this morning, we could not go too far down this other path.

"Yes." Michael said, as if he did indeed know all that had just passed through my mind. His eyes were dark, deep, and full of feeling.

Then he cleared his throat, not so much of necessity but as a signal that he was in a way changing the subject, our discussion was moving on.

He said, "I'm concerned about your being in this house alone."

"Mary is here," I responded.

"Two women alone in a large house, from which another has recently been lured or driven outside to her death? I am still concerned. I think I should move in."

"I'd love to have you here," I said earnestly, "but in truth that would be frowned upon before we are married. I think I have a solution to this problem." I told him about Ralph and Myra Porter, how I needed to talk

to them anyway, how I planned to offer them their old
jobs back.

Meanwhile Mary came in with a fresh pot of coffee
and took away the remains of the breakfast we'd finished some time ago.

When she had gone back into the kitchen, Michael
gazed toward the hall doorway and said, "I keep thinking the police will come at any minute. In fact, I'm
rather surprised they haven't been here already."

"So am I," I agreed.

He leaned close to me, and for a moment I thought
we might kiss. But then I looked into his eyes and saw
there not a hint of amorousness. He whispered, "I think
you should give me back the gun I gave you yesterday."

I blinked in surprise and said somewhat more loudly,
"I'll do no such thing! I need it now as much as I ever
did. Maybe more."

"The police will only take it from you if they find it,
Fremont."

"They will have to find it first, and for that they'd
need a search warrant, for which they have no cause!"

Michael shook his head, not satisfied. "That little revolver was one of mine, and if I take it back no one
need know you ever had it. You'll be much safer, believe
me, without it at this point."

"Oh. I didn't mean for you to give me your own
gun—I thought you'd buy one for me."

He shook his head. "Buying one in a town where one
does not live cannot be done so quickly, but that is not
the point. I have another gun with me anyway—the
small one I gave you is an extra. The point, my dear, is
this: The police are going to consider you a suspect in
Augusta's murder."

"Me?" I was astounded.

Michael nodded; his face was more than grave, it
was positively morbid.

After I had swallowed hard and forced myself to it, I
conceded: "I hadn't thought of it, but I do see it might

come to that. Not necessarily right away, though. Maybe it will take a while, and who knows, if Searles Cosgrove and William Barrett—"

"And the Forrest sisters and that lawyer, what was his name, Carraway, and your maid all keep quiet—"

"Then," I finished up for both of us, "the police may not realize I had a motive. Mary doesn't count, by the way. She would never come down on any side other than mine in any situation. But anyway, the police aren't going to know all that right away. Meanwhile I have work to do, and for that I will feel much more confident if I have your gun. So you still can't have it back!"

Michael grinned. "You're incorrigible."

"Yes, and irrepressible too."

That was when he did kiss me, and for a little while we both forgot everything.

TWO DETECTIVES of the Boston police came to the house before noon. They spoke to each of us separately, even Mrs. Boynton, although she had not been present during the night. When the three of us—Mary, Mrs. Boynton, and I—compared our experiences with the detectives later, we'd each noticed the same thing: They were preoccupied with keys. Of course, we each had keys to front and back doors, but that meant nothing. Half of Boston could have had keys to the house for all I knew.

I had the locks changed that very afternoon.

TWENTY

BECAUSE TODAY WAS a Saturday, I thought Ralph and Myra Porter might be at home. They were not on the telephone, so I could not call ahead, and must take my chances as I'd done with some success when visiting the nurse, Sarah Kirk.

The address Mr. Sefton had given me for my family's old employees was in Cambridge near Central Square; I went there in a carriage hired from the same company that had been providing carriages to us at Pembroke Jones House for various purposes over the past several days, including our entries in the funeral cortege. This continuous patronage had an advantage in that they were willing to accommodate me at short notice, but it had the disadvantage of costing money that was being, in my opinion, unnecessarily spent.

As the carriage rolled across the Harvard Bridge, I thought again about getting my own automobile. Somewhat to my dismay I realized I would require the assistance of the bank in order to make such a large purchase—I could not just walk into some auto showroom and walk out with the auto of my choice. If I were a man, I might have been able to do it by writing a check, but a single woman, alone, buying an auto? The

salesman would laugh me out the door—up his sleeve if
not in my face.

I did not like this state of affairs, but there was nothing I could do about it. Worst of all, I knew I'd be well
advised to confront William Barrett and have it out
with him, for if he and I could not come to an understanding, then I should feel it necessary to take the
money that was now mine to another bank. That, after
Father's long association with Great Centennial, would
be a shame.

The Porters lived in one of several medium-sized
clapboard-sided apartment buildings on their block.
Each of these was four stories tall, neat and simple, and
the street was clean if crowded. The arrangement for
mail and doorbells was quite up-to-date with an electric
buzzer for a bell. I pushed the buzzer by the name
Porter, one of eight apartments, and soon a woman
came to the door.

I recognized her by her shape even through the sheer
curtain, which she twitched aside to check who'd rung
the bell before she opened the door. It was Myra, grown
a little more stooped through the shoulders, her hair
perhaps a little grayer, but her wide smile and friendly
broad face still the same.

"Miss Caroline Jones, is that really you? Oh my
goodness me—"

She went on like that, and I got tears in my eyes
while acknowledging that yes I was indeed myself although I'd been answering to my middle name for so
long now I might not respond if called anything other
than Fremont. In a burst of spontaneous affection,
Myra forgot herself and hugged me, and I forgot myself
and hugged her back . . . and then I really did break
down and cry.

Fortunately, by this time she had shown me into the
tiny living room of their apartment and had presented
me to Ralph, who seemed almost as overcome as Myra.
When I went on my crying jag Ralph excused himself
and went to make tea.

"You know that Father died?" I said when I was able to compose myself once more. By then Ralph had ventured back into the room.

"Ralph saw it in the newspaper, didn't you, dear?" Myra said.

He silently nodded his agreement, put down a plate of cookies on a little end table, and went back to the kitchen.

"He was right upset." Myra shook her head as soon as her husband had gone. "Not that I can blame him, I was upset too. Wanted to come to the services for Mr. Leonard, but didn't think *she'd* consider us welcome. If I'da known you was back, Miss Fremont, I'da insisted we go whether Ralph liked it or not."

"I would have been happy to see you," I said honestly, "but the truth is that whole thing was such a hard time, I'm just as glad to be with you now instead."

"So what brings you here today, Miss Fremont?"

"If you think you can call me Fremont, without the 'Miss,' I might tell you," I teased.

"All right, so it's Fremont, you always was a independent little thing. Well, maybe not so little, either. A tall, fine girl you turned out to be."

We chattered on in that vein without either of us saying anything of substance. I was waiting for Ralph to return, which in a few minutes he did, bringing with him all the tea things on a tray and one of those little tray tables with the folding legs tucked under his arm.

Before Myra could do anything I jumped up to help Ralph; they would have allowed it without a thought if I'd been younger, but now they both fussed and clucked until I told them to hush.

"Thank you for the tea, Ralph," I said when we were all settled again.

He beamed at me—something he very seldom does.

Ralph is very much the quiet, sober New Englander. He's a big-boned man in his fifties, broad-shouldered and, I would guess, still strong for his age. His hair is brown, cut short, and he has a mustache that looks like a brush—with a good deal of gray in it. Growing up, I had always felt I could rely on him, and I was finding to my great relief that I felt the same way still.

At last I embarked upon the major purpose for my visit:

"Two things I must tell you so that you can fully understand why I'm here. First, Father left the house on Beacon Street and most of his estate to me. There is also a small bequest for the two of you—if you haven't yet had a letter from Mr. Elwood Sefton, a lawyer at the bank where Father used to work, you will have such a letter soon.

"The second thing I must tell you, you may most likely also read in tomorrow morning's newspaper: Augusta Simmons Jones was shot to death early this morning. Her body was discovered in the Public Garden by someone walking a dog, that person called the police, and they came for me to identify the body."

Ralph and Myra exchanged long, meaningful glances—and I, who was not in on the meaning, hoped I could soon persuade them to let me in.

"What you're sayin' is," Ralph said slowly, "Mrs. Simmons Jones was murdered."

"Yes."

"Oh my stars!" Myra exclaimed.

Ralph unselfconsciously put his big hand on his wife's knee.

"I am here in Boston with my business partner, Michael Archer Kossoff. I of course am staying at the house on Beacon Street, while Michael has taken a suite at the Vendome. He and I were planning to be married here in Boston so that Father could be present, but his sudden death, and now Augusta's murder, have—well, the thing is I don't know for sure when we'll be able to have the wedding.

"What it all comes down to right now is a situation in which I need help. I'm living in Pembroke Jones House alone, except for a maid named Mary Fowey. I doubt you ever met Mary—she's good at her job but quite young."

Suddenly I was embarrassed, horribly aware of what enormous presumption I'd had to come here like this, with no notice whatever, just assuming these two people who had always been so wonderful to me would jump at the chance to come back to work and live on Beacon Street. I felt the heat and color climb into my cheeks, and I couldn't go on.

Myra shook her head and clucked. "Poor lamb."

That was what she used to say to me when I would fall down and rip the knees out of my cotton stockings, something I did with great regularity until I was about twelve.

I smiled at Myra and decided to go on and say my piece; after all, the worst that could happen was they could say no. And one does not die of embarrassment— though there have been times in such situations when I have certainly wished I might disappear by some means short of death.

"Ralph and Myra, I want you both to know how shocked I was to ring the doorbell at my old house upon my arrival a few weeks ago, and have someone else—someone who was neither of you—come to let me in. I don't know what the circumstances of your leaving were, whether you left because Augusta asked you to, or whether you simply didn't want to work at Pembroke Jones House anymore, but what it comes down to is this: I want so very, very much for the two of you to come back. To live at the house again, with complete security, for the rest of your lives. To run the house for me when I'm not there, which could be as much as six months out of any year. And perhaps most important of all, to help me now get everything back to what it once was."

I did not say "before Augusta," but that was what I meant and I was sure they both knew it.

I made light, made a joke of something that was not

quite true—laughing, I said, "Why, Ralph, I don't even
know how to wind the grandfather clock and make it
chime again, so you see how much I need you!"

Ralph and Myra smiled at each other, and then at me.

"She never could stand that clock," Myra said.

"And he always loved it," said Ralph, "which in a
way you might say was the start of their problems."

WE TALKED a long time and drank the entire pot of
tea. Myra told their story with occasional verbal nudges
from Ralph when she ventured too far into the extrane-
ous. It was about what I'd expected: the first year of
their marriage, Father and Augusta were in an almost
embarrassing state of honeymoon-like bliss. They went
on a lot of trips. Father was home a lot, he showered
her with presents and so on.

But when he was not there, gradually Augusta's
snappish, selfish nature began to come out with Myra
and Ralph. By the second year of the marriage, Augusta
had insisted they move back up to the little rooms on
the fourth floor, and that they stay out of sight as much
as possible, use the back stairs, and so on.

"Seemed like," Myra said, hitting the nail on the
head I was sure, "she wanted your father all to herself.
Anybody else around was too much, anybody at all."

"When she convinced Mr. Leonard to close the stables, get rid of the horses and the carriage, well then
that was half my job right there, wasn't it?" said Ralph.

"What was the reason for that, do you know?" I
asked, because it truly baffled me.

"Pure spite," said Myra, "because neither of the two
horses liked her."

"Animals 'r like that," Ralph said, "they sense things
about a person, sometimes an animal can see things a
person can't. But anyway that wasn't the whole there
was to it."

"Tell her the rest," Myra urged her husband.

"I'm gettin' to it," he said in his patient way. "The

other thing was, Augusta, she wanted a new carriage, somethin' spiffier, and your dad—well you know how he was, Caroline."

I didn't correct him, because I was thinking back to my youth when I'd been just Caroline, and I knew exactly what Ralph meant. I said, "He liked the old better than the new, and he'd insist it be kept in good condition, no matter whether the old item was the grandfather clock or a pair of leather shoes. Father would buy the very best there was and then expect to be using it for the next hundred years. Especially something big, like a carriage."

"You betcha." Ralph nodded.

"But not Miss Augusta; she was the exact opposite, always a-wantin' new things. She'd figured out," Myra said, "she could have the very latest carriage and the handsomest horses to go around town in and show herself off, if she was to use hiring stables and always insist on their best."

"So she made a fuss," I guessed. I could see, and hear, her doing it. Just as I could see in my mind those magnificent black horses with the plumes on their heads, pulling her carriage for Father's funeral. No wonder I, using that same hiring stable, got such prompt service.

"Well," said Ralph, "it was the way she did it, made us quit. You tell her, Myra, I ain't got the heart for it."

Myra's kind eyes filled up with tears. "Mrs. Augusta said one of the horses bit her. She had a big bruise on her arm, with teeth marks—the skin weren't broken but the marks were there—and she said the gray horse, what was his name, Ralph?"

"Bill."

The other one was named Bob, I remembered now; Bill was the gray and Bob was a chestnut.

"She said Bill bit her, but he never did such a thing. So help me God, I don't know how she got them marks on her but that horse didn't do it. Your father, he believed that evil woman just the same as he always believed her—begging your pardon, Caroline, I mean Fremont, but I swear she could be evil—and Mr. Leonard told Ralph he had to put the horse down."

"Yep," Ralph confirmed, nodding somberly. "Perfectly healthy horse he was too."

"Oh, no!" I gasped, then covered my mouth with the back of my hand.

Somehow to hurt an innocent animal seems almost worse than to do something similar to a human being—I suppose because we humans can usually fight back.

I added inadequately, "I'm so sorry."

"We said to each other, didn't we, Ralph, we was glad you wasn't there to see it. That was when we decided to leave. Much as we didn't like to go off after all those years and leave Mr. Leonard . . . well, he had *her* didn't he, and she was what he wanted."

"Yep." Ralph first nodded, but then he slowly, sadly, shook his head.

I wondered if my father had continued to want Augusta all the way to the very end. I wondered if infatuation—I refused to call it love—could be that blind; and in a way, I hoped it could, because otherwise Father must have died an unhappy man.

IT TOOK very little persuasion for the Porters to say yes to my offer. Of course, Ralph had another job now where he would have to give two weeks' notice, but Myra wasn't working. She could move in right away at Beacon Street, and so could Ralph sleep there at night. They understood both my not wanting to be alone and my concern that no gossip be started about me and Michael. In fact, they said they would come that very evening to spend the night, and would start to bring over their things next day. Together we would restore their former quarters in the back of the third floor.

The sun was setting as my hired carriage crossed the Harvard Bridge going back the other way; its declining light made a golden wash across the mostly frozen surface of the Charles River. In mid-bridge, when for a few moments I could look straight down, I could see cracks in the ice and the river's waters moving beneath. Spring was coming soon.

I myself felt hopeful for the first time in what seemed like a long while; I was returning to Beacon Street with a sense of accomplishment. One wrong had been set right, at least: the Porters were coming back where they belonged. It was only one thing, a small step, but in the right direction.

TWENTY-ONE

—◆—

THE NEXT DAY, being Sunday, should by the well-known tradition have been a day of rest. I, however, did not rest so much as I found myself restive around the house, feeling there must be something worthwhile I could do to further my investigation into Father's death.

Michael had left on the train for New York City, where he intended to begin an investigation of Augusta's past by questioning her son, Larry Bingham, if in fact Larry could be found. Then Michael would move on to question the other Binghams—oddly enough there had not been a single Simmons—whose addresses he had taken from Augusta's address book. As I recalled, one was in New Jersey; the rest were in Connecticut, all easily reachable in a few hours by train.

For a moment I reflected upon how different this is from California, a state so vast that the urban Northeast would fit in only a part of it. Somehow my old environs had shrunk during my four years of living in San Francisco—especially the corridor from Boston to New York and the towns in between.

Soon after Michael left—that is to say, around ten o'clock on Sunday morning—I received a telephone call from a detective of the Boston police, McLaughlin by name. My memory being rather sharp after days of that not being the case, I thought to inquire after his health and that of his partner, Detective O'Neal. These two had been at the house yesterday. I found it quite encouraging to have my excellent memory back, but Detective McLaughlin seemed singularly unimpressed. In point of fact he was downright grumpy. He proceeded to ask me for about the tenth time if I could not tell him the whereabouts of "young Mr. Lawrence Bingham." I felt like saying that if I knew I would hardly have sent Michael off looking, as it would be much more pleasant to have Michael here, but of course I could not say any such thing.

I could only reiterate the same thing I'd said the day before—that is, that Augusta's son had been concerned about keeping his job and so had gone back to New York the day before my father's funeral. I insisted I had not seen him since, which was of course true; and I said again I believed he was a reporter on the *New York Daily News*. Surely, I asked sweetly, they could contact him there? This was not what McLaughlin had wanted to hear but he rang off, and so, to my great relief, I was rid of him. At least, for a while.

As I hung up the telephone, I knew it would be only a matter of time before McLaughlin and O'Neal came to search Augusta's room themselves. They'd be wanting that address book, and a diary too; and being of a somewhat suspicious nature myself, I was very worried they might think I had stolen the diary. They weren't likely to believe a diary did not exist; I would've had trouble believing it myself if I hadn't known Augusta.

The first search of her room, conducted on the day of her death, had been done by police officers of the rank and file while I was answering questions for the two detectives downstairs—a time-saving measure, no doubt, on that initial day of the investigation. I supposed it would be something of a coup, or at any rate something they could congratulate themselves on, if the two detectives were to find something the uniformed officers had missed.

If I were to put the address book back now, they
need never know I'd had it; further, they might well be
more likely to believe me when I said I had never
known Augusta to keep a diary.

Yes! I really was functioning much more like my
usual self. Such a relief!

Nevertheless, I wouldn't put the address book back
without making a copy of it for myself. It was unfortunate that I had no way of knowing which of the many
names and addresses might be of use, beyond the family
names Michael had already copied. I should have to
copy all of it, which I subsequently did, and it took a
good deal of time.

Meanwhile Ralph and Myra Porter, who had both
stayed overnight in one of their old rooms on the third
floor, had departed once more for Cambridge to tend to
their affairs, which included giving notice on their
rented apartment. Mary Fowey, who was religious, always had Sundays off to attend her church and to see
her family in South Boston. I presumed she was Roman
Catholic but had not actually inquired.

So I was alone in the house. I did the copying in the library, where I was more comfortable than in any other
room of the house; indeed I wished I could sleep in the library too, with the sound of the grandfather clock ticking, its pendulum swinging in the tall case just down the
hall. Ralph had set it back in working order first thing.

More than once as I worked I started at some unexpected sound. Many of these came from out-of-doors:
although today the sky was slightly overcast, the
weather continued to warm and the spring thaw was
under way, with its inevitable sounds of things cracking. Icicles dropped with a crash from under the eaves.
An occasional tree limb, weakened by long bearing
the weight of winter snow and ice, now tossed by the
strong March wind, broke and plunged to the ground
like a bomb.

Some hours later, when I had finished my copying
task and was climbing the stairs to return the address

book to Augusta's bedroom, I realized the wind was making me anxious. Surely it was the wind?

What with all that had been going on in this house, I had not paid more than superficial attention to the weather. But, now I thought back on it, this March of 1909 was conducting itself backward. It had come in like a lamb, but now it seemed determined to go out like a lion.

It was very distracting, all these noises at every door and window, wind moaning and squeaking and groaning, with the counterpoint of cracks and crashes from the melting snow and ice. Drips too. I began to wonder if all the sounds out there were from natural sources; had I possibly heard someone trying to work an old key in one of the new locks?

One by one I went to the doors—first listened through the door, then looked out a nearby window. Up close, I heard nothing on the other side. I didn't see anyone lurking suspiciously near the house, or running as if to get away; and further, there were a lot of people walking up and down the sidewalk on this side of Beacon Street. When the weather is fine, that is to say sunny (wind does not count in an assessment of whether the day is fine or not), Bostonians are fond of strolling—it is one of our principal entertainments.

Sunday is a major strolling day. I did not really think anyone would try to break into the house in the middle of the day when so many people were about. Nevertheless, after checking to be sure that front, back, side, and basement doors were locked from the inside, I went around to all the downstairs windows to be sure they were locked too.

After I had done that I could think of nothing more to do. Because it was only two o'clock in the afternoon and Ralph and Myra could not be expected to return for another two or three hours, and Mary not until after dinner, I went upstairs to take a nap.

It was no use. I could not possibly sleep. So what worthwhile investigatory thing could I do on a Sunday?

"I know!" I said aloud in a burst of inspiration. I practically ran down the stairs—so quickly that I almost stumbled and had to remind myself to slow down—toward my goal, the telephone alcove. This little room with its single purpose, to hold that newfangled instrument, had been cleverly created out of a broom closet in the space beneath the staircase. I switched on the light and seized the telephone directory.

I was in luck! Martha Henderson, Father's daytime private nurse, did have a telephone, and her address was listed. More luck: She lived in Back Bay, not too far, I could walk. I called to be sure it was the right person, that she was in and would see me, and upon receiving all replies in the affirmative I felt thrice blessed.

"IS IT MISS or Mrs. Henderson?" I inquired.

Even though that was not my favorite question, and I doubted it was hers either, one must be polite.

"It's Miss, but please call me Martha."

Ah, I thought, a woman after my own heart. I smiled.

"And do come in," she added.

"Thank you, Martha."

She lived at the back of a tiny mews, or pedestrian alleyway, off Newbury Street between Exeter and Fairfield. Her little house looked as if it might at one time have been the servants' quarters to the large edifice of golden stone in front. Perhaps the owners of that one had an unusually modern attitude and were renting this out. If so, the nurse was reaping the benefit, because her place was charming.

Or, I thought suddenly, it could be the other way around. Both large and small houses could belong to her, and due to whatever circumstances, she had chosen to live in the former servants' quarters—if so, then more than likely she supported herself at least partially by renting out her own large house. It was something I might have done, if necessary.

"This is a lovely little house!" I said enthusiastically. "I have always liked Newbury Street."

"Yes, I think my little house has turned out quite well. I grew up on this street, in that stone house out front. When my parents died I moved in back here, and now I let out the big house for the income," Martha said.

And I thought: Aha! I was right.

"Would you like some tea?" she inquired.

"Yes," I agreed, "I believe I would. We could have it in the kitchen if that would be more convenient for you. I am quite fond of sitting around the kitchen table with tea or coffee and friendly talk."

Martha Henderson was a tiny woman, barely five feet tall, with bones so small she put me in mind of a bird. Yet I knew she was very strong, because I had seen her help my father out of bed and do other nursing tasks that required strength.

I had the most striking feeling—almost a premonition really—that Martha Henderson and I were going to get along famously. Even more, I felt that she would somehow be of great help to me, even before we began to talk.

Once we did get to talking it was hard to leave aside socializing, for here I had found a woman much like myself—even though she had not quite the same degree of education and our parents had not moved in the same circle, which accounted for why we had not met before. Martha had trained and worked as a nurse because she wished to make a contribution to society and to be self-supporting. She cared not a whit for ostentation. And she continued to do nursing on a private basis, when the opportunity came along, not because she required the money to survive—living as modestly as she did, the rental of her house provided her sufficient income—but because she felt the work in itself was valuable and rewarding.

I told her about Michael's and my detective business in San Francisco; this was an aspect of me she'd known nothing about. In the days she'd worked at nursing Father, Martha had seen me only as the daughter of a prominent man in one of those Beacon Street houses that of themselves tend to set up certain expectations. But now, knowing more about me, she too felt our sisterhood, as it were, under the skin.

"But you did not come here to talk about these things we unexpectedly find we have in common, I think," Martha said.

"No," I acknowledged regretfully, "I did not, but I'm still glad that we've had this opportunity to become acquainted. And I hope, when this business at hand is resolved, we can be friends."

"Well, then"—Martha sat up straighter and folded her hands on top of the table—"let us get the business at hand over with, by all means. How may I be of help? On the telephone you said this concerned your father. You are aware, of course, that I only nursed him for those few weeks I came to your house on Beacon Street."

"Yes, I am." I looked into her eyes, which were a light hazel brown with streaks of green shot through them, both warm and lively. Except for the unusual eyes, her face was actually rather plain. I said, "Martha, may I take you into my complete confidence?"

"Yes, of course you may, Fremont."

I wriggled in my chair, feeling a touch of that anxiety I'd felt earlier in the afternoon. "It would be easy to misunderstand what I'm about to tell you, but somehow I think you will not misunderstand."

"I'll try my best."

"Very well. I have come to believe that my father's final illness, which came over him gradually through a course of about two years, was not from natural causes. I believe he was being poisoned, and I suspect his wife, Augusta, of being the poisoner."

Martha raised her eyebrows but said nothing, merely waited for me to go on.

"In part I believe this because Father did improve

once he was put into the hospital—but he wouldn't have been put into the hospital if I had not contacted someone at the bank where he used to work and insisted that something be done for him. I was, I guess one could say, stuck in California at the time."

"Yes, you must have suffered some fairly recent trauma. I've observed the slight hitch in your gait, even when you're using the cane."

I smiled. "You're very observant. I had both legs broken, and a head injury, but that is another story. To return to Father: While in the hospital he did improve, but only to a certain point. Dr. Cosgrove still expected him to die, and so sent him home because that is supposed to be the best place for it." I paused, for emphasis, then continued:

"At this point, Martha, please make a mental note of the fact that Augusta always came to visit Father in the hospital at the time of the evening meal."

"Noted." She gave a sharp nod.

"Now, I was not in favor of bringing my father home to Beacon Street. I feared we would only be putting him back in Augusta's clutches, though of course I could not say so. Therefore, I did the only thing I could think of: I asked Dr. Cosgrove to provide private nursing care for him at home. That was when he hired you and Sarah Kirk."

"A wise decision." Martha nodded again.

"You began looking after Father in the daytime; Sarah Kirk at night. You were both most assiduous in your duties and did not leave him alone for any appreciable length of time, including at meals. Under your constant care Father made a dramatic improvement. I know, for instance, that he had not a single hallucination after we brought him home, though he still had them sometimes in the hospital. In your care his appetite returned and his color improved, as anyone could see. I began to think Father might survive after all."

"That's so. I said the same to Dr. Cosgrove, that

I thought perhaps we had been mistaken as to Mr. Jones's illness having reached the terminal stage."

"What did Dr. Cosgrove say?"

Martha blushed a bit. "He said nurses are not diagnosticians, and I should keep to my place."

"That sounds like him."

"That sounds like most doctors, but once in a while one will surprise me. Not every single doctor considers the nurse his personal servant."

"Do tell," I said dryly. "Now, Martha, I have no proof of any of this, which is why everything I say must remain confidential. Without proof, which believe me I am trying to gather, there is nothing I can do. However, reasoning from the facts as I have presented them thus far, this is what I believe. First, that Augusta was poisoning Father with some agent—I regret to say I do not know what—that for a long time only weakened him and made him less able to function as vigorously as he previously had done."

Martha nodded but did not interrupt.

"Then gradually she increased the dosage, or perhaps the illness progressed on its own; either way he became more and more dependent on her. He lost his former zest for life. He was not able to go out socially anymore. Eventually he had to stop working. Slowly Augusta isolated Father until finally he was at home alone with her all the time. I believe that is what she most wanted, that he should be entirely dependent upon her until, at last, he would die. The problem was, Father had a strong heart. He kept on living and finally I was able to intervene."

"A strong heart," Martha mused, "yet he died of a heart attack, or heart failure. Cardiac arrest. That was what Sarah Kirk told me over the telephone when she called to say that I should not come in, because your father had just expired."

"What time was it when Sarah called, do you remember?" This was a key fact, which I'd wanted to get from Martha, and she was giving it to me without my having to ask.

"It was early. About seven o'clock, I should think. I was awake but not really up yet. As you've seen, your house on Beacon was for me an easy walk so I could afford to lie in for a little."

I shook my head. "Father could not have 'just expired' at seven A.M. I found his body myself at shortly after three. But wait, this is getting the sequence of events mixed up. Let me go back."

Martha nodded. "Don't worry, I'm following you just fine."

"My theory is that Father improved so dramatically because with you and Sarah in constant attendance, Augusta could no longer administer the poisoning agent on a regular basis. She must have gotten a little frantic—she couldn't have him getting well, or even just well enough to keep on living as a semi-invalid, not if people were going to be coming to the house and his daughter getting married, possibly staying in Boston—"

"Oh, are you doing all that? Excuse the interruption, I could not resist."

"Well, yes, I am marrying my business partner, but where we will live after the marriage has not been settled yet."

"I do hope you will be here so that we may continue our acquaintance, but please go on."

"There is not much more to say. I do not know how she did it, but I think Augusta also administered the final dose of poison and made it look as if Father had died of a heart attack."

"Hmm," Martha said. She got up from the table where we both sat in her cheerful kitchen with its yellow walls and white-painted cabinets, refilled the kettle, and set it on again to boil.

"There's a problem with some of that, but I think I can help," she said.

"Precisely why I'm here."

"Your father's long illness was characterized by gastrointestinal symptoms. The delusions or hallucinations can come on when the body is sufficiently malnourished. Likewise his liver had begun to fail—but the liver is a remarkable organ and can regenerate itself. Apparently your father's liver failure was fairly recent and not too far advanced. That would be why his color improved rapidly once Sarah and I began to look after him. This is strong support for your poisoning theory, Fremont. The liver processes toxins out of the body; once that toxin or poison was no longer administered, working his liver too hard day after day after day, the organ began to make a recovery."

Now it was my turn to nod.

"I must say, though, your father's cardiac arrest cannot have been caused by the same poison. It had to have been a different one. The poisons that could cause a heart to stop are all so toxic that even given in small amounts, his death would come within days if not hours."

"You've confirmed something I suspected, but really I know nothing about poisons. My partner, Michael, was going to look into it but right now he is occupied with another matter. From your own expertise, Martha, have you any idea what poisons may have been used, and how Augusta could have obtained them?"

The teakettle, which had been rumbling on the burner, then seized by a brief silence, now erupted into a whistle. Martha took advantage of the subsequent teapot-filling interval to think silently. As she brought the teapot back to the table she shook her head.

"I really can't say. You should have asked for an autopsy, that's the only way to tell, and even then it isn't always possible."

"I tried," I said, twisting my lips into a bitter approximation of my feelings on that score. "But Augusta was Father's legal next of kin, only she had the right to ask for an autopsy. Searles Cosgrove informed me of this fact when I went to ask his help. He was no help at all, by the way. In fact, he rather surprised me, because at our first meeting some weeks earlier, his attitude had been considerably different. Or so I'd thought."

"Hmm," Martha said. She poured tea, a third cup for each of us, then slowly stirred sugar into hers. "Well, I can give you a little information but I'm not sure how much good it will do. Incidentally, if I haven't said so before, I think you are right to be concerned and thinking along these lines. I was very surprised by your father's sudden death. In fact, his whole illness did not follow any predictable path I've ever seen before."

"Thank you. Any help you can give me at all will be much appreciated."

"All right. About the poisons: the ones that could cause an illness of long duration are not that hard to obtain, because they're in things most people have around the house. Such as rat poison and many different kinds of cleaning agents."

"Cleaning fluid?" I perked up, recalling the bottle I'd found in Augusta's room.

"Certainly. Much harder to obtain would be whatever caused your father to die suddenly. There are several poisons that mimic heart attack, but in their natural state—I mean things like plants, the leaves and berries and mushrooms and such—they're not strong enough to kill quickly or reliably. For that your poisoner would almost have to have the substance in refined form. Which suggests it was obtained from a druggist or a chemist. Not everyone could do that."

Our eyes met.

"In other words, Augusta had an accomplice," I said.

"You think it may have been Searles Cosgrove?" Martha asked.

"He's one possibility."

"If you would trust my discretion, I may be able to find out some more about Dr. Cosgrove's behavior in recent weeks by talking to Anna Bates," Martha offered. "I have a feeling she would welcome someone to confide in about now."

"Oh?"

"Um-hm. Shall I try?"

"Yes, please," I agreed.

"All right, I will. Now if I do that for you, perhaps you will tell me something in return, and in advance: What does all of this have to do with something I read in the *Boston Sunday Globe* this morning, about Augusta Simmons Jones having been fatally shot?"

TWENTY-TWO

———◆———

MARTHA HENDERSON'S QUESTION, which was a straightforward and simple one, brought me up short. The reply I gave was woefully inadequate:

I said only, "I'm not sure."

While that was the truth, of course it didn't satisfy her. Nor had I expected it to; what she really wanted from me was a fuller, personalized account of what I knew about the murder, and so I told her.

Even then, I knew it wasn't enough. I didn't really know the answer to her question, because I hadn't thought about it. I hadn't *wanted* to think about it. As long as the police didn't suspect me of shooting her, I didn't *care* who'd killed Augusta Simmons Jones—that was the awful truth. I tried to explain this to Martha in a way that didn't make me sound like a completely horrible person.

"My problem is," I said, "I know from experience that I cannot concentrate on more than one investigation at a time. If there's a connection, I'll come across it. Meanwhile I have to find out if Augusta really did poison Father, and if she had an accomplice, who that person was."

Martha then said something wise: "If the woman

was doing something like that to your father, most likely she has done other nefarious things, and it is not too surprising that someone would want her dead. One way or another, Fremont, there is likely to be some connection."

I said she had given me food for thought, and shortly afterward we made our goodbyes. Martha promised to be in touch when she'd had a heart-to-heart with Nurse Bates, and I went off home to Beacon Street.

MONDAY BROUGHT newspaper reporters to the house, and gawkers, and old friends calling. I should have anticipated this happening, but I hadn't, which put me quite out of sorts with myself and wreaked havoc on my plans for the day as well. I could hardly rush out the door saying, "So sorry, can't stay, I'm going to buy a car." Short for motorcar, of course—it's the shorter form I prefer—it sounds somehow much better than auto for automobile.

I talked briefly from the steps to the reporters, waved to the gawkers, then put aside everything else in order to receive the callers as they trickled in one or two at a time. After a while, I began to be glad to see old friends, both my own and the family's. Truly, in the weeks since my return I'd begun to think I must have alienated everyone when I left Boston for California, and that was why no one had come to call.

Most but not all of the callers had been here just three days ago for Father's funeral. This morning they were simply curious, and some were wanting, however awkwardly, to pick up our friendship, wherever we had left it off long ago.

They all said the same thing: It was a shame, or worse than that, quite horrible really, what had happened to Augusta (they couldn't bring themselves to say the word "murder"), but still, it would be so much easier to come to the house now that *she* was out of the picture. When each caller left I said, as was expected, "I hope you'll come again," and they said of course they would. The surprise for me was I'd meant it, and I hoped they did too.

Eventually midday came, and with it the usual cessation of social visits as all women went home for the noon meal. For some, their husbands would come home and this would be the main meal of the day; for others, it would be a lighter luncheon—followed, for the women, by an hour of rest, and for the men by a return to work. Briefly I wondered how it had come to pass in puritanical Boston that women of a certain class got to have naps after lunch.

While I was wondering about this, I went on to wonder if women have better instincts for understanding people than men do. Of course, there are exceptions like Michael, and certain men who make a profession out of understanding others, but in the main it did seem to me that women are able to see with a clearer inner eye. Every single woman who had been to my house this morning had seen through Augusta, perhaps not as deeply as I did, but they hadn't liked or trusted her.

I wondered what made the difference? Because in social situations Augusta would have been charming to the women too. She wouldn't want to be socially ostracized—would she?

Hmm. I wondered which had come first, her isolating herself with my father or the ostracism? Was it like the conundrum of the chicken and the egg? Would I ever know?

I WAS FINISHING UP my lunch when Mrs. Boynton, the cook, came into the dining room. She was wearing her coat and hat, and although it was rather late in the day to be going to the market I assumed that was what she had in mind. But I was wrong.

"Miss Jones, seeing as how you've Myra Porter here

now and little Mary as well, you won't really be needing me. So I'm givin' in my notice. Startin' now, if you please."

I put down my fork. "Mrs. Boynton, sit down for a minute, won't you? Let's talk about this."

She looked uncomfortable—in fact, she inspected a dining chair carefully as she pulled it out, as if she were judging whether or not it had been sturdily enough made to hold her weight. Mrs. Boynton was a large woman, but not that large. To my relief, she judged the chair worthy and sat, then looked at me warily. Her hat was flat, like a rather large porkpie, an unfortunate mauve color with a feather dyed to match that stuck straight up.

"Did something happen that has made you want to leave?" I asked.

"Well, I should think so, oh my yes. The woman what hired me got herself shot right across the street, that's what happened! I never had to talk to no police before, never in all my born days, and that's a fact. I just want to go on mindin' my own business and stay out of trouble, that's all." She nodded emphatically.

"And you believe you cannot stay out of trouble if you continue to work here, is that it?" I was, as they say in the courts, leading the witness, but why not—there were no lawyers present to object.

"Where there's smoke, there's fire," she said, nodding again.

Whatever that meant.

Mrs. Boynton knew something she hadn't told the police and it was bothering her, I had picked up that much, but how I would get her to tell me I had no idea. I could only, as it were, go fishing.

"Well," I said with a smile, "we should start with the most important thing first: How much are you owed in wages? I will of course pay you whatever you were promised by Mrs. Augusta, and I think for the extra trouble you should have a bonus, don't you?"

She shook her head. "No need. I been paid through

the end of the month. I don't believe in takin' bad money nohow."

That stung, although I didn't think she'd meant to wound me. "I'm sorry. I don't know what you mean. How do you come to the conclusion that my money is bad money?"

"It's all Jones money, isn't it? It's what *she* wanted, the Jones money, and now she's got herself killed and all, I want no part of it. You seem like a nice woman, Miss Fremont, you always been nothin' but kind to me, I never even heard you raise your voice to nobody. But Mary—well, Mary heard Mrs. Augusta being ugly to you on the very same blessed day your daddy was laid in the cold ground, and it was about money. Another time I heard Mrs. Augusta with my own ears be ugly to that boy of hers, and that was about money too. When we was in church yesterday the priest gave his homily on Money Is the Root of All Evil, and I got to thinkin' he's right."

"I hate to think my family's money is tainted," I said.

"Wash it in the blood of the lamb," Mrs. Boynton said, "there's the ticket."

That made a charming mental picture! I said, "I beg your pardon?"

"Give it to the church. Take the curse off'n it."

"Mrs. Boynton," I said, suddenly inspired, "if you don't want a bonus on leaving your employment here to keep for yourself, perhaps I might give you a sum of money you could contribute to your church?"

She tucked her chin down, which had the effect of trebling it, had herself a good think in that position, and finally said, "I guess that would do all right."

I excused myself and went into the library to write a check, which I made out to her name in case she should change her mind later. Actually I myself would rather have seen her buy a new hat with the money than wash it in the blood of the lamb, but we all have our differences.

Back in the dining room, Mrs. Boynton had apparently been uncomfortable sitting at the table by herself, because she was standing again, somewhat uncertainly. But at least she hadn't left yet. I handed her the check, which was of course a bit of a bribe, and just as her fingers closed on it I asked, "Can you remember exactly what Mrs. Augusta said to her son when they were having that argument about money?"

"Oh, she was bitter, she was powerful mad at the poor boy. Anybody can see he's just young, he'll be better when he's older. I got a boy too like that, can't keep things straight—it doesn't do to expect too much of 'em till they're all growed up, y'know."

"I agree. Mr. Lawrence will no doubt improve as he matures. What do you suppose she had asked him to do, that he messed up?"

"Well, they was having this argument in the pantry, so I think 'twas something to do with some food or drink, like he was sposed to have got somethin' special for the evenin'—most likely 'twas drink, because even if I'm not here evenins, which I'm not, if 'twas food she'd've asked me to cook it ahead and leave it. Anyways, the poor boy, he musta got the wrong thing, on account of she was yellin' at him somethin' fierce."

"Please, Mrs. Boynton, this could be important: *exactly* what did she say?"

The cook rubbed her nose, and her eyes took on a faraway look, as people's eyes will do when they are listening to something inside their heads. "She said as how he had to be awful stupid to bring her the wrong stuff all the way from New York. If he couldn't get it right, why'd he bother to come, and she'd have to do it herself now, and would he please tell her why, when this whole thing was finally over, she should share all the money she'd get with him, if he was too stupid to do his part right."

My heart beat faster as Mrs. Boynton put words to my suspicions. She was as near to a witness as I was likely to find! "And what did you think she was referring to when she said all that?"

"Why, I thought it was for makin' your father a special treat, most likely that hot drink he likes to have before he goes to sleep of a night. Since it was to come all the way from New York, I thought maybe some kind of fancy chocolate."

I WENT UPSTAIRS and lay down, but I have never been very good at taking naps, and so I was soon back downstairs again. Rummaging around in Father's desk drawers, I found a notebook in which only a few sheets had been used; I tore these out, saved them under the blotter because they were in Father's handwriting; then I used the notebook to record my thoughts about this investigation. It was highly appropriate, I thought, to be writing such notes in a book where he had written with his own hand not long ago.

I have the ability of total aural recall, which is similar to that of some people who have what is called a photographic memory—they can recall exactly anything they have seen, as if their mind has taken a photograph of it; I can recall anything I have heard word for word if I wish to write it down. I do not know how long photographic memory lasts, but my aural recall will not last forever. I must write down what I have heard within a day or two or it will be gone.

First I wrote down what Mrs. Boynton said she'd overheard between Augusta and Larry. Then I wrote down what Martha Henderson had said about poisons. After that I wrote a few of my own speculations, including a reminder to myself that I should give the bottle of cleaning fluid I'd found in Augusta's dressing room to Michael when he got back, so that he could take it for chemical analysis to the same place he'd taken that horrible tonic.

As I was writing that, I heard the doorbell ring, and shortly Mary came into the library with a cream-colored envelope in her hand.

"For you, Miss Fremont. It was brought by a messenger and he said he's to wait for your reply."

"Oh." It had been a long time since I'd had such an urgent communication, with a messenger waiting and all.

No one could have been more surprised than I was when I read it:

Dear Fremont,

I do not know if you can ever forgive me, but I have made the most dreadful mistake and wish to explain myself, as well as make amends.

I would be very grateful if you will join me for luncheon tomorrow at Locke's, at which time I will tender my apology and my explanation in person. Please send your reply by the messenger—if it is in the affirmative, I will call for you at Beacon Street just before noon.

> *Your obedient servant,*
> *William Barrett*

Locke's! He had certainly tipped the scales in his favor by dangling this plum before me. Locke-Ober's establishment is a fancy bar and restaurant for men only, with private dining upstairs where women may enjoy a meal once a week on what is called Ladies' Day. Of course I would go—even without the incentive of a meal in an excellent and usually forbidden spot, I was too curious to know what in the world William could possibly have to say for himself to turn him down.

My answer, which I wrote on an ordinary sheet of lined paper that I tore out of the notebook, was brief:

William: I will be delighted to have luncheon with you at the time and place mentioned, but do not call for me. I will meet you at the bank instead, as I have some other business I must attend to—

> *Fremont*

I put my sheet of inferior-quality paper into the thick, creamy envelope—which I had observed bore the name and embossed seal of Great Centennial Bank on the back flap—then I crossed out my name on the front and wrote his instead.

"Mary, will you kindly give this to the messenger? And if there are any dimes for tips out there on the hall table, please give him one of those as well."

"Yes, miss," she said, and did her little dip. Both of these are things I dislike, I would vastly prefer to be called Fremont instead of "miss," with no dip, but they'd been trained into her and I did not think I would ever be able to train them out.

I returned to recording my speculations in the notebook.

A few minutes later Mary was back, this time with a telegram that did not require a reply. It was from Michael, and it was brief, without even the usual salutation:

FREMONT STOP LB NOT AT NY ADDRESS STOP NOT
REPORTER ONLY OFFICE BOY NYDN STOP HAS NOT
RETURNED TO WORK STOP BE CAREFUL STOP NOW
PROCEEDING NJ AND CONN STOP WILL RETURN SOONEST
STOP LOVE MICHAEL

I took this rather cryptic telegram to mean Larry Bingham was not who or where he was supposed to be, and that Michael was now on his way to check out Augusta's other relatives. But why now, especially, was he warning me to be careful? I mean any more than I was being careful already.

I was not particularly surprised to discover that Larry was not a reporter but an office boy. Many office boys did work their way up to be reporters eventually, I had heard.

I was less happy with something Michael didn't know, and that was what Mrs. Boynton had told me about Larry's bungle and his mother's subsequent anger. Yet in a way, that bungle made me happy too, for it seemed typical of Larry that he would want to do something to please his mother but in the end couldn't quite do it right. I liked to think perhaps he couldn't quite do it because deep down inside himself Larry Bingham had known it was wrong. And so he had saved himself from himself by making a mistake.

He would have saved my father too, if only Augusta had not found *herself* another accomplice. Surely that was what had happened?

I intended to prove it.

TWENTY-THREE

———◆◆◆———

JUST WHEN I thought I might get away to visit an automobile dealership or two—they could hardly laugh up their sleeves at me if I were only looking, I could always say I was looking in order to persuade my husband, they should like that—my plans were thwarted again. This time by Detectives McLaughlin and O'Neal, who had finally decided they needed to search Augusta's two rooms themselves.

When they were done with that, they asked if they could take a look around the rest of the house, and I gave them permission. If they found my gun inside the muff, well then so be it; there was not much I could do to stop them from searching without making them suspicious. I asked if they were looking for anything in particular, to which they replied they couldn't say, which was what I'd thought they would say, but I'd had to try.

Everything I know about policing, I know from Wish Stephenson, who used to be a policeman in San Francisco. However, one does hear that police departments can vary from town to town; also I myself had heard rather often that San Francisco, like the West in general, is fairly corrupt as far as public officials are concerned. I did not know if this was true of Boston as well, but so far these two detectives were much milder examples of their breed than any I'd ever encountered in my City by the Bay.

Of course, they were somewhat winning me over by the fact that they didn't seem to suspect *me*—which had to mean no one had told them about Augusta's threatening to challenge Father's will in court. I'd been quite certain Searles Cosgrove would tell, even if William Barrett didn't. Why hadn't they told? It rather bothered me. I supposed I would find out about William when we had lunch tomorrow, but Cosgrove . . .

How was I going to handle him? I certainly didn't know—though I supposed I had better think of a way soon. Yes, Dr. Searles Cosgrove was definitely a problem.

Finally, after what seemed an inordinately long time, the two detectives came back downstairs. They asked about a diary. I said if Augusta had kept one I was not aware of it; I said further that she was not an introspective type of person and so I would not have been surprised if she hadn't taken the trouble, as a daily entry in a diary is a bother, which I could attest to, as that was why I did not keep one myself.

I wanted to add that it was a myth that all women who have had a certain degree of education keep diaries—a myth no doubt perpetrated by males because they think we are such idle creatures we have nothing else to do except embroider or perhaps play the piano—but that would have been going too far and so I did not.

They asked again about keys. I told them I'd had the locks changed on all the doors, and now I knew precisely how many keys there were and who had them, and would be happy to supply them with a list. This did not impress the detectives as much as I had thought it would—I mean to say, I had been efficient, I had been precise, did I not deserve at least a minor accolade? A "Yes, give us the new list," if nothing else?

Apparently not. McLaughlin, who was the primary asker of questions, looked at O'Neal and O'Neal looked back at McLaughlin, until I wondered if these two had been working together for so long that they had learned to communicate without speech. Then O'Neal said, "Tell her."

Yes! I wanted to scream at them: Tell me! So that we can be done here because I have places to go and things to do; and besides the police make me terribly nervous.

McLaughlin said, "We think the person who murdered Mrs. Jones entered the house with a key, more than likely by the front door, then left both doors—that is the door to the vestibule and the door to the outside—open. In the event he needed to make a quick getaway, it would take an intruder too long to get through both doors. He'd want to leave them open.

"That would be what happened with Mrs. Jones. She heard the killer—either she's a light sleeper or else she hadn't been to sleep yet—and she got out of bed and was able to run outside through those doors he'd left open."

"Or she," I couldn't resist saying. But then I could have kicked myself, lest it get them suspecting me. Still, police detectives or private detectives shouldn't assume a woman is not just as capable of killing as a man. Because, I assure you, we are.

"Or she," McLaughlin said, giving me a look. "See, you'd have the same set of circumstances going if the killer had hidden in the house."

"Hidden in the house?" That was something I hadn't thought of, and it gave me the willies.

"You had a lot of people here earlier in the day, didn't you, after your father's funeral."

"Yes, we did," I agreed. That afternoon seemed a hundred years ago now. But the grief was ever-present, and as soon as I heard the word "funeral," tears pricked my eyes.

I said, to keep the topic moving, "But I don't think anybody hid. I saw them all leave, said goodbye to them on their way out."

Surely I'd seen them all go, hadn't I?

"We don't think anybody hid either," O'Neal said, for once taking over from his partner. He was the shorter and rounder of the two, balding; McLaughlin had a square face and a lot of dark hair. "What my partner here is taking forever to say is, the crucial point here is Mrs. Jones was shot *outside* the house, not inside it. She had time to run down the stairs, out the door, and all the way across the street before she was shot. That couldn't have happened, we don't think, if the killer hadn't come in the front door and left both those doors open."

"And"—McLaughlin took over again—"we think he—or she—had a key, because the lock hadn't been forced. These big doors on these old houses in this part of town, and their locks, have been painted and spit-and-polished to a fare-thee-well. They'd show the slightest scratch, and believe me, ain't nobody been opening these doors with anything but a key."

"I see your point," I agreed. It was actually a sharp piece of reasoning, and I was moderately impressed.

I continued: "I'd love to help you, but ever since my father married Augusta Simmons, I have been living in California and she has been running the house. From what I've seen in the few weeks I've been back here, Augusta was only a passable housekeeper. She didn't keep a list of who had keys. My father would have had such a list—he was a widower for a long time before marrying Augusta, you understand—but once she was in charge she could have given keys to any number of people and we would never know. I do not even know the names of the servants she has had since I've been gone, except for Mary Fowey—and she has only been here a few months."

They had a few more questions about servants, about Myra Porter, whom they'd found upstairs, and about Mrs. Boynton's leaving, which Mary had told them about when they were looking around in the kitchen.

Eventually McLaughlin declared himself satisfied

with my answers, O'Neal concurred, and they left. As I closed the front door after them, I found I was satisfied too; their visit had gone a long way toward relieving my mind of some lingering anxiety.

I had changed the locks. The killer had come from outside, and he had come only for Augusta. He wouldn't come again, that was over now; he wouldn't come for me. And even if he did, with the new locks on the doors he couldn't get in.

I privately thought Augusta had been killed by one of her lovers. She'd had at least one, perhaps throughout my father's long illness, I felt sure. But none of that was my problem. I needed only to prove that she had killed my father.

IN THE WEE SMALL HOURS something awakened me. I was still in that guest bedroom on the back of the second floor. With Ralph and Myra's help, I was planning to refurnish and redecorate Father and Mother's room at the front of the house for myself and Michael, but that would take time. Also, the detectives were not thrilled right now about the prospect of my touching anything in Augusta's two rooms, and so that rather put me off doing much—therefore I was still at the back of the house.

The sounds I heard, very faintly, were coming from the walled garden out back.

I got up and went to the window. I had to feel my way because it was quite dark in the room, only the faintest light from the gas lamps out on Beacon Street filtered back this far.

But this state of affairs had its advantage: by the time I reached the window my eyes were fully adjusted to the darkness, and when I pulled back the curtain I was able to see out. And I did see something!

The problem was, I could not be sure what I'd seen. It was like seeing a ghost—you blink, and it's gone. One minute it's there and the next minute it isn't.

I stood there looking and looking, staring until I knew if I didn't stop I would end up conjuring something out of the darkness that wasn't really there. So I let my vision go all blurry and concentrated instead on remembering the sound I'd heard.

The sound that had awakened me had been a thud. Not a big thud, but a soft one. Like . . . someone jumping over the back garden wall and landing on both feet, in soft shoes. And then smaller sounds, nothing definite or definable, very hard to hear—as I've said, the house has thick walls and sounds don't carry well.

While I'd been feeling my way to the window, I'd heard something more, though: scraping noises, like something being dragged across a rock. And then I could have sworn I'd seen a white face turned toward the house when I first twitched the curtain back—but I'd blinked and it was gone. Just completely gone.

From all this, what could I conclude?

Either someone had climbed over the wall into the little garden, tried and failed to get into the house with a key that no longer fit the lock, and then had a rather difficult time of it climbing back over the wall . . .

Or I was sleepwalking and seeing ghosts—take your pick, Fremont Jones!

"YOU WOULD THINK," I said to William conversationally, as a waiter who was older than God led the two of us past the Men's Bar and Cafe toward the stairs to the two upper floors, "that they would realize if they opened the whole place to women all the time, instead of just the upper floors on Ladies' Day, they'd make a great deal more money."

As I said this, the waiter's ears turned pink. He was too well trained—and probably too set in his ways—to turn around and glare at me for my impertinence but I am sure he wanted to.

The waiter needn't have worried; William, like any

prosperous businessman on Tremont across from the
Common, had learned chapter and verse of the
Locke-Ober Bible. Locke's, you see, is on Winter Place,
which is a little alleyway between Winter Street and
Temple Place. In other words it's about half a block
from Great Centennial Bank; Locke's has been in this
same place since before I was born—and probably with
this same waiter.

Being therefore well prepared, William immediately
recited the appropriate verse in response to my plaint:
"Locke-Ober is not about making money, Fremont. It's
about tradition and excellence."

"Um-hm," I said, watching the waiter's ears turn
back to normal.

The interior at Locke's is all dark, gleaming mahogany, imported from someplace in the Caribbean and
carved by New England cabinetmakers. From past
experience I could attest to the excellence of the
mahogany wainscoting along the stairway, and in the
ceilings, and around the walls of the private dining
rooms; I used to come here with Father on Ladies' Days
as often as I could pester him into it.

When I was fifteen or sixteen I had fantasies of getting past the various watchdogs and into the Men's Bar,
where no women are *ever* allowed to go. I have heard
tell the mirrors and glass in there are from Paris or
Venice or someplace exotic like that, and there is a large
nude painting of a woman behind the bar, and another
nude woman in brass, a statue that they use for hanging
their hats. These things I have heard about for most of
my life, but never seen.

As William and I settled into our private dining
room, which was quite small and perhaps even a little
too private, I had a naughty thought: What if I were to
dress up like a man, as I had done a few times for un-
dercover work in San Francisco—would Michael accompany me to Locke's famous Men's Bar so that I
could see that nude painting for myself, just once in my

life? Not to mention hanging my hat on some part of the bronze woman's nude anatomy. Now that would be a coup.

William had asked me a question while I was having this fantasy. I recovered his question from the part of my mind that conveniently records these things when I am not otherwise paying attention, and answered it:

"Yes, I've been here a number of times with Father," I said, "and I am familiar with the menu. I will have the Lobster Savannah."

"An excellent choice," William said.

He was beyond nervous. I was glad when the food had been ordered and the ancient waiter—who was quite the most efficient and polite waiter I had ever had anywhere even if he didn't approve of me—had produced a half bottle of wine for William. I had ordered beer with my lobster, which may not seem refined, but I prefer that combination. It is, I believe, a Yankee thing. I got my beer too, in a lovely tall glass. And then the waiter left us until it was time to bring the first course.

"I'm waiting," I said pointedly. I did not intend to spare him, for I felt William Barrett had dealt me the worst sort of betrayal. He had, as it were, gone over to the enemy.

He swallowed so hard that I could see his Adam's apple move above his tight white collar. He said, "I— I'm humiliated. All I can think of is to thank God there weren't that many people present to hear what I said about poor old Sefton—"

"The Forrest sisters were there," I reminded him peskily, "and they will repeat it to everyone, you know."

"Yes, but no one pays any attention to them."

That was true enough.

"Of course," William said, leaning forward so that his tie dangled perilously close to his crab soup, "none of what I said is true. I can't think what came over me. Elwood Sefton is just as in command of all his wits as I am."

"In fact," I said acerbically, "he may be *more* in command of his wits than you are. Let us cut to the chase, as they say in the melodrama: Are you trying to tell me that Augusta Simmons bewitched you and caused you to say things you didn't really mean?"

"Yes! That's it, that's exactly what happened!"

I gave him a hard look and began to eat my soup slowly. The first taste was excellent, sharply fishy as good crab should be, the cream smooth as velvet would be if one could put tongue to velvet—but after that first taste I was really too busy controlling my anger to enjoy the food.

I simply ate. Without comment. Letting William stew in his own juices, lie in his own bed, which he'd made, all the clichés that apply; there are thousands of them for situations like this one. He couldn't stand my silence—I hadn't really thought he could; I'd thought my silence would get him to talk, and I was right.

He blurted, "When I heard, I mean when I saw in the paper that she'd been, well, shot—well, she was gone then, wasn't she? I mean Augusta of course."

I merely raised my eyebrows and kept on eating.

"I swear to you, Fremont, it was as if the woman had put a spell on me, a real witchy spell, that was broken just as soon as she died. Really, it was exactly like magic—well, I mean like one hears magic is, because of course I haven't really had any experience of magic. Other than this. What I'm trying to say is, it was exactly like magic because as soon as she was dead, it all fell away. All the madness, all my . . . my obsession with Augusta just simply disappeared. It was gone, poof! Just like that!"

"And you went to Harvard," I said, slowly shaking my head, "graduated and everything."

He blushed. The waiter brought our main courses. I asked for more beer, which of course the ancient fellow did not like, but he brought it to me anyway, and I began to enjoy the sweetness of my lobster together with the dry-tasting bubbles of the beer. I am sorry to say that poor William went along for quite a while in that ridiculous manner of claiming Augusta had driven him temporarily out of his senses.

Finally he got to the apology part—he said he was sorry he'd agreed to support Augusta in her legal action to break Father's will. "She'd need someone inside the bank, you see."

"Um-hm, of course she would. To get information that should have been kept confidential, no doubt," I said, lifting my lovely tall glass and taking a sip, "or perhaps even to plant misinformation in places where it did not belong? Had she gotten that far with you yet?"

William looked baffled.

"No?" I asked. "She would have."

"Fremont," he said, all the color draining from his face, "*you* didn't shoot Augusta, did you?"

"Oh honestly, William, of course I didn't. The police think it was someone from outside the house, who had a key. Their theory is quite sound, really. I suppose *you* could have done it, if she'd spurned you for Searles Cosgrove. I'm sure she gave you a key to my house on Beacon Street. Well, did she or didn't she?"

Now he looked uncomfortable again, and the color once more began to build in his face until he had red blotches on his cheeks. This was William Barrett's medium stage of embarrassment. It came to me that I had known this man too well for too long—but there are advantages to that, too.

"Are you going to answer me, or not?" I was merciless.

"Very well. It's not the kind of subject I would think a lady would want to discuss, but I do owe you a great debt and so I will answer any question you wish to put to me. First off, I didn't have to be jealous of Cosgrove, it was the other way around. Once she met me, and we became—er—involved, he . . . Dammit, I can't talk about this with you."

"Yes, you can. I am a grown woman soon to be married, and I am not inexperienced, shy or squeamish. We're talking about a woman who at the very least slept with, *had sexual relations with* . . . You might as well not look so shocked, for I believe it is better to call a thing by its right name. Where was I? Oh yes, Augusta had sexual relations with other men while she was married to my father. You've just admitted you were one. You've also suggested that Searles Cosgrove was another, and that does not surprise me in the least."

"Well, it certainly surprised me, I can tell you that!" William said very grumpily. "The man hates my guts because I took her away from him."

"I don't see how that's possible. How could you take her away from him when you both met her at about the same time? In fact, you must have introduced them! You wrote to me about it, how you went to the house first, and were so shocked by what you found that you called in Searles."

"Yes, that's true. What I didn't know then, but figured out later through something I overheard, was that Searles and Augusta had been lovers for at least a year before I ever came on the scene. I gather their, uh, liaison had nothing whatever to do with Searles treating your father—they didn't have their meetings at Beacon Street, so it's quite possible he really didn't know how ill your father was. Unless, of course, Augusta told him, which apparently she didn't."

Hah! I thought, bitterly.

The waiter came back. Just for spite, because I wasn't the least bit hungry anymore after having consumed more food than I normally eat in a whole day, I ordered the Sultana Roll for dessert.

When we were alone again I said, "William, it would be very helpful if you could explain something to me— you said this luncheon was about explaining, remember. What it is about Augusta Simmons that attracts men like you and Cosgrove? Not to mention Father. Cosgrove is also married, isn't he?"

"He's married, but nobody ever sees his wife. I suppose she's ill, or shut up in an insane asylum or something. What is it about Augusta? you ask."

He mulled for a while, and then said, "I think, in the main, it's this: When she's with you, you feel there is no one else in the whole world who matters to that woman but you. She hangs on your every word. She will do anything you ask, anything. In fact, most of the time you don't even have to ask, she just . . . somehow . . . knows what you want. Something extraordinary happens. It's like anything, *everything* you want she gives you—and then all of a sudden it's turned around and you're wanting to give everything to her instead. Do you see?"

I did, but yet I didn't.

William had been right, it was hard to talk about this, hard for me to listen to it. I nodded, just to keep him talking; and all the while I was cutting up Sultana Roll into little pieces, rather viciously, and not eating a single one.

EARLY IN THE EVENING Martha Henderson came to the house, after calling first. She had entertained Anna Bates, Dr. Cosgrove's nurse, at some length when the latter got off from work.

Anna, it seemed, was in love with her boss—the old cliché, the nurse in love with the doctor. She had run his office for years, and had been having an affair with him quietly for almost as long. She had passed up opportunities that might have led to marriage in favor of continuing her relationship with the married doctor.

This story, like that waiter at Locke's, was older than God. And it always ends the same. Poor Anna.

I heard out the end of the story from Martha, but I already knew from what William Barrett had told me how it would end. At some point in the last couple of years, Cosgrove met Augusta Simmons Jones, and he preferred her, and Anna was just out of luck.

"Martha," I said suddenly, as the idea occurred to me, "you don't suppose Anna shot Augusta?"

Martha was silent, thinking. "I don't like to believe a good nurse would do that, and she is a good nurse. But I can tell you, she's still in love with Searles Cosgrove. She's relieved that Augusta Jones, her competition, is dead."

Now I was silent, thinking too. I had a bit of a problem seeing how everything I had learned today might come together in a way I could use. Finally I said, "How did Anna find out in the first place that Cosgrove was having an affair with my father's wife?"

It was odd how the very thought of that hurt me. I hadn't liked her, yet the idea that she could betray my father, who had loved her so much, was like a knife to the heart.

"Apparently Anna figured it out in part from the medical record. Soon after your father stopped coming to see Cosgrove, the doctor began taking off certain blocks of time that he had not taken before. What Anna thinks is that when Dr. Cosgrove decided your father's impotence was incurable, he made overtures to Augusta, and she accepted them. You see, in a sense he preyed upon her, Fremont. She must have been ripe for the picking, if you'll pardon my saying so."

"No, with that pair, I do not believe either one preyed upon the other. I think they were well suited, and his caring for my father—once I began to insist from afar that Father needed to be cared for—was nothing but a sham. Oh, Cosgrove got Father into the hospital. But I think he also helped kill him."

TWENTY-FOUR

———◆◆◆———

I HAVE NOTICED before in the working of an investigation—and both Michael and Wish confirm that this is true also in their much greater experience—that there comes a time when the obstacles to truth just seem to fall away, until suddenly the truth stands revealed.

So it was that no sooner had Martha Henderson left than Father's other private nurse, Sarah Kirk, rang the doorbell at Beacon Street. Mary Fowey had already gone upstairs, as it was after 8 P.M. and the Porters were presumably happily ensconced in their room, so I answered the door myself.

"Sarah!" I said, recognizing her. "What a pleasant surprise. I had not thought I would see you again."

This was not quite true—I'd had every intention of seeing her again, but I thought I would have to be the one to go to her. I had certainly not expected her to come to me.

"I work nights, you know," she said, "because that's when I have someone to watch Edwin. And I have a new job up the hill on Chestnut Street, so I thought maybe you wouldn't mind too much if I just stopped by, even at such an hour?"

"No, of course I don't mind. Please come in."

Sarah was formally dressed in her white nurse's costume, complete with an elaborately pleated cap and a blue cape that appeared to be part of the outfit, for it had a little insignia on the collar that matched the one on her cap.

"May I take your cape?" I offered, closing the inner front door.

"No, thank you," she declined. "I won't stay long. It's just—I have something to tell you."

"By all means. Let us sit in the library, where I have a fire going."

Poor Sarah looked exhausted. My heart went out to her and I said impulsively, "I know you didn't come here to talk about your own situation, but I wish there were something I could do to help with your son."

She nodded gravely. "I know you have a kind heart. That's one of the reasons I'm here. The other reason is, it's the right thing to do. About my son, there's nothing to be done—the only merciful thing would be to hasten the end of his life so that he doesn't suffer any more. But—"

Suddenly she bit her lips together in the manner I'd come to know from our previous visit, and she turned her face away. I witnessed her painful struggle to hold back tears, wishing there were something I could do, even just to ease her speech, and helplessly knowing there was not.

"That was why I did it, you see," she said, despair stark in her eyes. "They promised me, Dr. Cosgrove and Mrs. Jones did, that if I helped your father end his suffering by giving him the powder in his drink, Dr. Cosgrove would give me the means to end poor Edwin's suffering too. And I did give it to your father, and Dr. Cosgrove did give me enough of the powder for my son, but then I couldn't bring myself to give it to Edwin anyway!"

Sarah broke down, sobbing. I sat stunned and dry-eyed.

Finally my voice came back to me. I don't know how long we'd been like that, me stunned and the nurse sobbing; it could have been seconds or it could have been much longer.

"What was the powder?" I asked.

It took Sarah a few tries before she was able to pull herself together enough to answer. "Digitoxin. It's a distillation of digitalis, from foxglove. In a large enough dose it stops the heart."

I digested this information. "Is it . . . a relatively merciful way to die?"

My question unleashed another flood of tears. "I'd thought so, but then when it was my turn to give it to my Edwin, and I couldn't do it, I—We don't know, do we, what's right! We don't want them to suffer, but life itself is—it's—it's so hard to let go! And to make that decision, to let go, for another person . . . ! I couldn't do it for my Edwin. I don't know how Mrs. Jones could do it for your father."

"So you believed it was a mercy killing?"

"Yes, of course. And I said I would do it because if I did, then Dr. Cosgrove would give me the same medicine to, to kill my son."

"You didn't think Father would ever get well, even though he was so much better?"

"Not well, no. He might have lived on like he was for much longer, though. Didn't I tell you that when you came to see me, didn't I agree with you how much better he was?"

I didn't reply; I couldn't. I just bowed my head in an acquiescence of sorts.

"Oh, Miss Fremont, the truth is I was so upset that day, I can't even remember what I said to you. I was eaten up with guilt!" Sarah cried. "What I did was wrong, and I know it, and I'll take the punishment. It's just that Edwin will die soon, I know he will, but until then he needs me. Could you please wait and not tell the police what I did until my boy is gone?"

I lifted my head. "I just have one more question. You were asleep when I came into Father's room and found him dead. If you were the one who gave him the fatal dose, why were you sleeping? I thought they'd drugged you so that one of them could get to Father."

For a moment Sarah Kirk covered her face with her hands. Her voice began as a whisper: "I'm so ashamed."

Then she raised her head, sat up straight, and the strength one must have to follow her profession took over and sustained her: "I had to give your father the dose in his nighttime drink. That way he wouldn't think anything was different. It took him first with vomiting—I'd expected that—and I cleaned him up, sat him up for a minute to put a clean nightshirt on him. The sitting up, that sudden change of posture, made his heart drop out; he convulsed once and died. So it's fair to say he didn't suffer long. I made sure he was clean and peaceful, tucked him in, all the sheets were clean too, and I put a clean spread on the bed.

"But then I had to sit there in the room until Mrs. Jones could come in and find him, because that was what we'd agreed. It was to look as if he'd died in his sleep, the two of us witnesses that he'd died quietly between the last time I looked at him and whenever she came in. Oftentimes she'd look in late, around midnight, but that night she didn't. I don't know why she didn't. And I—well, I just couldn't stand it, being there alone with your father dead in the bed. I think I'd already begun to realize how wrong it was, not the act of mercy it was supposed to be. So I gave myself a sedative, and that was why you found me sleeping."

She looked at me, her eyes pleading, and I nodded, not quite sure yet what I was going to say. But a conviction was growing within me.

"I'm sorry," Sarah Kirk said. "I know it's not enough, but I *am* sorry, and I *will* take my punishment. If only we could wait until after my Edwin is gone."

I went over to Sarah and placed my hand on her shoulder. First she jumped, and then, as she felt the warmth of the message I wanted to convey through my touch, she began to relax.

"Sarah," I said, "I don't blame you for my father's death. You were only the instrument, you gave him the fatal dose the same way a gun delivers a bullet. Nobody blames the gun when a person is shot. The real killer, that's the one who ordered the dose, or the one who pulled the trigger—that was someone else, not you."

I drew her to her feet and put my arms around her, just briefly. "Go now, and try to forget. Take care of your boy as well as you can. Don't worry—I'll never tell anyone what you've just told me. Dr. Cosgrove won't tell anyone because he's more to blame than you are, and he knows it. And Augusta Simmons Jones—shall we call her the one who pulled the trigger?—is dead herself. There has been enough of death, and of killing, and of sorrow. Let this be an end to it."

IMMEDIATELY, before I could lose my resolve, I called Martha Henderson on the telephone.

"Since you left I've been thinking," I said, "and I've decided to be satisfied with what you learned about Dr. Cosgrove. That, plus the information I had from my friend Mr. Barrett, is enough for me. I think it would be best now to leave this matter in the hands of the police. They do seem to be doing a good job of investigating the murder, and who knows what they'll turn up in the process."

After a slight pause Martha said, "If you're sure."

"I am."

At the other end of the line, she sighed. "In that case, I think leaving this to the police is the wise thing to do. Good night, Fremont. I hope we will see each other again soon."

I echoed the same sentiments, and then we both hung up.

* * *

AROUND MIDNIGHT I dressed in my full mourning gear, the long black cloak over the black dress I'd worn all day long, black shoes and stockings, black leather gloves. I took my small revolver out of hiding, spun out the cylinder to check that all the chambers were loaded even though I didn't think I'd have to use it. I weighed it in my hand for balance—I had not fired this type of gun except in training with Michael, but it was actually easier to handle than the antiquated Marlin I'd left back in San Francisco. Then I shoved the gun into the right-hand inner pocket of the cloak. Lastly I put on the black hat and pulled down the veil. A glance in the mirror assured me that I could not have been more shrouded and live.

I went down the front stairs because the Porters were less likely to hear me, their rooms being at the back. I assumed they were asleep and hoped they would stay that way. After letting myself out the back door as quietly as possible, I settled down to wait invisibly on a bench in a shadowed corner of the walled garden.

"Let this be an end to it," I'd said to Sarah Kirk. But it is not so easy to let go of anger, and the desire for revenge. I had found the perfect antidote, though, if any such thing existed: Every time I felt my anger rise up and I wanted anew to find a way to avenge my father's death, alongside these feelings there also rose up a vision of Sarah Kirk with her tragically ill son wrapped around her, his huge head lolling out of control and her thin-boned yet strong hand going up to support that head. I would never have my revenge—I *could not,* because if I brought down Cosgrove, he would bring Sarah down with him. I wasn't going to allow that to happen.

No, it was a much better decision to let my anger go. But oh how hard it was to do. If Augusta were still living, I knew I couldn't have done it.

I was not particularly cold inside my warm cloak.

The night was a little foggy. Wispy tendrils of mist drifted up the Charles, worked their way around the base of Beacon Hill, and crept over the garden wall. In Boston as in San Francisco, a misty or foggy night is warmer than a clear one.

I'd waited for a while, I don't know how long but probably more than an hour, when scrabbling sounds from the other side of the garden wall broke through my reverie. I reached inside the pocket of the cloak and brought the gun out into my lap, just in case. If my hunch was right, I would not need it.

He came over the wall slithering like a snake, on his belly. No thuds tonight—he'd learned his lesson the other night, when he'd seen my face at the window just as I'd seen his. Had he recognized me then? Or had he thought what I'd thought, that I was a ghost?

He crawled along in the shadow of the wall toward the house, his eyes fixed on the doors and windows. It never occurred to him to examine the corners of the garden—and even if it had, he might not have seen me.

Sometimes burglars or thieves will blacken their hands and faces so that their white skin does not reflect light at night. As I watched Larry Bingham crawl closer to the house, I did not think he had blackened his skin on purpose; rather I thought he'd been living rough, extremely rough.

I watched him crawl up the back steps and try his key in the door. I wondered at the tenacity of desperation—what is it in the mind that brings a person back to try again where he has failed before, hoping against hope? The key did not work of course, any more than it had worked on any other night he'd tried it.

I was determined to help this young man, whether he wanted help or not. He, at least, could be saved. He could have a future. Augusta Bingham Simmons Jones—however many other names she may have had—must not be allowed to ruin every single life she'd ever touched.

From the shadows where I sat, I spoke his name gently, knowing he would not expect it.

He turned around, not so gently, and with something I did not expect: the flash and report from the muzzle of his gun.

TWENTY-FIVE

HIS SHOT WENT wide; he hadn't aimed but had fired his gun in a reflex action. I had my revolver in hand beneath my cloak, and I was fairly certain I could see him better than he could see me—though behind my heavy black veil it was like seeing through a glass darkly.

I could have fired back but I didn't want to, for a lot of reasons. They all raced through my mind: with a small gun I should shoot to kill or not at all; my first shot would give away my location and if I missed I'd be sorry I'd given myself away; I didn't want to kill Larry Bingham. The cloak was voluminous, it relied on its many folds to keep the wearer warm and had only one point of closure, at the collar. I held the revolver ready with my finger on the trigger. A revolver has no safety, and with one sweep of my arm, the cloak would fall back. Yes, I could wait.

"Where are you?" Larry called out in a hoarse voice. "I didn't mean to shoot! Honest, I didn't mean it."

Something in the quality of his voice rang like a warning bell in my mind. I didn't move.

"I know you didn't mean to shoot," I said, injecting warmth into my voice, although it is difficult to feel truly warm toward someone when you are holding guns on one another.

"Show yourself!" he pleaded—and I thought: Ah! So he cannot see me after all.

"Please," he said, "let me see you."

"Soon," I said, "you'll see me soon. You know your mother's dead, Larry?"

"Dead! Yes, dead. I know. I did it, I know! I did it did it did it!"

"You shot your mother?" I took a step forward. I hadn't meant to move, it was involuntary, I was drawn by his confession, not wanting to believe it, hoping I'd misunderstood what he said.

Larry didn't reply. He stood on the back steps, the arm with the gun still raised, out in front of his body, in the dim light looking like a dark cutout of a man up against a dark cutout of a tall house with doors and windows. Everything was outlines and shadows.

I took another step, encouraged by his silence and wanting to be able to see the expression on his face so that I could use that as a clue to how I might proceed.

"Why?" I asked. "Why did you do it?"

He raised the arm with the gun higher, though it trembled visibly, and pointed it at me. "*You* know why," he said. "Because you're evil, you had to die. You're a thing from hell now, you stay away from me!"

Omigod! In a flash I understood: To Larry I loomed like a specter in that huge black cloak, for I am a tall woman; with the hat and the long black veil, coming out of the dark of night, I must have seemed a terror to behold. He thought he was seeing the black, vengeful ghost of his mother.

I said no more. I stood stock-still perhaps twelve feet away. I was afraid if I spoke or moved even a fraction of an inch, he would empty all his shots into me, even if he did think I was a dark ghost.

"I'm not doing it anymore, you understand, you got that?" Larry was weeping desperately. "All my life, that's all I was good for. I was a boy, I could do all the dirty things, the nasty things. You taught me, you know you did, you made me do it. I stole for you, I hurt people for you, I *killed* for you, I even went to *jail* for you, and did you care? No, you didn't, you just said I'd get out in a couple of years because I was a kid. I got out all right, but you don't know—"

Larry broke off, sobbing. The arm with the gun had begun to droop, and as he swiped at his streaming eyes with his other hand I tensed my muscles, wondering if I could run at him, catch him off balance, bring him down.

But then I remembered why I had my gun—I couldn't run anymore, my legs weren't strong enough yet.

"You don't know!" Larry's voice rose to a scream. "What they do to you in jail, it's horrible, they *hurt* you!" Now his voice came back down to a normal pitch, and was somehow all the more eerie for its seeming normality. "They hurt you like you hurt me, like you made me hurt other people. I didn't want to do it anymore when I got out."

He noticed his gun was dropping and he brought it back up, stood taller, seemed to gather himself—then slowly he moved his gun arm straight out to his side. "I got that poison for you the one time. The one *last* time, because you said it was so important and I wanted to do it for you. But then I made a mistake, one lousy mistake, and you treated me like dirt.

"Maybe I am dirt," he said firmly, "but you're not going to haunt me for the rest of my life."

Larry Bingham crooked his elbow, bringing the gun to his temple, and shot himself through the head.

TWO DAYS LATER Michael returned from New York, New Jersey, and Connecticut with a whole briefcase full of information about Augusta née Bingham—for that was her maiden name—Simmons Jones. He was obliged to share the material with Detectives McLaughlin and

O'Neal without delay, for it illuminated and confirmed Larry Bingham's disjointed confession, which I had written down for them in all the detail I could recall.

As it happened, the detectives themselves had begun to look into Augusta's past, for as they went around our Beacon Hill and Back Bay community on their interviews, not a soul had had much good to say about "the new Mrs. Jones," and this made them suspicious. They surmised she might have made an enemy here or there, but like me, they had not suspected her son.

The only bad part about Michael having dug up all this information was that he had to tell the detectives about our private investigation agency, so that they could understand not only why Michael and I had taken so much on ourselves but also how he'd had the expertise to pull it all together. Of course, Michael didn't say anything about having the names and addresses of all Augusta's relatives, which had made everything a good deal easier. That, along with public records and newspaper archives in the towns concerned, had done the job.

Augusta Bingham had two sons out of wedlock at an early age, possibly incestuously. Her one and only advantage was that she was from a "good" family determined to cover up their sins, and part of the cover-up was to act as if nothing unusual had happened, Augusta continued with her lessons and so on. The family arranged to have the older boy raised by an aunt and uncle and passed off as their son, her nephew. (Presumably this was the nephew I rather narrowly escaped being forced to marry—though nothing could make me believe Father would really have forced me if it had ever come to that.)

But when the younger boy was born, Augusta had refused to part with him; instead she ran away from her home in New Jersey and went to live in a small coastal town in Connecticut, taking her baby with her. This baby grew up to be Larry Bingham. Whether Larry Bingham would have been different if he had been raised, like his older brother, by someone other than his mother is impossible to know.

What is known from reports of the Simmons family (into which Augusta married when Larry was eight years old) was that Larry was always a peculiar child. He had few playmates, animals shied away from him, he was the sort to pull the wings off flies and legs off beetles and to delight in their deformity, and so on. He got in trouble at school. He stole; often he stole the way a cat kills, to take the prize home to Mother. When he was sixteen years old he was sentenced to prison for having set fire to an abandoned house. Unfortunately, a man had been in the house and burned to death; Larry claimed he didn't know the man was in the house and so had received the minimum sentence.

Also around this time, Mr. Simmons died after a lingering illness.

After Detectives McLaughlin and O'Neal made note of that, and remarked on my father's also having had a lingering illness, Michael told them about the benzene.

The chemical analysis of that bottle of Dr. Zahray's Hercules Tonic for Males came back the same day Michael returned from his trip. The chemical that was present without authorization, as it were, in the tonic was benzene. It just so happened that the "cleaning fluid" in that large brown bottle I'd found in Augusta's room was also benzene. Father's symptoms were consistent with long, slow poisoning by benzene.

A maliciously clever woman, she had put it in the tonic that Father had consumed by the truckload in his futile attempt to please her sexually. Only God knew what else she had put it in—other than his food at the hospital.

The Simmons children in Connecticut subsequently had their father's body exhumed and examined. He had died of arsenic, probably from rat poison, also in a long-drawn-out manner.

I never told anyone, not even Michael, about Sarah Kirk and the digitoxin. I said I was satisfied to know

BEACON STREET MOURNING   269

about the benzene and did not want Father's rest disturbed. There was no need to take it further.

In April, Dr. Searles Cosgrove began quietly to close down his practice. In May, he left Boston. Martha Henderson told me that Anna Bates went with him as a private nurse in charge of the semi-invalid Mrs. Cosgrove. Some people never learn; I suppose that is because it does seem there are always some people who get away with it.

Then again, some do get caught; and that is where Michael and I are continuing to make our contribution. We are still the J&K Agency . . . we are still partners. But still I have not married him.

AFTERWORD
AN AUTHOR'S NOTE

I have attempted to be as accurate as possible in my fictional re-creation of Boston in the year 1909. Streets, landmarks, and public buildings when mentioned by name are for the most part real places that did exist then (in which case they are described as they were then in historic photographs), and may still exist now. Examples are the two hotels mentioned by name, the Parker House and the Vendome.

There are, however, a few exceptions: Great Centennial Bank is my own creation. Pembroke Jones House is my fictional amalgam of the handsome houses that still stand on Beacon Street in the location described, where they have stood since the early nineteenth century. Boston Priory Hospital is fictional; but Mount Auburn Cemetery is still, and always, completely real.

—D.D.

ABOUT THE AUTHOR

DIANNE DAY spent her early years in the Mississippi Delta before moving to the San Francisco Bay Area. She now lives in Pacific Grove, California, where she is at work on a novel of suspense based on the life of Clara Barton. Fremont Jones has appeared in five previous mysteries: *The Strange Files of Fremont Jones,* which won the Macavity Award for Best First Novel, *Fire and Fog, The Bohemian Murders, Emperor Norton's Ghost,* and most recently, *Death Train to Boston.*

APRIL
1863

*I confess I am confounded, literally speechless
with amazement! When I left Washington
everyone said it boded no peace, it was a bad
omen for me to start. I had never missed of
finding the trouble I went to find, and was
never late—I thought little of it.*

—from the unpublished diary of Clara Barton,
dated "April 7th, 1863, Tuesday"

ONE

———◆◆◆———

HILTON HEAD ISLAND

H ere," I said, just loudly enough to be heard over the cries of seagulls and their bass counterpoint, a continuous throbbing hum that comes from all the unseen life hidden in these marshes. I raised my hand until I felt the boat slow, then pointed a finger to indicate that I wished us to move deeper into the cover of the seagrass, which even now at high tide loomed above my head.

I gave my directions serenely, without turning to look my man Jack in the eye; he was at the moment out of favor with me. I had no need to look—I could feel his sullen acquiescence behind me just as easily as I felt the small boat creep into the grasses at the merest pointing of my finger.

I know Jackson obeys me only because he fears me. I've given this man a home and work to do for which I've paid him wages, even back before Emancipation, when he was nothing but contraband. He didn't understand the value of money, so I taught him how to spend it wisely. Yet if he was not afraid of me he'd run away in a minute.

I can't allow the man to run. I need him because he's strong, healthier than most, and he knows these Low Country marshes so well that he can navigate the creeks even on a dark night—a skill they say must be learned from an early age or it cannot be acquired. Then too, I need to keep him close because he's seen too much. If I let him leave he'll carry tales—and his tales would be of only one side, the more gruesome side, of my work. Of course that gruesome aspect is why he fears me, and so I must let it be; but sometimes it pains me to be so misunderstood, even by a poor black man.

Jackson can't be expected to comprehend the grand purpose, the noble aim of my life's work. How could he, with his lack of education, understand when my own professional colleagues did not? No one else has my clarity of vision, not to mention the sheer level of my skill. They could not keep up with me; therefore they excluded me.

I am accustomed to feeling alone.

Yet after all I've done for Jackson, one would think the man could give me devotion, if not love. Not so. Instead, he has so little sense that he mourns after his former owners, who abandoned him. I deserve better.

I have always deserved better than I get; such is all too frequently the curse of having a brilliant mind.

Jackson called me a monster not two hours earlier this day. He was talking to a woman outside the freemen's clinic in Beaufort, and I overheard him say that word, *monster,* an appellation I truly abhor. Of course I had to put a stop to that kind of talk right away, and I did. As a result, his fear of me has been reinforced, and that is a good thing.

Even as I raised the spyglass to my eye and trained it on the military settlement at the northwest end of Hilton Head, I wondered fleetingly if my man Jack had loved that woman. She was pretty, if one measured her looks only in comparison to her own kind. A pity I could not have saved her head, as it was the most attractive part of her, but I had no use for it.

The parts I can use are in my black bag, here in the bottom of the boat not far from Jackson's bare feet. He knows all too well what is in the bag. I do not think he will call me a monster ever again. I have taught him a lesson.

"Jackson," I said politely, as I generally do him the honor of calling him by the longer version of his name, "can you move us any closer without our being seen? I'd like to know what's going on over there."

Some kind of ruckus had arisen over at the military base. I couldn't quite make out what. Though I doubted if it could have any relation to the matter that had brought me here spying this day, any disruption of normal routine on the post was interesting and bore watching.

"Yassuh," Jackson said and pushed off, using his long oar like a pole.

The boats these Gullahs fashion are sharp-prowed and flat-bottomed. They part the tall sea grasses with a swish that can be eerie or silky, depending on one's mood. My mood was silky this afternoon, despite that brief disruption to take care of Jackson's woman friend. Dismemberment, the way *I* do it, is hard, exacting work—but in its wake it leaves a sense of the greatest satisfaction.

I returned my attention to the activity captured in the glass.

For some months now Hilton Head Island has been headquarters for the Union Army's Department of the South. All the sea islands to the south of Charleston were abandoned by the plantation owners about a year ago, when Union ships found their way into Port Royal Sound—the white gentry just took off. They left almost all their possessions behind them: mansions, furniture, field slaves and all. On the mainland near the coast it was the same—every house in the rich old town of Beaufort had been left empty of people but fully furnished. And everything—*everything*—including the abandoned field slaves, became contraband. Beaufort and all the sea islands, as far south as Savannah, all were seized and occupied by the Union without so much as a single shot having been fired.

As for me, I came here to the Low Country by luck, at one of those times in life that reinforce the truth in aphorisms such as: It is always darkest before the dawn. I've always been a lucky man, though I do not mean with gambling and cards; rather I am supremely confident that luck will in time make things break my way. I do not believe in a loving God who watches over us, because I am a scientist; but Lady Luck is the goddess who takes a special care of me.

Therefore I was not at all surprised to soon find, through my spyglass, the small figure of the very woman for whom I sought over there on Hilton Head. In town I had heard that she'd arrived, and I'd said to myself: *Ah, she has come to me.*

She stood on the long veranda that runs across the whole second story of the former plantation now known as Headquarters House, looking down on that ruckus of unknown origin. I could not see her features, but by her dark hair, slight stature and neat appearance in a wide-skirted black dress I knew her. Her identity was further confirmed by the simple fact of her standing there, as if she had every right to be the only woman in a company of soldiers—she alone among the hardest of men.

I sharpened my focus, yet still could not make out her face.

Never mind—from secret observation at Fredericksburg four months past I remembered her well: Her face was piquantly pretty, with an indentation at the point of her chin; her eyes were large, dark and lustrous; her cheekbones wide and prominent. Before Fredericksburg, at Antietam (the first time she got in my way), I'd lingered long enough to learn her name: Clara.

My Clara.

I had always known I would see Clara again someday. Now luck had brought her to me, without the slightest effort on my part. Idly I wondered how much time I'd have with her, how long I'd dare to keep her before she had to die.

"Whatever is going on over there, it seems to involve a number of your people, Jackson," I said.

They couldn't have found that woman's body already, I thought. *They aren't likely to find it until it starts to stink.*

*　　*　　*

COLONEL JOHN ELWELL bit his lip. His mind was not on pain, and he was able to stay his hand only with difficulty.

He wanted to stroke her dark brown hair *now*, this very minute, while her attention was focused on his leg wound; wanted to touch her before she could see it coming or sense his intent, and with a frown or the merest narrowing of her eyes, shame him into stone.

For a moment John fantasized: *If I were to touch her just once, even the merest, lightest touch, then like magic the attraction between us would take hold—must take hold, for it's truly irresistible—and so we should be forgiven, also like magic, whatever might come next!*

But then Clara did something that caused such a sharp twinge in his thigh that he gasped, and groaned as the twinge dissolved into an only slightly lesser wave of pain that traveled all the way down his leg into his very toes. And up the other way as well.

She tilted her head and looked over her shoulder with a little worried frown, at the same time applying a gentle pressure on his wound that brought relief.

"I'm sorry, Colonel," she said, "but I have to change the dressing, and it was stuck. I should have warned you this might hurt."

"You just changed dressings yesterday," John grumbled.

"I know," she agreed, gathering up some strips of cloth that he had to admit did look rather nasty, "but I've observed that wounds heal faster, the cleaner they're kept."

Clara whisked the old bandage out of sight and produced a clean length of cloth that she began to fold expertly, without looking. Instead she smiled, her brown eyes with a mischievous glint. "It's like kitchens."

"Kitchens?" John felt his own lips twitch in amused response, though he had not the slightest idea what she was talking about. Who could resist this woman, who was not much taller than a child, yet had the hands of an angel—and to boot, a wicked wit?

"The best-tasting food comes from a clean kitchen,"

she said, "and the neatest, fastest healing comes from a clean wound."

John thought about this as he watched her bind that white bandage around his thigh, over the angry, red, raggedly-sewn-together edges of a deep hole where the broken bone had poked through. She had not done the sewing, of course, because she hadn't yet arrived; he was sure she'd have made a much neater stitch. It was true that soldiers and their male nurses tended to ignore dirt. There was something manly, in fact, about the ability to ignore the muck and the mud along with all the other hardships.

Clara's insistence on cleanliness seemed a purely feminine thing—and she'd saved his leg, against a lot of odds. If there'd been a surgeon available when his horse fell on him, most likely he wouldn't have that leg anymore. Amputation, then cauterization, was the preferred method of treatment when a broken bone pierced the skin. But to the Colonel's everlasting shame, his was not a battle wound—for there was no battle in the area yet, and so no medical personnel on Hilton Head Island. He'd only been out pleasure riding and his horse had stumbled; he'd lost his seat and landed wrong, and so had the horse. A sickening snap of bone was the last thing he'd remembered before blacking out.

John suspected he might have lost not only his leg, but his life as well, if Clara Barton had not arrived a week ago and seen how things were for him. She'd immediately taken over his nursing. He'd been too weak and wracked with fever to protest that no lady should have to tend a man whose wound was in such an intimate place as his inner thigh.

She touched *him* all the time. Her touch itself was healing. He fancied—or was it mere fancy?—her touch was not always impersonal.

Yet John, being a gentleman, had never allowed himself to touch her at all.

It's not fair, he thought grumpily.

"There!" Clara said with a note of satisfaction. She pulled the afghan back over his lap and straightened up. For a few more moments she bustled about, washing her hands, tidying things, putting a small bag of refuse outside the door.

Then from one of the pockets inside her voluminous skirt, which seemed to contain any number of wondrous things, she produced a small bottle of some sweet-smelling cream. This she proceeded to rub thoroughly into her hands, taking time to go between each finger.

Aha, John thought, enchanted, *that is how she manages to work so hard yet keep those little hands so white.*

At last Clara looked around and asked, "Now, where is that book of poems we've been reading?"

It was the moment he'd been waiting for all day.

"DID YOU HEAR THAT?" Perhaps half an hour after she'd begun to read to the Colonel from his favorite volume of Keats, Clara paused in mid-poem. She lowered the book to her lap and cocked her head, listening hard.

John Elwell frowned. "It sounds like some sort of disturbance outside."

"I'll go see what's happening, shall I?" she offered, unable to keep an eagerness from her voice, yet so immediately ashamed of it that she forced herself to remain in her chair. It was not Colonel Elwell's fault that the War seemed to have come to a halt on the sea islands, making Clara feel as if the Army must have sent her—and more important, all the supplies she'd gathered for the fighting men—to the wrong place.

"If you like," John said, "but it's not necessary to trouble yourself."

"Oh, it wouldn't be any trouble," Clara said, biting her lip and keeping her seat. Her whole body suddenly seemed to itch and she wanted to fly out the door to see what was happening.

"Go and find out, then come back and report to me," John said at last, in a tone somewhere between command and his usual soft-spokenness.

Even as Clara rose—slowly, so as not to hurt his

feelings—and handed him the book, the noise grew louder: Many voices cried out, haphazardly different in tone and pitch, sounding all together as if they must be working up to something, perhaps some sort of riot.

But not a battle.

"It's some domestic thing, I'm sure," she said, as much to herself as to him. Nevertheless he'd given a command of sorts and, grateful, she was on her way to the door. She flung it open, stepped out and left the door standing wide, momentarily not thinking about drafts and their possible effect on the Colonel's fragile state of health.

At Headquarters, the former plantation house had been divided so that the working offices of the Quartermaster Corps were below on the first floor, and the officers' living quarters were on the second floor, which was accessible only from the veranda that ran across the whole façade. As Commandant, Colonel Elwell occupied the two best center rooms, so Clara emerged midway on the veranda.

She stepped quickly to the railing and looked down. The enclosure on the grounds below, usually sedately patrolled by silent guards, was now a mass of motion, swirling with noise and color and people the likes of which she had heard about, but never seen before.

Their thin arms waved above their dark heads like a writhing thicket of naked, blue-black branches. Their bodies too were thin, clothed in splashes of color that made an exciting contrast to the somber uniforms of the soldiers who stood aside, warily looking on.

Gullah, Clara thought, *they are the former slaves, now freemen and women, called the Gullah.*

Her first few contacts with the Gullah, she'd been warned, would not be easy—their language was difficult to understand and almost impossible to speak, though the words were a dialect of English. Sure enough, though she tried hard, she couldn't make out a single intelligible word rising from the crowd below. But the syntax and cadence of the Gullah speech were exotic, melodious—in fact bewitchingly beautiful—in spite of the sense of urgency she felt coming from them.

They chanted and keened incomprehensibly, and all the while a sense of grief, of mourning, ebbed and flowed in a palpable rhythm, as if through a heavy vocal sea. Most of the voices were high-pitched, the cries of women . . . and one woman stood out from all the rest.

Swaying near the center of the crowd, she was taller, her uplifted arms rose higher, and she was dressed in all white, even to a turban headdress. The tall woman threw her head back and howled—momentarily a hush fell—and then she broke away. The others parted to let her pass as she rushed toward the staircase.

Soldiers followed, brandishing their bayonet-tipped rifles and yelling "Halt! Halt!" But the woman was already halfway up the stairs, propelled by her own great momentum.

"Let her come!" Clara yelled down, "I take full responsibility!"

The soldiers, though their heads jerked up as if in surprise, responded either to the tone of her voice or to the words "full responsibility." They backed off and arranged themselves in a barrier at the foot of the stairs before anyone else in the crowd could follow.

The woman who emerged onto the veranda must be nearly six feet tall, Clara judged by making a swift comparison to her own height, which was just under five feet. And the woman was so thin that she seemed even taller. Her eyes were enormous, their whites having a clear bluish cast against her dark skin, and she carried her head in the white turban with an exotic grace, like the queen of a far-off land.

Yet this queen became an immediate supplicant, bending double, babbling and imploring in words Clara could scarcely make out.

George, she thought she heard, and *cunnel,* no doubt for colonel.

"Shush for a moment," Clara said kindly, holding out her hands with the palms up in a pleading gesture, "please, I want to help but you must speak more slowly."

Twice more she repeated both her plea and the

gesture, before the woman's words tumbled to a halt and she raised her head. Clara was finally able to ask, "Can you tell me your name?"

The woman, calmer now, unfolded to her full height. "Annabelle," she said.

"And who is George?"

One large tear spilled from Annabelle's right eye and rolled down her cheek, leaving a silvery track on ebony skin that glowed with a purple sheen. "E mah boy," she said.

"Something has happened to your son, George," Clara interpreted. She understood the tone, the facial expression, the outpouring of sorrow all too well— these were a common language that needed no words.

Annabelle drew in a sharp breath and nodded. "E don' binnah los'," she said.

"And you've come to see the Colonel, is that right?"

Annabelle nodded again.

"Colonel Elwell has been injured, he is hurt, do you understand? His horse fell on him and broke the Colonel's leg bone, high up above the knee." Clara tapped her own thigh, though her full skirt and petticoats made the gesture fairly meaningless. "It hasn't been healing right and he's confined to his room."

Confined to his bed, and in a weak and precarious state of health if the truth be known—but generally it was not. The Colonel could not leave his bed to receive this woman, nor would it be at all seemly to show her into his bedroom, and so Clara did not know what to do.

Annabelle hung her head, clasped her hands tightly together and brought them to her lips. Whether she was thinking, praying, or crying, was impossible to tell. All three, perhaps. Within the enclosed grounds below the other Gullah still moaned, their voices rising and falling as if in an agreed cadence, with occasionally a single wail that soared high and chill on the winds of afternoon.

Clara reached into the deep pocket of her skirt and took out a palm-sized notebook and a lead pencil. Making notes was second nature to her, though most often she did it in a field hospital, or walking the battlefield to find soldiers still alive among those who'd been left for dead.

She flipped past pages of names of sons, fathers, husbands, lovers, all of whose messages she had promised to deliver and someday she would—until finally she found a blank space and in it she wrote: *Annabelle*. Then she drew a two-headed arrow, and at its other end she wrote: *George, son*. Along the shaft of this arrow she wrote *missing*.

Then Clara moved closer, tipped her head to one side and looked up into Annabelle's face. Above the Gullah woman's clasped hands her cheeks were shiny-wet with tears, and the skin around her eyes was creased with sorrow.

"Is George the only one who's lost?" Clara asked quietly, urgently compelled by some sort of sixth sense she had about people who'd gone missing. "Are there others?"

Annabelle did not reply. Instead she closed her eyes and began to sway ever so slightly forward and back, forward and back.

"Do you understand what I'm asking?" Clara pressed.

The tall woman stilled herself, opened her eyes and wiped her cheeks with the back of her hand. Slowly she shook her head back and forth—a negative reply.

"George don' binnah los'," she insisted. "Uh tole oonuh. Dem tek um. E don' binnah onlies' dem tek."

Clara bit her bottom lip in frustration—now she was the one who did not understand.

THE COLONEL SHOVED his elbows back hard against the pillows and struggled to raise his shoulders and neck off the bed so as to see through the doorway. He hated not knowing everything that was going on.

Damnation! He still couldn't see.

Beads of sweat popped out on John's forehead as he tried harder, leaning all the weight of his upper body first on one elbow, then the other, until at last he'd dragged himself more or less upright. Then he bent forward from the waist—a position that produced an instant nausea in the pit of his stomach—reached back, and quickly balled the feather pillows up behind him for support.

Aaah! Better.

Sitting up he felt less like an invalid. Though he still couldn't see her—she'd moved out of range. By craning his neck to the left, he got a glimpse of her black skirt. And he could hear some anguished-sounding outpour of the Gullah language, in a woman's voice.

It would be good experience for Clara to handle it as much as she could, whatever it was—even though he was jealous of his time with her.

Within two days of her arrival, John had freed up a room beside his own in the big house and assigned it to Clara. He'd raided some of the officers' rooms to provide her a rocking chair and some other, smaller luxuries; he'd ordered that a handsome chest of drawers with parquet inlay from his own room be moved into hers, as well.

All without her knowledge. If he'd asked, she might have declined, and he wasn't taking that chance. He was the commanding officer, he could give what orders he liked, and if the men made rude remarks behind his back about all this fuss over a woman (he was pretty sure they did), well then, let them.

John's next step had been to assign David Barton, Clara's brother and travel companion, to share Sam Lamb's quarters. Both men already shared the rank of major—they might as well share a suite of rooms.

Better two officers together than force a brother and sister to live in a two-room cabin that had been assigned before their arrival, in the mistaken belief that "David Barton" and "Clara Barton" were man and wife.

Anyway, that was the rationale of the new arrangement, and there was no one entitled to complain about it—no one except John Elwell's occasionally aching conscience.

Rumor had it that the two majors were not entirely happy, but they had no choice other than to obey orders. Major Lamb was Colonel Elwell's second-in-command, and what with the Colonel out of commission, he had too much to do. So John had made Major Barton Samuel Lamb's assistant. It had seemed a good idea, but was not working out, and their living together only exacerbated the situation.

The Colonel grimaced when he thought of Clara's brother. He didn't like the man, who was much older and yet had so little experience as a soldier that John wondered how he'd earned his rank. Of course John also didn't like that David was always watching Clara. . . .

Which was why John had put him in a room on the other side, where it was much harder for him to know his sister's every move. Smiling at his own cleverness, the Colonel again craned his head to see as much as he could of the pair on the porch. Clara had bent toward the Gullah woman, a motion that set the hoop under her skirt swaying and provided a rare flash of ruffled petticoat.

That's the trouble with war, far too few petticoats. John was appalled by the frivolousness of his own thought . . . but it was nice to smile for a change.

Clara's reputation had preceded her, along with her clearance papers—but she'd turned out to be far different from what any of them had expected. She had her own permits issued by the U.S. Congress, including a battlefield pass that allowed her to go anywhere, even to the front lines, to distribute her supplies and to assist the medical corps. No ordinary citizen got a battlefield pass that circumvented the whole military chain of command, especially not a woman. Such a thing was unheard-of. So they'd anticipated some sort of amazonian bluestocking, and got an energetic little angel instead.

Clara Barton's battlefield pass was legitimate—John had seen it with his own eyes.

Amazing woman! Smiling again, he shook his head.

Amazing or not, it was time he offered to help in the present situation. He'd been listening, thought he'd recognized the voice of the Gullah woman, who was a kind of leader in their community. And now, he'd just heard Clara say his name.

John cleared his throat and called out: "Clara! Miss Barton!"

After a beat or two there she was, a small woman in a skirt so wide she took up the whole doorway.

"Yes, Colonel? I'm sorry I forgot to close the door. I hope you're not feeling a chill."

"Nonsense." John felt himself smiling. It must be years since he had smiled so much. "I'm enjoying the fresh air. I've been cooped up in here for far too long."

"I'm sure that's so."

"Bring the woman on in. I think I know her, and I'd like to help."